THE SECRET ADVENTURES OF SHERLOCK HOLMES

Ciaran Murray

ORANGE PIP BOOKS

Hardcover ISBN 978-1-80424-707-5
Paperback ISBN 978-1-80424-708-2
ePub ISBN 978-1-80424-709-9
PDF ISBN 978-1-80424-710-5

Published by Orange Pip Books
An imprint of MX Publishing
335 Princess Park Manor, Royal Drive,
London, N11 3GX
www.mxpublishing.com

Cover design by Awan

CONTENTS

ONE

THE TREASURE OF THE BLACK TAJ

Readers of these memoirs of mine concerning Mr. Sherlock Holmes will be aware that the records of certain of his cases were, for reasons of discretion, placed in a tin dispatch-box in the vault of my banker's, Cox & Co., at Charing Cross, to await publication in some unimaginable future. To these were added records of his own which even I have not perused, but which were delivered to me sealed. The happiness of families in some instances, in others the exigencies of politics, have made it imperative to put off to a later date – if Holmes does not in the meantime decide to separate and destroy them – the publication of some of his most intriguing adventures. In the case which I record here, these factors are intensified by another which makes it unlikely that it would be received by the present age with anything but uproar and execration. Indeed I myself have hesitated to place it upon record, and it is only at Holmes' urgent insistence that I take up my pen to describe what may well be the most mysterious of all the adventures in which he was involved.

Summer had descended upon Baker Street with an unmoving, enervating heat that left both of us prostrate and listless. Parliament was up, the newspapers were empty, and no client had written or called over all the weeks of the strange, subtropical season.

As it wore on, the slightest mental effort became impossible to Holmes. In this stagnation he gave signs of wishing to revert to that unfortunate addiction which had been

1

a matter of so much concern to me in the past. It was, therefore, with a stirring of hope that I heard the doorbell ring as the sun began to sink over the rooftops across the way. Holmes groaned cynically. 'A lost tourist, no doubt, seeking directions to Madame Tussaud's', he murmured. It was with a shock of surprise, therefore, that he sat upright as a heavy tread shook the stair. 'I know that step. But what the devil can Lestrade want with me?' His back was turned resolutely to the door as our visitor, after knocking, entered, and remained turned as he remarked, 'Help yourself to some brandy and soda, Lestrade'.

'Ha, very clever, Mr. Holmes. No doubt you were peeping out the window just now'. The Scotland Yard detective's oft-stated scepticism about my friend's abilities was matched only by the inevitability of his applying to him once his own investigations had failed. But Holmes was too exhausted for a rejoinder, and waved him wearily to a seat. 'State your difficulty'.

'Well, it's like this, Mr. Holmes', began the official, with a gulp and an appreciative glance at his glass. 'We all know at the Yard that you can go where we cannot, and use methods denied to us'. It was characteristic that he should put Holmes' successes down to trickery at the very moment when he was appealing for his help. 'As it happens, that's something we need just now. It's this Simpson case – you know, the Dorset brewer'.

Holmes laughed shortly. 'And the next Home Secretary, from what I hear. That rather complicates matters for you, does it not?' Lestrade's hangdog look showed that he had hit his mark. 'The fact is, Mr. Holmes, I cannot afford a mistake on this one. And as things look at the moment, whatever I do will result in one'.

The case was coming back to me. There had been little enough of interest in the papers, and the item, though brief, had stuck in my mind. Ezekiel Simpson's nephew, a young cavalry officer home on leave from India, had disappeared in London, and his Indian servant been arrested. Further details were promised, but none had so far been provided, and Lestrade had few to give. The young man, by the name of Crutchley, had come back on leave to his family home in Dorset, where he shocked all who knew him by the evident decline in his health. 'Looked as if he had put on thirty years in three, from what I hear', said Lestrade. He was accompanied by his servant, one Desai. After a single night at home, the two had set off on the first train to London, without giving any notice to the family. A number of witnesses testified to an altercation between them at the local station. Nobody could say what it had been about: the exchange had been conducted in undertones; but all agreed that the gestures and expressions of the two were indicative of some violent disagreement. After their arrival in London, the young man vanished, and the Indian was apprehended while attempting to book passage back to his own country. 'But I cannot get anything out of him', the official concluded.

'I expect', said Holmes with some asperity, 'that you handled him with your customary tact'.

'Nothing illegal, Mr. Holmes. Told him he'd best own up, or things would go badly for him. Clammed up on the spot, he did, and refused to say another word'.

'Have you had any leads on young Crutchley?'

'Nothing, Mr. Holmes. We have checked the passenger lists of all the shipping lines, and there is no sign of him. He is still in England – if he is alive, that is'.

'You have reason to believe that he is not?'

'What else can I believe, Mr. Holmes? I reckon the servant lured him to London, and made away with him here'.

'For what reason?'

Lestrade shrugged. 'Money, I dare say'.

3

'Have you found this money on his person?'

'Concealed it before we caught up with him, I don't doubt'.

'And on this monumental lack of evidence you keep him in custody?'

'Can't do any other, Mr. Holmes. He's our only lead; if we were to let him go, Mr. Simpson would have my head, he would'. Lestrade's dilemma was that he could not hold the Indian indefinitely without material evidence, nor release him, as the only link to the disappearance, without incurring the displeasure of an influential politician.

'Perhaps you would consent to interview him, Mr. Holmes? He will say nothing more to me'.

'Very well', answered Holmes, who had begun to show signs of throwing off his lethargy. 'But I must insist upon interviewing him alone – unless you would accompany me, Watson'. I was glad of anything that might absorb Holmes' attention, and we rattled away through a city to which the deepening darkness had brought a welcome lowering of temperature. It was evidently less welcome to the Indian, who lay shivering under a thin blanket in his cell, his dark face pale and strained. When he saw Holmes he turned away. 'You are an agent of that man Lestrade', he said listlessly, in an educated English of which only the lilt betrayed his origins. You too wish to prove me an assassin'. 'On the contrary', said Holmes. 'I know of no evidence that a crime has been committed, still less that any has been committed by you. I see no reason to believe that you have made away with young Crutchley'.

The Indian's face brightened as he sat up. 'You are absolutely right, Mr. Holmes. I tried to save him'.

'From what?', demanded Holmes, his eager, aquiline face leaning forward in the light of the lamp. 'Save him from what? Tell me! I can have you released!'

The Indian paused for a moment, irresolute. For an instant he seemed about to confide in us, then he shook his head and subsided, with a hopeless gesture of the hands. 'It is no use. I cannot tell you. I might just as well let them hang me on the spot'. And, for all of Holmes' pleadings, he refused to say another word.

Lestrade received the news with insolent satisfaction. 'Told you so, Mr. Holmes'. His face changed abruptly, however, as Holmes whispered a few words in his ear, scribbled some addresses in his pocket-book, tore out the page, and handed it over. 'Try these', he said. At once the official was all fawning submission. 'I'll see to it immediately, Mr. Holmes'. Holmes ignored his protestations of gratitude. 'We will work from the other end. Good night'.

Holmes sat in silence through the drive back to Baker Street, where he riffled through the pages of a railway timetable. 'We leave tomorrow morning, Watson', he said, a hint of the old alertness about the eyes. 'Can I count on you?'

'Absolutely', I replied, my spirits lifting at the prospect of an escape from Baker Street, and of any occupation for my friend's too-active brain, however futile it might prove in the event. 'But do you really imagine you can solve the case from there?'

'I have already solved the case, Watson. What I seek in Dorset is confirmation'.

'Already solved it! But how?'

Holmes dropped himself onto the sofa and waved me to a chair. Then he ticked off the points on his fingers. 'One. We have indisputable evidence of a quarrel between master and servant. Lestrade takes this as evidence of the servant's guilt. But – two – the servant insists: "I tried to save him". This may of course be the standard protestation of innocence. But consider point three: "I might just as well let them hang me on the spot". No guilty man would have made such an admission'.

'He may have let it slip by accident'.

'Perhaps, Watson. But my instinct tells me to trust this man. There is an honesty in his eye, and a note of genuine sorrow in his voice, which compels it'.

'What, then, do you make of the case?'

'Simple. Opium, or some such narcotic. The sudden deterioration in young Crutchley's health, attendant upon a return from the east, the abrupt departure for London, the quarrel with the servant, combined with the latter's claim that he wished to save him. What other conclusion can there be?'

'Why then the admission of guilt?'

'I can only conclude, Watson, that the servant had at some time been responsible for supplying his master with the drug – perhaps had introduced him to it. I have instructed Lestrade to search every known opium den in the East End, and provided the addresses of a few he may not be aware of. We, meanwhile, will seek further enlightenment through those devious methods in which, as the good inspector avers, we excel'.

The following day dawned with the inimitable rose-colour of an English summer morning touching the faces of the buildings opposite, and we were on our way to the station before the heat of the day had begun to bear down on the city streets. As our train thundered westward, gusts of air rushed through the lowered windows, which, though mingled with wafts of coal smoke, made a welcome contrast to the unmoving air of the capital. While we swayed along the tracks, Holmes read aloud from the volume of *The History and Antiquities of Dorset* that he had snatched from his shelves as we left. 'Hmm, Crutchley', he mused, as he ran his finger down the index, and quickly turned to the page indicated. 'Seat of family of same name. Sir Guy de Crutchley, first of the line, brought back from the Crusades a relic of the True Cross, from which the village was named, and founded a convent to house it with treasure captured from the Saracen. The convent, with the relic, was destroyed at the Reformation, its lands reassumed by the family. A descendant, Sir Hugh, sailed with Raleigh in his search for the gold of the New World, and perished on the Orinoco. The Crutchleys served on the royalist side in the Civil War, forfeiting great part of their estates, but recovered them at the Restoration. In the eighteenth century, the manor was rebuilt in Palladian style by Sir Mortimer Crutchley, a noted gamester and rake, who perished in a duel over a lady's honour. The estate had been much reduced by his extravagances, and the house fell into dilapidation; but it was restored on the marriage of the present baronet, Sir Joseph, to the noted heiress Miss Judith Simpson, sister to Mr. Ezekiel Simpson, M.P., by whom it has been improved in the modern taste. And what might that be, I wonder?', queried Holmes as he tossed the book aside. 'Well, Watson, you know my views on heredity. What do you make of this young man's predispositions?'

I shrugged. 'I scarcely know what to make of them. Idealism, venality, self-sacrifice, dissipation: they are a mass of contradictions'.

'Precisely, Watson. We have some pointers; but in the absence of further evidence, it would be foolish to say more'.

From the station, we took a trap towards the wooded hillside which towered over the village. An imposing gateway marked the entrance to the estate, its piers surmounted by heraldic dragons, newly gilded, each grasping in its claws a shield on which a cross was displayed. A noble avenue wound upwards through the woods, until at last we emerged within sight of the manor. A pillared mansion in the style of the last century, which one might have expected to be grey and lichen-coated, had been freshly covered with a gleaming white stucco which made it resemble nothing so much as a seaside hotel. The effect was underlined by blinds of red and blue, creating the impression of a gigantic and deranged Union Jack. On the slope in front of the house, an enormous flower-bed had been planted to form a portrait of the Queen; but a recent storm had left Her Majesty in a sorry state of bedragglement.

Holmes burst into incredulous laughter. 'Behold the "modern taste"!'.

Further evidence of the occupant's loyalty presented itself after we had been admitted, and our cards taken. The hallway had been turned into a kind of museum, recording the fact that, in the course of an excursion from Osborne, Her Majesty had made a halt here, and accepted a cup of tea. The cup and saucer stood under glass, while enlarged photographs of the occasion, and a huge portrait of the sovereign in oils, competed for space on the walls. We were shown into an adjoining chamber, mercifully free of decoration: for every inch of space, from floor to ceiling, was taken up by books. A gallery, reached by a spiral staircase, ran around the upper part of the room. The books, to judge by their bindings, were rare and old.

'What a wonderful library!', I exclaimed.

'On the contrary', said Holmes, 'it is a perfectly dreadful library'.

'My dear Holmes!'

'In its own way, Watson, it is no better than the hall we have passed through. It is a veritable museum, in this instance of the book. If you have glanced at the shelves, you will have noticed that there is nothing there more recent than the last century. Nor is there any evidence of study: see, the inkwell is dry, the remains of the ink clotted and cracked. And should one wish to read, it would be impossible. Seated at this table, one's eye would constantly be distracted by that glimmer on the horizon'.

I walked to one of the windows, from which I enjoyed a splendid view. Over the woods through which we had ascended was a band of sea from which the light was blinding. At its verge, on a clifftop, was a circular temple.

I heard Holmes observe: 'Everything in a library should conduce to inward vision. There should be no distraction – none. But no man of spirit could get through a single page before such a vista as this. See the sails pass and repass in the Channel. Surely they call to adventure: the light that breaks through those upper branches and is scattered as they move, revolving through the cut glass of the inkwell as through a prism, darting over the gilt of the bindings – is it not a standing memorial to the vanity of books?'

Holmes' reflections were interrupted by the entry of a servant. 'Her ladyship will see you', he announced gravely, but with what I could not but perceive as a suppressed smirk. We were led, not to a lady's boudoir, but to a large drawing-room fitted out as an office. The shelves were packed with parliamentary reports, directories, and other volumes of a practical nature. On the antique desk in the centre sat a telephone, and behind it a woman of middle age and imposing proportions. The unnatural sheen of her bright red hair, proclaiming it newly dyed, and her dress, of an electric blue, proclaimed the source of the improvements we had so lately observed. 'I am Lady Crutchley', she said, keeping to her chair and offering us none. 'Which of you is Holmes?'

My companion bowed.

'What is your business here?'

'We have come at the request of Inspector Lestrade. He feels...'

'I have no interest in his feelings. If he cannot do his work, he ought to be replaced. And will be'.

'I was about to say, madam, that it was his opinion that as a private investigator I can work in a confidential capacity which, as a public servant, is denied to him. However much he might desire to, the Inspector cannot conceal the secrets of families'.

'You think there are such secrets to conceal?'

'I do, madam'. And Holmes proceeded to explain the hypothesis he had outlined to me. 'I wished, therefore, to ask if you had noticed any behaviour which might bear upon this theory, and whether I might look through the young man's luggage'.

In the course of Holmes' relation, Lady Crutchley had at first turned white, and then the colour of her hair. 'Unthinkable', she muttered, as if to herself. 'Intolerable! How could he...' She jumped to her feet, eyes starting from her head. 'Absolutely not', she shrieked. 'And if you do not leave this house at once, I will set the dogs upon you'.

'I have no wish', said Holmes in his most ironic mode, 'to precipitate an action so far beneath your ladyship's station'. And, with a grave, mocking bow, and waving me ahead of him, he retired.

After he had closed the door behind him, Holmes doubled up in a fit of suppressed laughter. 'You will have observed, Watson', he remarked, 'the lady's well-developed maternal concern... Hullo?'

A door had opened in the corridor through which we were passing, and a wizened little man hissed: 'In here. Quick!' He hurried us into a smaller version of the office we had just vacated, but in which the papers were yellowed and in disarray. An ancient calendar hung at a crazy angle. In the wastebasket beneath a cheap desk, on which stood a half-empty glass, was piled a collection of discarded bottles. His breath exuded a heavy odour as he extended a shaking hand and muttered nervously, 'Crutchley. You must be the people sent by Lestrade. You can do nothing here. Try the rectory'.

'The rector?' asked Holmes in puzzlement.

'No, no, the daughter. Now go. Quick, or *she* will catch us'. And he pushed us through the door.

'The proprietor of the manor', laughed Holmes, as we stepped out into the sunshine, 'no less than his property, appears to bear the imprint of this extraordinary personality. But now we seem to have a new direction in which to work. I had no idea there was a young lady in the case'.

We walked down the avenue to the village, where the spire soon led us to the churchyard. As we entered, a scraping and scratching drew our attention to a trench by the apse of the church, out of which shovelfuls of gravel were emerging and falling onto the path. Looking in, I expected to find a gravedigger, but instead saw a middle-aged gentleman in clerical collar and shirtsleeves, with iron-grey hair and shrewd eyes. He smiled in response to our greeting and pointed to a layer of brickwork which he had begun to uncover in the lower courses of the wall. 'Roman', he said, with a tap of his shovel, 'Indisputably. That shape is unmistakable'.

'The Rev. Horatio Ponderby, M.A.?' queried Holmes politely.

The cleric looked puzzled for an instant, then with a look of comprehension pointed his shovel back along the path. 'You have read my notice-board'.

'Exactly', said Holmes. 'But in fact it is a young lady we have come here to see'.

'Ah, my daughter', said the parson, as he climbed out of the trench. 'For a moment I dared to hope you were visiting antiquarians. For some time I have suspected that the church rested on ancient foundations: that Mars, perhaps, was venerated here before St. Michael'. He rolled down his sleeves and retrieved his jacket from the churchyard wall as Holmes introduced himself, telling us that his daughter was taking her afternoon walk by the seashore, but he expected her back shortly. He then led us into the building and up the nave.

11

Holmes drew his attention to a carved and painted Jacobean tomb showing a kneeling gentleman in a ruff: 'The companion of Raleigh, I presume?' 'A cenotaph', murmured the vicar. 'The body was never found'. Beyond lay a number of effigies, culminating, in front of the altar, in a chain-mail clad figure whose crossed legs proclaimed a pilgrimage to the Holy Land. 'Sir Guy?' queried Holmes in an undertone. The cleric nodded, and led us to the rectory, where he seated us in a parlour with stiff chairs. 'Am I mistaken', queried Holmes, 'or is there no monument to Sir Mortimer?'

'There is none in the church, Mr. Holmes. The locals would have it that he was refused burial there. The fact is, he was laid to rest elsewhere at his own desire. You have noticed the temple on the cliff? That is his creation. He had a passionate love of the beautiful'.

'So I understand', said Holmes drily.

'No, no, Mr. Holmes, there was far more to Mortimer Crutchley than legend would allow. His gaming was not excessive by the standards of the time; any extravagance was reserved for his architectural projects. He had visited Italy, and belonged to the Society of Dilettanti. Nor did he conform to the standard image of the rake. There was one lady only, who had been married against her wishes during his absence, and to whom his attentions were subsequently resumed. The lovers were surprised one evening at the temple, and he died in the duel which followed. I have seen drawings he made from his collection of antique statuary that suggest a sensitive artist. The quest for beauty takes many forms, Mr. Holmes; as does that for truth'.

'I am not sure that your preoccupations are shared at the manor'.

'Not by its mistress, certainly. Judith Simmons was part-heir to the Simmons brewery, which at the time of her marriage was a small though solid business, run quietly over generations by a family of dissenter stock. She, however, had ambitions: it was well known that she married Crutchley for his title and the access to society which this provided. The prosperity of the business under her brother's management is attributed by many to her advice. Rumour has it that she is currently engaged upon a search for aristocratic ancestry, in preparation for his eventual ascent to the House of Lords'.

'Hence the protestations of loyalty', observed Holmes slowly. 'And no doubt, also, the terror of scandal'. He went on to recount the details of our interview.

'Oh yes, scandal, Mr. Holmes. The classical sculptures were removed from view in the current pursuit of respectability. Joseph Crutchley, spineless though he may be in other respects, dug his heels in against a proposal to sell it. Though I must say it took all my persuasion to keep him to his principles'.

'*Your* persuasion?' echoed Holmes, with a slight lift of the eyebrows. 'I cannot but consider that a somewhat unusual attitude in a man of the cloth'.

The rector shook his head impatiently. 'We live an age of evolution, Mr. Holmes, the Church with the rest of society. What changes is not what we believe in, but the manner in which we do it reverence. I should have no hesitation, for instance, in describing Mortimer Crutchley as an essentially religious man. I will admit, however, that my opinions are not popular among my colleagues, which is why I shall probably end my days in this...'

The door opened, and there walked into the parlour one of the most beautiful young women I have ever seen. Her face had a full-lipped, sensual beauty made still more attractive by its air of steady determination; while her eyes, though lustrous, were calm and unwavering. She was in the act of removing a straw hat, and shaking loose a luxuriant mass of rich auburn hair, when she noticed us.

'My daughter, Anna', said the vicar simply. 'Anna, this is Mr. Sherlock Holmes and his friend...'

'Dr. Watson', said the young woman, relaxing into a smile. 'I have read every one of your accounts of the exploits of Mr. Holmes with the greatest interest. You have made him so vividly present to us that one feels one has always known him'.

I bowed, flushed with pleasure. It was not often that my sketches, so sardonically depreciated by Holmes, received such praise in his presence. 'And I have long wished to meet you, Mr. Holmes', she went on, taking him by the hand and gazing into his eyes. 'Mental capacity is a power that I admire without reserve'.

The attentions of the female sex were normally abhorrent to Holmes; but it seemed to me that in this case there was a tinge of hesitancy in the manner in which he disengaged his hand. He recovered immediately, however. 'Madam', he murmured coolly, with a curt inclination of the head.

'If you will come in here to my study, Mr. Holmes, we can speak more at ease'. The rector shook hands with us both, while the daughter led us into a simply-furnished room in which a broad window looked out across the glebe to the manor. An ancient overstuffed sofa sat in front of it; the young woman gestured us to this, while she seated herself on a deal chair behind a bench, which a covering of oilcloth had converted into a desk. On it were a scratched typewriter, some books of shorthand, and piles of notes. A shelf behind held the works of George Eliot and an assortment of books and pamphlets, many of them of a radical tendency, as well as more general magazines, amongst which it gave me satisfaction to see some well-worn numbers of *The Strand*.

'Let me say at the outset, Mr. Holmes', she began, 'that I consider myself partly to blame. I wished to help him, but at the time – there was so little of it – I could not see how. If only... but I must not fall into the practice, which I know you so greatly reprehend, of telling my story out of sequence'.

Holmes smiled at this, and she resumed. 'Jason and I were brother and sister to each other from the start. As a child, his one impulse was to take refuge from his dreadful family – his parents quarrelled bitterly – and he found a second home here. Though he used to say it was the first he had ever known. He loved my father's tales of his ancestors, and it was these, I feel, which gave him the courage to believe that he might add another chapter to their chronicles. At any rate, when he came down from Oxford, his mother wished him to follow his uncle into the family business, and eventually succeed him in the House of Commons; but he refused, and instead took a commission in India'. She halted, with a faraway look, and, almost imperceptibly, sighed.

Holmes gazed at her over steepled hands. 'Brother and sister, I think you said?'

The young woman flushed slightly. 'I see that you do indeed possess the qualities which Dr. Watson attributes to you, Mr. Holmes. Yes, so it was at first. But there was always some adventure in his mind, whether of action or of imagination. We would walk along the shore, and he would tell me of his dreams, so that he made me, too, impatient for a wider world outside this village. I recall vividly his saying to me: "It is not death I fear; it is not having lived". Once, while we walked along the shore where the cliff is steepest – where it is crowned by the temple – I wondered aloud if anyone had ever climbed it, and he immediately began to do so. My heart stood still for him, Mr. Holmes, until he waved to me from the top. It was at that moment that I realised that – well, that...'

'And was this feeling returned?', asked Holmes, with a rare gentleness of tone.

'Oh yes, Mr. Holmes. When he was leaving, he said to me: "There is only one person in the world who could keep me

15

from what I am doing. But she is the one I can best trust to understand it". I knew, indeed, how he felt: that in some fashion he had to prove himself. He promised to be back in three years. Every month since then he has written to me, until just before he was due to return'. She paused reflectively, then resumed in a more sombre tone.

'When I saw him again, it was there'. She pointed to the window behind us. 'I heard a sound outside and looked up. I am not given to superstition, Mr. Holmes, but for a moment I thought it was his ghost. He face was death-pale and hollow, as if he suffered from some wasting sickness. When I let him in, he staggered to that sofa, where you are now sitting. "For God's sake, save me!" he pleaded'.

'"From what, Jason?" I cried. "Save you from what?"'

'"From myself", he replied in a hoarse whisper'.

'You can scarcely imagine my astonishment when he pleaded with me to marry him. This was something I could by no means agree to. When Jason first went away, Mr. Holmes, I read to fill the time and the empty space that he had left. Then I began to read out of interest. I learnt that there are great causes afoot, that there is much to be done in this world. I learnt to think and to formulate my own philosophy, and consider how I might express it in practice. I have written some articles for the magazines, but not enough upon which to live. I have therefore learnt typewriting and shorthand, to support myself when I go to London, as I intend. I am repelled by the idea of marriage as we know it, but should have no aversion to a partnership of equality. Jason, however, was in no fit state to discuss practical arrangements of any kind. It seemed to me that he was ill, either in body or in spirit. I pleaded with him to confide in me the source of his trouble. Several times it seemed he was about to, but could not get out the words. He left me, at last, in something like despair. His final words to me were: "It is too late"'.

'What did you understand by them?'

'I did not know what to make of them. I still do not'.

Holmes explained his own hypothesis. 'Did you observe any signs in him of such a condition? Come, be frank with me'.

'Frankly, Mr. Holmes, I know nothing of such matters. I can only say that he seemed to me possessed: by what, I cannot imagine. But since then, I have felt a growing certainty that I shall never see him again: that I was his last hope, and that I failed him'.

'Why, what could you have done?'

'I would have done anything for him, Mr. Holmes – anything'.

Holmes looked at her with a curious, appraising gaze.

'Yes, Mr. Holmes, I can answer the question in your eye. I have told you of my views on marriage. I would not and could not have married him under those circumstances. What I could have done did not appear to me at the time. Seeing him in that shocking state had confused me: I could not think clearly. And I have realised, since, that there was something else. Now I know that in my heart I was angry with him: that when he went away, I had felt abandoned. I had in the meantime built a new life for myself; I could not surrender it at his demand, and for what might have been merely a passing whim. But I know now that my anger was a form of love; and I know what I could and should have done. If I had that evening to live over again, I would offer myself to him. Yes, Mr. Holmes, I am sorry if I offend you or Dr. Watson, but if I could have helped him by it, I would have lived with him as what you would call his mistress. And now, if you will excuse me, I should like to be left alone'. Agitated by her confession, she hurried from the room. Holmes looked after her with undisguised admiration. 'If I were young again, Watson', he declared as he rose from the sofa, 'and in the shoes of young Crutchley, it would take a very great deal to part me from such a woman'.

For myself, I was too shocked to speak; and there was something in Holmes' manner which made it seem inopportune to do so. We returned to the station in silence, and in silence sat together until we arrived in London. It was a melancholy journey. The tale of the high-spirited young man, full of promise, whose life had been destroyed by some sinister addiction, held a particular menace in relation to Holmes, and for me as his physician and friend; and we were carried to the pulse of the train and the rattle of the rails in a strained silence.

But when we alighted at Waterloo, Holmes gasped in astonishment. He pointed with his stick to a poster behind wire mesh at a newsagent's. Here, in large letters, was inscribed:

THE TREASURE OF
THE BLACK TAJ
Officer Gives Evidence
in Crutchley Case

Holmes raced to the stall and snatched up a copy from amid the folded piles of paper. It was left to me to pay for it and quiet the profanities of the stall-keeper, as Holmes devoured the printed lines, oblivious to the mutterings of the stream of passengers that divided around him. I have the article before me as I write; here is what it says:

The matter of the mysterious disappearance of Lieutenant Jason Crutchley has been brought to a satisfactory conclusion through the tenacity of Inspector Lestrade, of Scotland Yard. From the outset, it was the Inspector's opinion that foul play was

18

involved. Startling confirmation of this theory has now come to light. From an interview with Captain Alexander Hopkirk, Inspector Lestrade has ascertained that, just prior to his return from India, Lt. Crutchley had interested himself in a search for the fabled hoard known as the Treasure of the Black Taj. Letters in the possession of Capt. Hopkirk show that the lieutenant had actually discovered this treasure, and believed himself pursued as a result. The treasure is said to be guarded by a ferocious sect of Thuggees, of which the lieutenant's servant, Desai, is thought to be a member. Desai, as the Inspector reconstructs the case, lured Lt. Crutchley to London, and into the hands of accomplices. Fears are entertained for the lieutenant's life. It is understood that serious charges are pending.

Holmes took a cab to Scotland Yard, where he found the normally furtive-looking Lestrade at his most offensively triumphant. 'You have your fine theories, Mr. Holmes, and I have my facts. You will not deny that this time it is I who have been proved right. Fortunately Captain Hopkirk turned up before we could set out on the wild-goose chase that you proposed for us'.

'You have informed Desai of your new evidence?'

'Yes I have, Mr. Holmes. Turned white as a sheet, he did, and refused to answer a word. Never saw guilt clearer on any man's face'.

Beneath Holmes' impassive exterior I sensed his suppressed agitation as in a resigned voice he asked the inspector for the captain's address. With a patronising shrug, Lestrade opened a file that lay on his desk. As he turned over its contents, a photograph came to the top. 'Crutchley?' asked Holmes. Lestrade nodded indulgently, and handed him a portrait of a man in his twenties, of undistinguished looks, but with a glow about the eyes indicative of youthful idealism and daring. When Holmes asked if he might borrow it, Lestrade treated me to a broad grin. 'Some of us just don't know when we're beaten, I reckon', he said good-humouredly, as he copied out the address. The following afternoon Hopkirk arrived in our rooms, tall, fair-haired and moustached, with an easy and athletic bea

'I am happy to give you my time, Mr. Holmes. I would do anything possible to help Crutchley – though I understand it may be too late for that. I will tell you exactly what I have told Inspector Lestrade.

'I was in a remote region of Scotland, settling the details of a minor inheritance, at the time of the lieutenant's disappearance. I did not see the London papers until my return, when I glanced over the back issues at my club. Immediately I telephoned the police.

'The facts, as far as I know them, are these. I first met Jason Crutchley six months ago, when his unit was transferred to Agra. He was a soldier's soldier, Mr. Holmes, and I took to him at once. One night when we had sat up rather late over our whiskies, and were, I suppose, a little the worse for wear, I told him the story of the Black Taj.

'The tale is that one of these old native chappies – the Shah of Japan, or something – '

'Try Shah Jahan', Holmes broke in severely. 'The Great Moghul, and builder of the Taj Mahal'.

The blond giant laughed without offence. 'Why, you are a wonder, Mr. Holmes. I have looked at that thing every other day for the past couple of years, but none of these names would stick in my head. I never was one for books, I confess. In any case, it seems he wanted to build another – why, I can't imagine – but they locked him up'.

'Precisely', answered Holmes. 'Having built the Taj in white marble as a tomb for his wife, whom he loved, he intended to build another for himself, in black and across the river. But he was imprisoned by his parsimonious son, and spent his last years immured in the nearby fort, gazing ceaselessly at his creation but unable to realise its dark replica'.

'Yes, that was it', said the captain. 'He had hidden some treasure for the building – a hoard of gold and jewels – and when he died the son came looking for it. But the servants had got in first, and made off with it. They are supposed to have built the replica, or part of it, somewhere else. This took most of the treasure, but a single jewel was left – the finest. This, they say, is lodged at the centre of the Black Taj, as it is called. It is said to lie under a curse. No-one has ever gone in search of it and come back: it is death to touch, or even to view it'.

'This was the tale I told Jason Crutchley, Mr. Holmes, and he listened in rapture. It is a yarn passed on to every newcomer at the station; but I had never seen anyone so entranced by it. When I had finished, he said in a kind of breathless whisper – more to himself than to me – "I will find it". It is the sort of thing a new man will say, and then forget about – until the next newcomer arrives, and he passes on the tale. I was a trifle nettled, though, by the way he said it – the sense that he was going to be the one to succeed where all others had failed – and without thinking I answered: "I'll wager you don't". It was a most unfortunate choice of words. Immediately he was for setting the amount, which we fixed at a hundred guineas. I was perfectly easy in my mind, Mr. Holmes: I thought he would have forgotten the whole business by morning. But from that day on, every free moment he had was spent in tracking down this treasure. It had become a point of honour with him – some of us thought, an obsession. It was as if I had sent him out on some crusade'.

'Perhaps you did', said Holmes quietly, and told him of Crutchley's ancestry. The young soldier whistled. 'I never thought his people were anything in particular', he remarked. 'Come to think of it, he never spoke of them'.

Holmes and I exchanged glances. Then the deetctive went on: 'Have you anything further to give us?'

'Only these, Mr. Holmes', said the officer, taking two envelopes from his pocket. 'Just before I was due to return here on leave, he told me he had tracked the thing to Benares. He took my address, and said he would keep me informed of his progress. Since then, I have had two notes from him. Here they are'. He unfolded and spread them out on the table. The first read:

> You will remember the matter of our wager. I have found the treasure! It is beyond description. More when we meet. J.C.

It was written in dashing, excited strokes, heavily digging into the paper, to which the second provided a remarkable contrast. This was spidery and very nearly indecipherable; it wandered all over the page. It said:

> The curse has begun to work. It pursues me everywhere. My very existence is threatened. Will tell you all on return. J.C.

'You are certain that this is his hand?' queried Holmes.

'The first, yes, Mr. Holmes. But I should not have recognised the second'.

'Oh, they are the same, all right. There is no doubt about that. But the second has been written under the influence of some powerful disturbance'.

'Surely it is obvious', said I. 'He feared for his life'.

The young officer shook his head with decision. 'No, Dr. Watson, I cannot agree. Fear was an emotion unknown to Jason Crutchley'.

'Be frank with me: have you ever known him to take opium, or anything of that kind?' said Holmes, in a tone of great gravity.

'No, Mr. Holmes, I have not; nor could I imagine him doing so'.

'How then do you explain this letter?'

Hopkirk shook his head. 'All I know is what you see. Since you speak of drugs, this rascal Desai may have drugged his food. In such a state, he may have been persuaded that he was under a curse. Certainly, it would have been easier to make away with him'.

'You speak of Desai as a rascal', said Holmes evenly. 'You have evidence on this score?'

'Actually no', shrugged the young officer. 'I have no reason to suppose him worse than any of the others. But I have a long experience of the native character, Mr. Holmes, and you would do well to regard them, one and all, as scoundrels'.

Holmes smiled benignly. 'I have little doubt', he remarked, 'that that is how they would describe us'.

The young man's forehead creased. 'I had no idea you were a radical, Mr. Holmes'.

'Nor am I', answered Holmes simply. 'I am as devoted to the Empire as you are. But I believe in it as a force for enlightenment. With it we have carried notions of right and liberty which will ultimately involve us in respecting those of others'.

'Too deep for me, Mr. Holmes', said the fair young giant, as he rose in a single deft movement. 'I have risked my life for the Empire, and would freely do so again. But if we were to think as you do, we could not hold India for a week.   Good day'.

Our rooms seemed shabby and middle-aged once the bluff young soldier had departed, and I could not but feel that he had had the best of the argument with Holmes.   But the latter seemed unperturbed as he drew the tobacco-slipper to him and began to stuff his pipe.   I sank into my own thoughts, which after some time he interrupted.   'No, Watson', he stated firmly.   'I cannot agree.   I do not consider that I have wronged him'.

'But...', I began angrily, then halted in disbelief.   So perfectly was Holmes' observation in accord with my own thoughts that at first I wondered whether I had spoken aloud. But such is not my habit.   'Holmes', I cried, 'this is preposterous'.

'Not in the least, Watson', he replied, waving his pipe in deprecation.   'Perfectly elementary.   When that young man left, you looked admiringly after him.   Your eyes watered over, and your gaze turned inward.   It was evident that you recalled in him some- thing of your own lost youth. Involuntarily your hand reached for your wound, and your head drew back in pride.   You were thinking no doubt of your service to our country, and perhaps of others who had made the supreme sacrifice.   You cleared your throat as if to speak, then thought better of it; but your jaw jutted and your lips tightened in your most obstinate mode.   It was evident that you disagreed with me.   I then spoke, and you answered'.

'I am all admiration for your acumen, Holmes.   But I must insist that I think you wrong in this matter'.

Holmes gripped me by the wrist.   'My apologies, Watson. As you well know, there is no man I would sooner have beside me in a situation of danger.   I know that in our Indian wars you have carried yourself bravely; no doubt this young man has done the same. But I too have visited our eastern Empire.

You have recorded how after my escape from the Reichenbach Falls, I travelled overland, and spent two years in Tibet. I did not tell you – it was still a matter of some diplomatic delicacy – of my journey south, at the urgent representation of the Viceroy, to look into the matter of the Simla assassination. While there, I took advantage of the opportunity to study our rule of India at close quarters. In that vast land, there is not more than one British soldier to every six thousand inhabitants. It is not military force which keeps the country ours, but moral; and that can only persist as long as it is seen as such. Imagination, Watson, will ultimately rule the world; action always fails before it in the end. I will admit that our young friend has forced me to modify my theory; but there is something gravely amiss with Lestrade's. A less likely Thuggee than Desai I have yet to encounter'. And he fell into a brown study, punctuated by puffs of his pipe.

In the days that followed, Holmes left the house in various disreputable guises, returning at unseasonable hours exhausted and depressed. Late one evening he confided to me, as he gulped some brandy at the sideboard: 'I have shown young Crutchley's photograph in every evil den, every haunt of corruption in this city, Watson; and all to no avail. It is as if he had vanished from the face of the earth'. As time passed, his equanimity forsook him, and his temper grew progressively shorter. I was familiar with the symptoms: the broken sleep, the endless succession of foul-smelling pipes, the snatches on the violin ranging from tenderness to agitation and, as often as not, abruptly broken off, the savage sarcasm of his replies to the most conventional greetings. I determined to take myself out of the house, and spend a day at my club, where among the leather-coated chairs and serene atmosphere I could settle into my *Times* in quiet. But here I found myself no less disturbed. I read of the rantings of the Kaiser at Berlin, of the boasts of his country's military and naval might, supported by a science and an industry which England could scarcely hope to equal, and returned home with a chill about the heart that the warmth of the late afternoon did little to dissipate.

As I approached our lodgings in Baker Street, a haunting tune echoed out of the open window. It was Holmes on his violin, in a melody that was a favourite of my own. It dipped and soared, hovered and fluttered, in what seemed to me a sound of good omen. But as I entered the hallway, I heard the instrument modulate into a series of savage chromatic scales, ascending and descending in dizzying sequence, and grating on the ear. In these frenzied assaults, mounting in intensity, I heard the nervous frustration that had dogged Holmes' recent days. As soon as he saw me enter, he laid down his bow. 'Pray continue', I besought him. 'Not what you were at just now; but I should love to hear the last tune again'.

'Tune? What tune? I have not the faintest idea what I was playing. I have sat here with my violin all afternoon, allowing my mind to roam at random, in the hope that it would somehow settle on the truth. Have you never felt that some realisation was just beyond your reach, buried within your mind but inaccessible, and that if only you could find the password, it would reveal itself to you of its own accord? So it has been with me today. There is some fact, some anecdote, some fragment of memory that holds the key to this mystery, and which somehow I seem to know or have known. But always it eludes me, and I seem only to go round in a maze. I am ready to desist for the day, but will gladly offer you an encore. I suspect that I have not been very companionable of late. What was the tune?'

'One of the loveliest of our English melodies, Holmes: "On Wings of Song"'.

'Lovely indeed, Watson, but scarcely English'.

'No? I was assured that it was written by the Poet Laureate, and set to music at the express desire of the Queen'.

'The music is indeed the work of the Queen's composer, Watson. But I fear we must renounce any claim to the good Mendelssohn. And the words are a translation from the work of another German, Heine. Indeed, had you known them, you might, applying my methods, have deduced while still standing in the street what question it was that agitated my mind'.

'You speak in riddles, Holmes'.

'No doubt. And yet it is very simple. The song is a song of flight, of the desire to carry the beloved to a land where – how does the English go? – "Where by the moonlit meadows, the silver fountains play"'.

'"Silvery"', I corrected.

'In the original, however', he went on, ignoring the interruption, 'the geographical reference is exact: *fort nach den Fluren des Ganges* – to the meadows of the Ganges. Now do you see? The German, Watson, is far more precise'.

'I do not wonder', I said with some warmth, stung by Holmes' exposure of my ignorance, and heated by what I had been reading. 'I have for some time held that the greatest threat to our empire lies in the mechanical cast of the Teuton mind. The Prussian worship of blood and iron will yet lead us into some terrible war'.

'Perhaps, Watson. I have only too much reason to believe that you are right. But in this instance, I am afraid, you are off the mark. The lyricist, no less than the composer, was of Jewish extraction. Indeed, I have often thought that, in terms of race-memory, the song might well be regarded as a hymn to the ancestral orient, a cry of longing to return...'

Here an extraordinary change came over Holmes. He stopped in mid-sentence with a choking cry, his thin face chalk-white with excitement, then smote his forehead with his palm. 'Of course! How could I have missed it? How could I?'

'Missed what?'

'The vital clue', he answered. 'You have placed it in my hands. But for you, Watson, I might never have grasped it. A thousand apologies, my dear fellow, if ever I have seemed to slight you. Now if only...' He raced over to his desk, extracted Crutchley's photograph from a drawer, thrust it into his pocket, and, taking the stairs in a series of bounds, was gone.

He returned late that night. When I saw him next morning, all he would say was: 'It has been as I expected. Now we wait, Watson'. On the following day, a telegram arrived, which he tore open impatiently. A look of dismay passed over his face, and he said gravely: 'There is only one chance more'. Standing over the table, he scribbled a reply, which he handed to the telegraph boy. I waited in trepidation, while another day passed. A second telegram was delivered; and Holmes' face grew grim. 'I very much fear, Watson', he said, 'that we shall never meet Lieutenant Crutchley'. Gathering up the messages, he hailed a cab and drove away. This time he returned in company. With him there stepped into our sitting-room the Indian, Desai, in far more cheerful spirits than when I had seen him last. 'Mr. Holmes has told me, Dr. Watson, of the part you have played in securing my release', he smiled softly, clasping my hands.

'Your release?', I repeated, uncomprehending.

'Certainly, Watson', said Holmes. 'Even Lestrade could hardly continue to hold him for the murder of a man who, since his arrest, has been seen alive'.

'Alive?' I gasped, still more baffled than before.

'Yes. The train of thought you started in me, Watson, led me to the conclusion that Jason Crutchley had returned to India'.

'But the ports', I objected. 'The passenger lists...'

'I was convinced', said Holmes, 'for reasons that will shortly be obvious to you, that he did not wish to be followed. I therefore brought his photograph to the shipping offices, where I enquired about last-minute bookings. I found myself in luck at the third: there I saw the name of one Josiah Crowley. It was a transparent alias: I produced the photograph, and the clerk recognised it'.

'I then sent off two telegrams. The first was to Bombay, where his ship was due to dock that very day. Back came word, however, that favourable winds had brought it in earlier, and that its passengers had already dispersed. My second message was to police headquarters at Benares, urgently requesting that a watch be kept for young Crutchley at the railway station, that some fellow-officers be sent to identify him, and that he be detained on any pretext. They were waiting when he came in; but as soon as he saw them, he backed away, and fought his way through the crowd like a tiger – their description, Watson. In a city such as Benares, it was impossible to trace him'.

'As to why he had gone back there, let me ask you to recall to mind the tune which you heard me play upon the violin. It is, as I observed, a song both of desire and of return, and this recalled to me a story I had heard in the course of my travels through India, but which, my sensations there being so crowded and intense, had slipped to some deeper level of the mind. Once recalled, it formed the final piece of the puzzle, the part that made sense of all the rest. What I now had, however, was mere surmise; what I needed was confirmation. And that this gentleman here has provided'.

The Indian bowed. 'You are absolutely correct, Mr. Holmes'.

Holmes nodded and went on. 'The tale of the treasure, in essence, was true. But what struck me most about those notes from young Crutchley was, not their content, but their postmark. They had been sent, as Hopkirk had led us to expect, from Benares. Now Benares is the sacred city of the Hindoos. The Moghuls, however, were Muslim. It seemed likely that the emperor's servants were Hindoo, which would explain their flight to that city. But why should they construct what is after all an Islamic monument there? That is what Shah Jahan's son did, and it is still an object of abhorrence to the Hindoos'.

'It was your observation that enlightened me, Watson. On my way from Benares to Bombay, I passed through Agra; and I shall never forget the sight I had there of the Taj Mahal. However often one sees it pictured, it takes the breath away. You enter through a gate of red sandstone, from which it is invisible, then turn into another, from the shadows of which its white marble form first reveals itself. I saw it on a winter morning, when a faint mist hung about the place, rising from the river behind. The pearl or teardrop shape of its dome, pointed up by the surrounding minarets, is set on an octagon whose alcoves were shadowed blue in the early light. It was as if it had been composed of sky and clouds: as if it were, in every sense of the word, ethereal. And all this was created in the name of love: it was desire itself made palpable'.

'The emperor's servants will have been intimately acquainted with his feelings. To them it must have seemed matter for wonder that a man who had lost an empire should sit dreaming over a lovesong in stone – for that, in effect, is what it is. In their sympathy with his wishes, and their determination to fulfil them, I suspected that they saw him in terms of some Hindoo archetype, and I thought that I knew what it was. Mr. Desai, here, has confirmed it'. Holmes motioned to him with a lift of the eyebrow.

'The goddess Kali', the Indian began, 'is known to Europeans largely for her cruelty. It is she who is patron of the Thuggees, who murder and steal from travellers, as they believe in her honour and by her licence. But more fundamentally she is nature in all its aspects, in its glory as in its terror. She rules over desire as well as death; and the besotted Shah Jahan might well seem to his servants to be, unwittingly, her devotee. When, then, they built the temple known as the Black Taj, they did so as a shrine to the goddess, and surrounded it with her rites. It was a ritual of terror, cloaked in a secrecy whose violation was punishable by death. That is why its existence has remained a rumour, and its location a mystery'.

'How then', I queried, 'did Jason Crutchley discover it?'

'For that I was responsible, Dr. Watson', returned Desai. 'I was not in fact his servant; but when an Indian travels with an Englishman, people assume that such is the case, and it seemed better not to upset that preconception. I am in fact a man of some wealth, a merchant in the silks for which Benares is famous. The legend which credits us with gauzes of such delicacy that they wear out in a single night is not altogether without foundation. Now it so happens that those who spin the thread are Hindoo, while those who weave it are Muslims. Disagreements, therefore, over trade not infrequently develop into the most acrimonious religious disputes. It was in the course of one of these, when four Muslims had me at knife-point in the corner of a Benares courtyard, that Lieutenant Crutchley came by, evidently exploring the city. When he saw what was happening, he drew his sword, and soon put them to flight. In my gratitude I offered to fulfil any request he might make, and which it was in my power to grant. Immediately he asked my help in finding the treasure of the Black Taj. He wished only to view it, he assured me – some wager he had entered into – and had no further designs upon it. I was terrified: I knew something of the peril in which he was placing himself; but I had given my word.

Through my connections in the city, I was able to secure an introduction for him to some who would lead him to the temple; but before he left me, I secured in turn an engagement from him. I had heard of men who had become deranged after viewing it, so that they wished to make away with themselves; I elicited therefore a promise that, should he survive the ordeal – for ordeal I knew it to be – he would place himself in my hands. He accepted, and I led him to the Golden Temple, a well-known landmark of Benares, where he was to be met by his guides'.

'This ordeal', I interrupted. 'In what did it consist?'

The other two glanced at each other, then looked away. Holmes took up the narrative.

'Benares is a labyrinth, Watson: a bewildering web of courts and alleyways, of mosques and temples, of stalls that barely contain their owners and the palaces of maharajahs. Crutchley was met at the Golden Temple and taken into the shadows of this maze. At some point he turned into a courtyard, and was taken through one of its doors. The heart of the building he then entered reproduces, under ground, the marble vault of the Taj Mahal, with the difference that its marble is black. It is adorned in all the richness of the most luxuriant Indian taste. And here, in the centre, at the spot where the tomb stands in the original, lay a bed. Upon it there waited the loveliest woman that Crutchley had ever seen. She was dressed, one must presume, in the celebrated silks of the city – that is to say, virtually unclothed'.

'My dear Holmes!'

'It could not be otherwise, Watson. She was more than the priestess of the temple. At that moment, and in that setting, she was its goddess'.

'A living idol!'

'Yes, Watson; and more. It is here that the story which has filtered to the outside world has become distorted – much like that of Crutchley's ancestor in the eighteenth century. That there was originally a hoard containing actual jewels we know. But this has become conflated with the purpose to which it was put. The young priestess was the centre of the subsequent cult. She was its innermost secret, the jewel in its crown. *She* was the treasure of the Black Taj. And that treasure was not placed in its subterranean setting merely to be viewed. In the hours that followed, young Crutchley learned what peril it was to the touch. That exquisite young woman became radiant for him, facet by facet, as she took him through a tableau of lovemaking such as he never could have imagined'.

All my civilised feelings rose in revolt. 'What a filthy practice!' Why, it is no better than the vilest prostitution!'

'On the contrary: it is a religious rite. I have seen, in India, a temple cut from the rock: chiselled out of the hillside, with the greatest deliberation, over the space of two hundred years. And at its core, in its innermost chamber, is represented the process of generation. The building is a masterpiece of the sculptor's art: unified, coherent, carried on over several lifetimes. The impulse which could sustain such a creation was clearly not the illustration of any biological process, still less the satisfaction of any pornographic urge; it was the sense that life, and its sources, are sacred. It is the same with this young woman. From earliest childhood, she has been dedicated to the goddess. In the view of her society, it is a high and noble calling'.

My brain was in a whirl. At one stroke the man opposite me, whom I looked upon as
mentor and friend, had with the studied calm of a pathologist stripped away every mask, every reticence, that distinguishes the civilised individual from the savage. That Holmes should say such things at all was shocking; but that he should do so in a tone suggesting that moral evil and moral good were mere local conventions was appalling. I grasped at what seemed

to me the one fixed point in this whirlpool of infamy. 'But what of the young man? What of his feelings, his beliefs, his...*standards?*'

'Oh, his standards', said Holmes, imperturbably, stuffing his pipe. 'These will have had nothing to do with it. He had given his word to go through with the matter, and we know what that word meant to him. Besides, he had, and had been forewarned that he had, no alternative: had he attempted to turn back, he would have been ruthlessly struck down'. He paused. 'But it is what happened afterwards that is significant. Upon awakening, he will have found himself alone, and fully clothed. The chamber will have been stripped. He will have seen only a vault of black marble, with the look and the feel of a tomb. The door, and those which followed it, will have opened to his touch, but, one by one, closed immovably behind him. Coming out again into the noises of the street, he will have been tempted to believe that what he recalled was no more than a dream. But it was here that his ordeal began'.

'Ordeal?' I echoed, feeling myself very stupid. 'Why do you speak of it as an ordeal?'

Holmes leaned forward intently, his smoking pipe held to one side. 'However far he might wander from that chamber, Watson, he never could leave it behind. The memory of the night that had passed would take hold of his being like an unassuageable fever, gathering in intensity until it reached the force of an obsession'.

'Do you mean to tell me', I exclaimed, 'that he fell in love in a single night?'

'I should not describe it as love, Watson. The person he loved was that admirable young woman whom we have met. No, this was something far more ancient, far less amenable to the higher powers. It is something that our society has done its utmost to bury; yet it bursts forth from the underworld, even here, like the eruption that overwhelmed the gardens and the painted villas of Pompeii. If you doubt me, only look at our newspapers. Young Crutchley was infatuated, besotted, enmeshed, as was intended, in a web of instinct which, because our civilisation has denied it, he was left without weapons to fight. Add to this his ardent nature, his involvement from childhood in historical romance, and the sense of dark mystery which surrounded the rite, and you will begin to understand the despair from which he besought his lover to save him'.

'It was diabolical', I gasped. 'A fiendish trap!'

'You know now', said Holmes, 'what Mr. Desai meant when he said they might as well hang him as demand the details. Knowledge of such a ritual would lead to a most dangerous state of feeling in this country: there would undoubtedly be a clamour for its suppression. And this in turn, should the Hindoos believe that one of their sanctuaries had been violated, could lead to a conflagration in India beside which the Mutiny would look pale. No, it was undoubtedly the highest wisdom in him to hold his peace'.

'As to fiendishness, Dr. Watson', interposed Desai, 'while the goddess is very powerful, she appears in many forms. The lieutenant had told me of the young woman who waited for him; and I brought him back to her as his only hope. He travelled in a state of near-insensibility, in which I kept him with the help of a plentiful supply of morphine. When his meeting with the lady went badly, I pleaded with him to persist. It is what we argued about at the station. But he was adamant on return; and in this city of yours, which is unfamiliar to me, he easily escaped. By the time I traced him, his ship had already sailed. It was then that I was apprehended by Inspector Lestrade'.

'Crutchley's tragedy', ccontinued Holmes, 'lay in the nature of his dilemma. To the torture of his obsession was added the torment of infidelity to the person he loved. I too

35

believe that young woman could have saved him; but in order to do so, she would have to have been told the truth. And, in Crutchley's eyes, she was the last person who could be told. To the chivalrous and idealistic element in his nature, she was still the conventional English girl he had left behind. He had no way of knowing of the mature and self-possessed woman she had become'.

'You speak of tragedy', I said, 'of an only hope, of a failure to be saved. What, then, has become of him?'

A deathly silence greeted this enquiry. At length Holmes knocked the ashes from his pipe and laid it down. His voice, when he spoke, was solemn.

'Once Crutchley escaped into Benares, word would swiftly be carried to the temple of the Black Taj. Sooner or later he would be accosted, and led back. No force would be exercised; none would be needed. The lieutenant would walk to his fate with the springing step of a lover returning to his beloved'.

'His fate?'

'Yes, Dr. Watson', said the Indian. 'The young woman of the temple is a priestess and, if I may say so, pure. She exists in a space outside society. She lives for one purpose, and one only: to glorify the goddess. When she has succeeded in doing this – when she has induced a young man to return to her – she has made of him a sacrifice. His second night with her would be identical with the first: save that this would be a marriage with death. Again she would weave her fascinations; again she would hold him enthralled. This time, however, there would be no awakening. When at last, emptied of passion, he would fall into a trance-like sleep, the priestess would strangle him with a silken cord. He would feel nothing. The body would be treated with all reverence, as befitted a voluntary sacrifice. Dressed in white robes, surrounded with the perfume of flowers, it would be carried to the riverside to be burnt. Nobody would notice: one body more or less in Benares would excite no remark'.

A great heaviness came over me, as I thought of that young life snuffed out before its time. 'You speak of his sacrifice as voluntary', I said. 'Is it not rather a taking advantage of human weakness? Why, he had no prospect of escape!'

'Good old Watson', said Holmes, 'always one for fair play'. His words were jocular, but their tone was sombre. 'I have said that his society left him without weapons; I have not said that none existed. There are arts by which young Crutchley, had he been in a position to avail of them, might have walked out of that chamber a free man. In my time amongst the Tibetans, I came to know of a curious practice amongst certain of their secret orders. It resembles that of which you have heard, but to entirely different effect. It is a participation in intercourse without the attainment of release. It is an ascesis of the most rigorous kind: the most powerful of all human impulses is subjected to higher control. Animal nature is transcended, in a triumph of the will'.

I felt utterly revolted. 'You speak as if you admired it!'

Holmes shrugged. 'Everything you know of me, Watson, should have led you to that conclusion. It is the victory of mind over matter. It is simply another manifestation of those practices of the yogin in which I gained some competence. There were times, in fact, when I was tempted to remain at the verge of my Himalayan cave, where the air was piercing and the sun blinding, the world below blotted out for me by clouds. But it was ultimately borne in upon me that a task awaited me in that world: a task I could not refuse, since it was something I alone could accomplish. It was that realisation, and that only, which induced me to return. Yet here, too, is the same reality. Mind over matter, Watson: it is the veritable history of the species, and its only avenue of advance. And on that road I am not convinced we are in the lead'.

The silence that followed was broken by Desai's rising from his chair, placing his hands before his face, and inclining his head to Holmes, who returned the gesture. The Indian repeated it to me; but I was too stunned to move. It was only after his soft footsteps had died away, and the door shut quietly behind him, that I found my voice again.

'What of this unhappy young man's family?' I asked. 'How are we to inform them?'

'I think, Watson, it will put an end to their curiosity if we give them to understand that he had formed a connection with a native. The father is in a state of near-insensibility; while the mother, it seems to me, is a person in whom social ambition has replaced every other emotion. She is unlikely to blazon what she will undoubtedly consider the family's disgrace. Lestrade, likewise, for all his doggedness, knows how to let go where his career is concerned. The young woman, however, must be told the truth. She is worthy of it; she has the spirit to face and to overcome it; and I shall be extremely surprised if we do not hear more of her in the future.

'But where you speak of unhappiness, Watson, I cannot agree. Nothing is more persistent, in the literature of the ages, than the ubiquity of desire. The greatest works of art have been fashioned to celebrate it; the most ghastly crimes committed to satisfy it. I have no doubt that the young man went to his death perfectly content with the exchange: that he felt himself never to have lived so completely as when he found himself once again on that threshold, and in the presence of the woman who obsessed him. He would, I suspect, have sacrificed himself a hundred times for that moment. And in a sense one might envy him. How much happier he was, Watson, knowing what he wished for and what he was willing to give for it, than we, who scarcely know what we want; or if we do, live unsatisfied, its realisation out of our grasp; or having grasped it, live to see the hollowness of our dreams'.

My unease at his words must have shown; for he went on: 'No, you need no longer be concerned for me, Watson. The spell of my lethargy has been broken. Besides, the summer is over: I feel a touch of autumn in the air. Pray be good enough to hand me my violin'.

TWO

THE LAST PRE-
RAPHAELITE

'I shall be extremely surprised if we do not hear more of her in the future', was the final judgement of Sherlock Holmes on the unusual young woman we met in the course of the adventure I have titled 'The Treasure of the Black Taj'. However, when we did advert again to Miss Anna Ponderby, it was not in such fashion as our previous encounter had led us to expect.

It was in autumn, after a night of equinoctial gales had lashed the house and set the windows rattling, that I was awoken early one morning by a hammering and pounding outside. As I returned to consciousness, I at first thought it a continuation of the storm; but I gradually realised that the wind had dropped, and that this was a drumming on the hall door. As I crawled from bed to throw on my dressing-gown, the sound ceased as abruptly as it had begun; and when I reached the bottom of the stairs, I saw through the open door the figure of Holmes stooped over the prone body of a woman in a dark hooded cloak, lying motionless upon the steps. 'Here, Watson – help!' he called; and after we had carried her upstairs, and laid her on the sofa, I forced a few drops of brandy between her lips.

She coughed and sat upright; and, as she did so, her cloak parted, revealing fresh bloodstains on the hem of the white dress beneath. 'Why, you have been hurt!' I cried.

'Not I, Dr. Watson', the young woman said in an exhausted voice. 'It is Sir Leoline. He has been...'

Until that moment I had not recognised, in the strained and suffering features, in their frame of luxuriant hair, now lank and tangled, the radiant young woman we had known.

'Yes, Watson', said Holmes, 'it is she'; and soothingly turned back to our visitor. 'What of Sir Leoline? What has befallen him?'

'He is dead, Mr. Holmes', she replied. 'He was murdered last night'. A look of recollection and horror passed across her face. 'And if I am not mistaken, the police will shortly be on my track, to charge me with the crime'.

Holmes placed the glass in her hands. 'Drink a little more of this', he said firmly, 'and then tell us, in sequence, what has happened'. She took a sip, laid the glass decisively on the floor, and began: 'You recall our last meeting?' We nodded.

It had been early in the spring of the same year, and bright splashes of leaf had begun to appear against the black of the tree-trunks in London's squares, when Miss Anna Ponderby called upon us in our lodgings at Baker Street. On the young woman's face were still traces of the earlier tragedy she had endured; but the shadows served only to give depth and gravity to the serene beauty of her features. At the same time, there was a sense of lightness in her movements which, like those signs of spring in the city around us, made it clear that her recovery was under way. Holmes, through a grateful client, had been able to place her with a journal devoted to society and the arts; and after some months in this position she had called to thank him in person.

'How good of you to visit us, Miss Ponderby', said Holmes.

'Potter, Mr. Holmes: I write under the name of Anna Potter. It sounds more practical, don't you think? I felt, also, that it would reduce the likelihood that anything I wrote would be linked to my father, and affect his career in the Church. Though on that score, as it happens, I need not have troubled myself'.

Holmes glanced at her quizzically.

'My father is no longer rector of Crutchley, Mr. Holmes. Soon after your visit, Lady Crutchley wrote a ringing denunciation to his bishop, charging him with atheism. The real cause of her animosity appears to have been that he offered support to a group of strikers at her brother's brewery. The theological opinions of a Lady Crutchley, however well-connected, are not normally taken very seriously; but in this case she gave a handle to his enemies in the Church, and he thought it more prudent to resign his benefice than submit to a long and humiliating investigation. Sir Joseph Crutchley, who in his intervals of lucidity had shown himself a good and kind friend, lived just long enough to will my father the temple on the cliff above his house. Like so many of the decorative "follies" of that age, it was designed as a dwelling: two rooms only, but ample for his needs. He has written to me that with his improved vista, and unbounded leisure, he at last feels free to write as he pleases. As do I, Mr. Holmes. Roger has been a wonderful employer: all understanding and encouragement'.

'Oh, it is Roger now, is it?', smiled Holmes.

'Yes', the young woman answered briskly. 'Once again I see that I can hold no secrets from you. He is also a dear friend. For a time, I thought he might become something more. Once or twice, indeed, I felt he was about to express feelings similar to those which I had begun to have for him; but on each occasion he halted on the brink of speech, retreating into silence. When I in turn have spoken to him with more warmth of feeling than I had intended, he has responded only with a thin, wan smile. There is, I feel, some threshold in him, which he seems to forbid one to cross. I expect that the death of his wife, coming in the terrible way it did, has left him in an acute state of distress, and perhaps distrust of our sex'.

Roger Clavinger's wife had died of poisoning, under circumstances which led to his being arrested for her murder. Holmes, however, through a meticulous examination of the evidence, had established that the woman's death was suicide, engineered, in a fit of derangement, to cast suspicion upon her husband. The late Mrs. Clavinger had been of a withdrawn and pathologically jealous nature, and the fact that her husband's work brought him into contact with more vivacious women, of a modern stamp, had led her to believe that he was on intimate terms with at least one of them: a charge without foundation.

'I have now', Miss Potter went on, 'resigned myself to the fact that our relations are likely to remain those of employer and employee; but of these I could hardly ask more. He has given me absolute freedom of expression. My first assignment was to investigate the working conditions of secretaries to large institutions – such a life as I myself might have lived, had it not been for you, Mr. Holmes. As you may have read' – here I nodded – 'I found these places, in the main, no better than our factories; and I am grateful to you and to him for having saved me from what, in effect, would have been the life of a galley-slave'.

Holmes inclined his head urbanely. 'And now', Miss Potter went on, with an animated air, 'to still better news. Roger – Mr. Clavinger's – next suggestion was that I portray the lives of artists' models. This brings together two themes which intrigue me: that of the social question, and that of art. I accepted the assignment eagerly, and have already filled two notebooks with material: the models' social background, their working conditions, their personal lives, and their understanding of the process of which they are part. These I have met at the major academies; and through the head of one of them I have received an introduction to Sir Leoline Knightleigh'.

'The great historical painter?', I asked.

'The historical painter, yes, Dr. Watson', she replied, 'though as to his actual greatness the critics are in some dispute. For some, he has recreated the rarefied, otherworldly beauty of the medieval imagination; while others have dismissed him, brutally, as mechanical in execution and insipid in effect. But whichever of these opinions one may incline to, it is certain that he is the last Pre-Raphaelite. Beginning as their model, he went on, some would say, to become their heir. At any rate, as the younger contemporary of Ruskin and Morris, of Rossetti and Burne-Jones, he is associated with much that is noble and beautiful in our art. For myself, he is at any rate a living link with history'.

This was the enterprising young woman, all aquiver with excitement, whom we had just discovered in a crumpled heap on our threshold. But from a face still ghastly with shock and dread, her eyes shone as she recollected her first meeting with the celebrated painter.

'I cannot describe to you how my heart pounded as I lifted the heavy iron knocker on his door. It is a great house in the medieval style – a castle, really – set in its own woods in the heart of Epping Forest. I stepped under a portcullis, and my footsteps echoed on a drawbridge as I crossed the shadowed moat. As the door creaked open, I found myself dazzled. An elaborate stained-glass window stood at the end of a lofty hall; and the morning sun, shining through it, filled the space with a glory of multicoloured beams, spilling over the tiled floor, and making the air itself jewelled and almost tangible. I felt as if I had strayed into some solemn and sacred romance.

'An elderly housekeeper informed me that Sir Leoline was with some clients, but that she expected him to finish presently. As she hobbled away, leaving me to sit on a carved wooden stool, I felt like a novice in some convent of long ago. I suspect I had come to believe myself so when, after what cannot have been more than fifteen minutes, Sir Leoline emerged from a doorway down the hall. With him was an older, expensively-dressed couple, with accents of the North; and my reverie faded as I heard them discuss financial arrangements in thoroughly contemporary fashion. It seemed that a very large sum of money was being spoken of. After he had seen off his clients with great suavity, Sir Leoline turned in my direction. He is – was – a tall man, of somewhat portly figure, but he moved with a soft, padded walk. His pointed beard gave him a tinge of melancholy, the more so as it had now turned to grey. He regarded me with an expression of the utmost graciousness, that as he came closer changed to one of astonishment.

'Guenevere!', he exclaimed.

'I am afraid there is some mistake', I stammered. 'My name is Potter – Anna Potter'.

'But of course – of course', he said soothingly, as he laid a hand upon my arm. 'You must forgive me, my dear young lady. I live so much within my *métier* that I have come to see all things in its light. I am now engaged on an Arthurian painting, which will require a Queen Guenevere. It seems that fortune has just propelled her in my direction'.

'I was speechless with excitement, Mr. Holmes, and it did not occur to me for a moment to refuse. To understand Sir Leoline's world by becoming part of it – to move within his vision of noble knights and ladies – was a dream I had not dared to indulge. And what better way to acquaint myself with the life of models than to live it myself? Though I little thought where that experience would lead me'. The young woman shuddered, and pulled her cloak more closely around her shoulders. She took another sip from the glass. Conflicting emotions seemed to chase one another over her face. 'There is something I do not know how to say, Mr. Holmes'.

45

'Will it help', asked Holmes quietly, 'if I suggest that all was not as it seemed with Sir Leoline?'

The young woman immediately looked relieved. 'Concerning a figure of such accepted probity, I found it difficult to express my own – very different – experience. I had little hope of being credited'.

'You need have no such fear with us, Miss Potter', said Holmes firmly. 'We both trust you absolutely'. I nodded my agreement. 'Besides, there have been rumours afloat concerning Sir Leoline for quite some time. They began when, as a boy, he served as model to an older painter. Given the older man's reputation, it was perhaps natural that such rumours should arise. But there have since been whisperings concerning Sir Leoline in his own right. Nothing has ever been proved, however, and they have not stood in the way of his acceptance by society. And now I must ask you to tell us exactly what it was that happened, however painful this may be to you'.

The young woman met my friend's eyes candidly. 'I will tell you everything, Mr. Holmes.

'Sir Leoline took me into the room which he had just vacated, and sat me at a long, dark, heavily-carved refectory table. Everything else there matched it: the walls were panelled in the same sombre hue, the furniture massive, elaborate and shadowy. The room ran to the back of the house, the right-hand wall broken into by five pointed windows with armorial glass, through which the sun was beginning to glitter. On the left, and built into the wall, was a series of bookcases with pointed arches, housing an impressive library of the Middle Ages. In the centre of the wall was a fireplace, from which a bright coal fire had taken the edge off the morning's chill; above this was a portrait of a helmeted face, which I immediately recognised as a younger Sir Leoline. Smiling as he intercepted my gaze, he reached towards a volume on one of the shelves titled *The Company of the Round Table*. As he pulled it towards him, a cabinet was disclosed, in which were a set of Venetian glasses and decanters, from which he offered me some excellent sherry. 'To Arthur and Guenevere', he said. Then, having carefully shut the decanter back in its hiding-place, he invited me to carry my glass to the room across the hall, which, as it faced north, was his studio. It was identical to the room we had left – the five pointed windows on one side, the fireplace on the other – except that the walls had been painted white, and the windows were of frosted glass, so that, left to itself, it would have suggested a classroom, or a village hall. But it resembled nothing so much as the property-room of some great theatre. Painted sets, costumes, weapons and ornaments, were scattered everywhere, whilst over all hung a pungent odour of linseed oil. In a cleared space in the middle were five wooden panels, three of which had already been painted. The central panel showed a glowing chalice, its rays reaching into every corner of a vast Gothic room: with a thrill, I recognised it as the hall I had just passed through. The two outermost panels had also been completed; and here, too, I received a shock of recognition. Each showed a kneeling figure, in pilgrim's dress, with faces dazzled by the light: they were the clients I had just seen with Sir Leoline'.

'A common practice of the Middle Ages', Holmes observed. 'The donors were frequently memorialised in their donation'.

'Sir Leoline then went on to explain the nature of his commission. His clients, as I had guessed, were from the North, where they had prospered considerably in the steel industry. Growing older, and being childless, they wished to be remembered in their native city for something more than the prosperity they had brought to it. Accordingly, having funded the restoration of its oldest church – a genuine masterpiece of the Middle Ages – they planned to adorn it with a massive altarpiece, to replace the celebrated Flemish work destroyed at the Reformation. Its theme – the adoration of the Grail – had, with its overtones of the Roman Mass, been such, Sir Leoline pointed out, as to attract the immediate rage of the Reformers.

'He then did something very strange. In front of the panels, on easels, there stood studies for the portraits of the donors. To my unutterable surprise, Sir Leoline took, first one, then the other, and cast them into the fireplace, where they were rapidly consumed by the flames. I cried out in horror. Each was a work of art in itself; each might have hung with dignity on the walls of some distinguished gallery. But he brushed aside my protests, explaining to me that between painter and sitter there was a confidence as inviolable, in its way, as existed between physician and patient. He had been engaged for an historical painting, and that he would provide. To derive any further profit, personal or financial, from the transaction, was in his view a breach of this unwritten contract.

'I was impressed, Mr. Holmes, by this evidence of the scrupulosity of his conscience. That is why I was perhaps less taken aback than I might have been when he asked me to pose for him in the nude'.

'The cad!', I exclaimed, beside myself.

'It was not so that he then appeared to me, Dr. Watson', the young woman replied. 'In fact, his proposal seemed eminently reasonable. He explained that he had to draw from the nude in order to attain a sense of the body when clothed; and this seemed to me to accord with his general working methods – his meticulous care over detail. As I had, moreover, attended some life classes in the course of my investigations, the idea was not novel to me. What brushed away any lingering hesitation, however, was pride: pride in my new-found career as a modern woman. To have refused, out of traditional notions of female modesty, would have seemed to me both philistine and unprofessional. I therefore accepted immediately.

'No sooner had I done so than I received another surprise. Remarking that there was no time like the present, he led me back into the hall. Taking a key from his waistcoat pocket, he unlocked a heavy door in the thickness of one of the columns. A cold draught came up from it, and I had to repress a shudder; but after I had followed him down a circular stair into darkness, I emerged, as it seemed, in another world.

'The room we stood in opened onto a courtyard in which a small but exquisite garden had been planted. An octagonal kiosk, flanked by a pair of fountains, stood in the centre. Behind were almond-trees, just then bursting into blossom, and behind these again a hedge of dark cypress. In front, beds of flowers alternated with cages in which colourful birds sang, their calls counterpointed by the soft splash of the water. The whole was surrounded by a high wall from which no window looked out. Enclosed as it was, the sunken court trapped the sun's heat, and had already given to the spring morning an unseasonal infusion of warmth.

'When I turned within, I was no less surprised. Here was a large room, built in the Saracenic or Moorish style, in which columns rose into horseshoe arches to support the ceiling. An ingenious system of indirect lighting bathed it in an even glow, by means of which I could see, on the facing wall, an exquisite tile-painting of the garden. I received yet another surprise when he informed me that it was the garden that was the copy, and the painting the original. It was genuine medieval work, he assured me, that had been brought from a palace in Damascus; and the entire room had been decorated to match, with embroidered silks, luxurious divans and mounds of cushions. Everything conduced to sensuality and repose; a more complete contrast with the ascetic gloom of the floor above it would be impossible to imagine.

'Sir Leoline, it appears, had anticipated the uneasiness which the place aroused in me. To tell you the truth, Mr. Holmes, it resembled nothing so much as a harem. But its function, as he explained to me, was quite practical. As he had become known for his medieval studies, he had sometimes received commissions for topics connected with the Crusades. After he had created a setting for these, he had discovered that it worked upon the spirits of his models, causing them to relax, and had come to use it for all of his studies in the nude.

'I was disarmed by his frankness, and went to disrobe. A small ante-room had been provided for the purpose. He informed me that his back would remain turned until I declared myself ready; and this I very soon did. The system of lighting was such that there was never any glare in the room. Again, a fire burned in the open hearth, rare incenses perfumed the air; and the divans and cushions were as luxurious to the touch as to the eye. One was, indeed, insensibly enervated; but this did not induce in me any feeling of alarm. Sir Leoline never came forward beyond his easel; nor did I ever observe what it held. Soon my taking off my clothes, and posing naked for him, seemed utterly natural. The only question that arose in my mind, and gave rise to some slight feeling of uneasiness, concerned some of the postures he requested me to adopt. These appeared to me unnecessary for his purpose; but as he always seemed to sense any hesitation on my part, he assured me that what he sought was a three-dimensional sense of the body so that, when he came to paint me in my clothes, he could proceed, as he put it, by instinct. He invariably offered to discontinue any procedure that caused me the least discomfort; and I, no less invariably, surrendered to what I thought his artistic purpose'.

'And in all this time, he never made any advances to you?' queried Holmes.

'Never, Mr. Holmes. Not even when I had begun to wish he would. As I have said to you, I had given up hope of Roger; and this man, in spite of the difference of age between us, gradually became invested for me with an aura of romance. Part of it, I am sure, was the place. Sometimes, I sat for him through the afternoon; and when I walked back through the hall, into which the lancets around the doorway filtered the setting sun, and passed through the imposing shadow of the entrance-gate, with its avenue of cypress be- yond, I felt as if the world itself, and not only a single day, were coming to an end. And when my session was fixed for the morning, the sun bursting from the east through that magnificent window gave me a sense of a new beginning, not alone to my life but to my spirit. My task came to seem to me something solemn, something consecrated.

'To pass from here to the room below gave me a deepening sense of intimacy, made still more powerful by its contrast with the building within which it is hidden. I see now that my first impression was right: that Moorish chamber *is* a harem, its sensuality enhanced by the convent-like quality of the Gothic above. It was our sanctum: for I had begun to think of it as ours. We were never disturbed. Sometimes I heard the echo of the servants' voices over the wall of the garden outside; but I never saw them. Sir Leoline told me that they boarded in the village. His concentration was precious to him, and he paid them well to do their work and leave. Meals were served at regular hours, announced by the tinkling of a small bell, and accompanied with fine wines, which he poured for me with the utmost courtesy. I sank gradually into this life of luxury, and I suppose had become corrupted by it, to judge by... But I had best keep to the sequence of my story.

'As time went on, we came to know each other quite intimately. My misgivings had long vanished; and I found Sir Leoline extraordinarily candid. He told me of the struggles of his early life, of his poverty-stricken childhood in East London, of his being noticed, as he begged on the street, by one of the great artists of the day, of his growing interest in the techniques of the painters for whom he modelled, of their support for his studies, and his establishment in his own career. He admitted freely that he did not think of himself as an originator, but a follower: the supplier of a demand which had been created by his mentors. He was aware that new and less representational movements had arisen in painting; but he regarded these as being outside the scope of what had clearly become a very lucrative practice.

'This admission rather endeared him to me than the opposite. I had long sensed something unsatisfied in him, something unexpressed, which seemed one of the springs of that melancholy which made him attractive to me. Another, undoubtedly, was the sadness of his life. I learned that, like myself, he had grown up motherless: his mother having died in giving birth to him, as my own dear mother perished so soon after my own birth...'

'One moment', interposed Holmes. 'Had you previously apprised him of this fact?'

Our visitor looked thoughtful. 'Now that you mention it, Mr. Holmes', she answered slowly, 'I believe that I had. Yes, I am certain that I did. Why do you ask?'

'Only this', said Holmes grimly. 'As Watson here will tell you, I maintain an informal, but highly reliable, network of connections in what is known as the London underworld. Through this I heard, some years ago, that our painter's name was not always Knightleigh, and that one of his reasons for altering it was that his old mother, then in the best of health, was the exceedingly prosperous manager of what is known as a disorderly house'.

'I am afraid that nothing I could hear of Sir Leoline would surprise me any longer', said Miss Potter ruefully. 'I suppose that the high-born lady he had set his heart upon, and who loved him in return, but who wasted away of consumption, is no less a fiction?'

'I have not heard of any such person. When was it he told you that you had taken her place in his heart?'

'Yesterday evening', the young woman sighed. 'He said that as he had come to identify himself with the burdened and solitary Arthur, so I had become to him what he described as his "blessed Guenevere". Indeed, I had begun to feel myself so. As I was drawn to this accomplished man, for whom art had become a high and a noble calling, but who seemed to carry some sorrowful mystery within, I felt as if I had been sent to soothe the troubles of his spirit. I began to believe that I could make him whole again'.

'These feelings were intensified by what he told me yesterday afternoon. Upon my arrival, he took me into the studio off the hall, where I saw that the altarpiece had been completed. The two panels which had formerly been blank were now filled with what for me were the most striking images in the composition. To the left were a young man and an older woman, writhing away in agony from the blinding light in the centre, and on their averted faces an expression of the utmost depravity. He told me that these were Sir Mordred and Morgana le Fay. To the right were Arthur and Guenevere, their hands clasped as their features were lit up by the Grail. It was as if Guenevere caught its full radiance, through whom it seemed to reach her weak and mournful husband: as if the vision, in inspiring her, had given her the strength to reanimate him.

'I had seen a good deal of Sir Leoline's painting – I have sought out every specimen on view – and I do not think I flatter myself if I say that this was the best thing he had done. Here there was an animation that is – so his critics aver – all too often lacking in what they describe as his "wooden" and "literal" representations. Here, it seemed to me, he had caught the essence of what had passed between us – he, in some fashion that I could not fathom, lost, and I bringing him back to himself – so that all that afternoon I sat for him in a dream'.

'I do not quite understand', said Holmes. 'You say that the altarpiece was complete. Why, then, did Sir Leoline continue to work on a study for it?'

'I asked him the same question, Mr. Holmes. His reply was that the study had a momentum of its own, that it needed to be finished before he could dispose of it – the word he used was "exorcise" – dismiss it from his mind so that it would be freed for his next project. This talk of ending, of discontinuance, left me in a very depressed state of mind. I felt a pang of loss. I now realised how complete a rapport had grown between us, and that I would do a great deal to ensure that it did not come to an end. I resolved, that, at the slightest opportunity, I would be frank about my feelings for him. I was all too conscious of the fact that I had failed to do this once before.

'When we had finished – I had resumed my clothes, and he was cleaning his brushes – he informed me in a nonchalant tone that our sessions were at an end, and that there was now no further reason for us to meet. He asked about my plans for the future; I replied that I had not made any. Gathering all my courage, I told him that these meetings had become precious to me, and that nothing could take their place. He confessed that he felt as I did, and said – these words were balm to me, Mr. Holmes – that there was no absolute need to discontinue them.   We spoke for a long time together, sitting side by side.   He was about to reach out, I sensed, to touch me, when a bell tinkled far away, and there came the sound of a slamming door from the hallway.   He glanced at the timepiece on the mantel with a look of irritation.   "I had forgotten", he growled.   "An appointment with other models". It was agreed that I should return the following day; my heart leaped at the thought.

'When I came out at the top of the staircase, it was dark in the hall.   A pair of candlesticks, on wooden chests, gave a dim light at the far end.   As I made my way towards them between the columns, I walked full into a figure which had suddenly emerged from the gloom.   She stumbled and fell.   I extended my hand to help her, with a murmured apology; but as she glanced up at me by the light of the candles, the words froze on my lips.   I was looking at the face of Morgana.

'Dashing my hand away, she scrambled to her feet. "Proper little daydreamer you are", she snarled.   Then she gazed at me more closely.   "Old Leo been up to his tricks with you, my pet?"   I was startled no less at her insight than at the uncouthness of her expression.   She must have seen the shock on my face.   "Don't suppose it's got much beyond kissing, then", she said with coarse amusement, and gave a short laugh. "Here", she went on, "I'll give you an education, my fine young lady.   Come with me".   And, taking the key from the stairwell door, she gripped me by the wrist and drew me across the hall to where there was an identical door in the corresponding column opposite.   Opening it, she pointed the way down.   "In", she hissed, "if you want to know what he is. And mind that you don't make a sound".

'My first impulse was to tear myself away.   I was horrified by what she had said, or rather hinted at.   But reason reasserted itself.   If there were no truth in her innuendoes, what had I to fear? And so, with dread in my heart, I stumbled down the stairs.

'The darkness at the bottom was absolute except for a faint point of light at the end of a passageway. Walking towards it as softly as I could, I saw that it came from a small opening in the wall, not more than an inch across. Pressing my eye against this, I found myself looking into the room I had so recently left. Sir Leoline was still sprawled on the divan, a look of the uttermost dejection on his face. I heard muttered voices from the dressing-room beyond, and then saw Morgana walk in. She was naked. Though in middle age, she was of striking figure, with a dark, saturnine beauty that suggested the south. Behind her, and also naked, came a young man of the same type – he tall and slender, and with dark, curling hair. I expected them to pose, as I had done; but instead the pair began, on the cushions that littered the carpet, to engage in a species of lovemaking of the most degrading kind. I call it lovemaking; but what was most conspicuous about it was the absence of any inkling of love. What alone inspired them, it seemed, was a delight in pain and humiliation. And over it all, from his divan beside the fire, sat Sir Leoline, watching, his eyes cold and impassive. I do not know how long I stayed there, wishing to flee from the spot, but at the same time unable to move. I wanted to fling myself out of that terrible house, but did not trust myself to walk away without betraying my presence.

'At length the orgy came to an end, and Sir Leoline poured wine for them. "To us", cried the woman triumphantly, holding her glass aloft; and, as she did so, looked directly at me. Draining the glass at a gulp, she began to unfasten the large silk tie which Sir Leoline wore, as was his custom, in a foppish bow. "Not tonight", he said wearily, as he pushed her away. "Our Leo's being naughty, he is", she said insinuatingly, but it seemed to me with an undercurrent of anger. "Haven't fallen in love, perchance, have we?" she went on.

"'I believe I have", he said, with an air of resolution, his eyes steady on her face for the first time.

"'And I believe I've heard those words before", she replied.

"'That was different…", he began.

"'Yes", she interrupted, fiercely. "I wasn't a lady, was I? But what I am you made me, *Sir* Leoline". She spat out the word in contempt.

"'No", he said quietly, "that was not what I meant. I have felt for some time that this must be brought to an end. She has given me the means to do so. She is innocent and trusting. With her I can begin a new life, away from all of…this"'.

'The woman had torn herself out of his grasp and, even as he spoke, strode to the painting he had completed that afternoon. "What's this, then?", she cried, in a shriek of exultation that sent a shiver along my spine. I could not see her where she stood, but she had evidently held the picture aloft, because the young man stared in amusement, then burst into scornful laughter. The woman joined in. It was a horrible sound – a long, low, knowing chuckle that arose as if from some sewer, and that made my blood run cold.

'Sir Leoline made a gesture of feeble protest. "I had meant to destroy it. Come, I will pay you double what we agreed". He left the room, and the other two also passed out of my sight. I heard the sounds of an urgent muttering from the dressing-room; then, to my great surprise, a panel slid open beside me. Silhouetted in the space was the woman I knew as Morgana, and she was holding a glass in her hand. "Here, duckie", she said. "Drink this down. I fancy you need it". I took the glass, and the panel slid closed again. I gulped gratefully at the contents – I was close to fainting – then realised that the wine held a peculiar taste. Some draught had evidently been mixed with it, for I felt myself grow dizzy and fall to the floor. As I drifted into oblivion, I seemed to hear voices swirling in altercation; then, as if from a great distance, a cry of terror. After that, I recall nothing but silence and sleep'.

The young woman trembled visibly, and drew the blanket I had given her more closely around her shoulders. Her eyes looked into the distance; then she came to with a start.

'When I awoke', she resumed, 'it was as if to some scene out of hell. It was not yet light, but by the remains of the fire, I saw that I was back in the Moorish room. I struggled to raise myself, and sat for a moment with a great heaviness in my head. When my eyes had opened fully, I screamed. In front of me, sprawled over the cushions, was the body of Sir Leoline. It was headless. Beside it was a great scimitar which had hung over the fireplace, and which, like the cushions, was covered in blood. I then noticed the head, which had rolled to one side. It was horrible, staring at me out of dead eyes which still held his final expression of terror. The cushions that I lay on were spattered with blood; the hem of my dress lay in a pool of it. I staggered upright, and as I did so a sight still more horrible came into view. Beyond the body, standing on the easel and facing me, was the painting I had sat for but never seen. It was a bestial picture, Mr. Holmes. It was not the attitude, which was degraded enough, but the face that appalled me. It was recognisably mine, but that of a ruined and abandoned voluptuary: as if I, too, had been a party to that vile orgy of the previous night. Most terrible of all was the knowledge that it rested on some foundation of truth: that Sir Leoline had ferreted out some possibility that lurked in the depths of my being...'

'We all have enough to answer for', said Holmes gently, 'without berating ourselves for what we might have been'.

'I am aware of that now, Mr. Holmes. But at the time I was overcome with horror; and without a second thought thrust the painting in the fire. I saw the oils bubble and hiss, and the flames run black across the canvas, with emotions very different from those with which I had watched the earlier conflagration. When all was consumed, I felt calm, but very weak. Somehow, I dragged myself to the station, where I caught the first train; and, as soon as I had arrived at Liverpool Street, took a cab straight to you'.

Miss Potter sat back, her eyelids drooping, exhausted by the reliving of her ordeal. I spoke urgently to Holmes. 'This young woman needs rest. She is in a state of acute shock'. Holmes nodded and leaned forward. 'There is one question I must ask you, Miss Potter. You said when we brought you in that you feared to be charged with the murder of Sir Leoline. Why?'

'As I returned in the train, Mr. Holmes, I struggled to make sense of what had happened. I could only conclude that I had been placed beside the body to implicate me, with the painting providing a motive. I realised that other evidence might have been left elsewhere, to point in the same direction'.

'Other evidence?'

The young woman shrugged listlessly. 'Some record of my sittings, perhaps. But I thought it best to continue my journey, and place the matter in your hands'.

'You have done well', said Holmes, clasping her shoulder in rare gesture of affection as he rose for his ulster and stick. 'I will set out for Epping Forest immediately. Watson, will you accompany me?' Ringing for Mrs. Hudson, he left Miss Potter in her care.

It was still early as we drove to Liverpool Street. Birds sang forlornly from the near-leafless trees as we crossed the deserted squares, or passed along streets upon which was to be seen nothing but the occasional milk-cart. From the station, a trap brought us to Sir Leoline's castle, concealed among its woods. The drawbridge was down, and the door yielded to a push. The building was silent.

Holmes began in the chamber of death. As he worked his way over the floor, examining every detail minutely, I strolled out on the terrace to remove the stench of blood from my nostrils. Even in the chill of the season, it was a miniature paradise. In the windless courtyard, beyond the fountains, the trees still held their leaves; while birds chirped, and flowers blossomed, as if at the heart of summer.

At Holmes' signal, I followed him back upstairs. There was nothing untoward in the studio, where the altarpiece stood as described by Miss Potter. In the reception-room, however, there were traces of disturbance. Holmes' sharp eye straight away caught something amiss with the picture over the mantel. Striding up the room, he pulled the frame forward. It swivelled outward easily, revealing a partly-open safe. It was empty. A massive desk which stood opposite was the next object of Holmes' investigation. Immediately he gave a low cry. I saw him descend to his hands and knees, painstakingly scrutinising some tiny fragments of wood through his lens. Having placed them in his pocket-book, he pointed to the central drawer. I saw that it had been forced. Carefully, he eased it open. It contained documents that might have been of value to the owner, but certainly not to anyone else. There were honours, commendations, accounts of the opening of exhibitions, favourable notices from the journals. With these were two leather-bound notebooks, the first stamped 'Clients' and the second 'Galleries'. In the first were entered all of Sir Leoline's commissions, with their subjects, the names and addresses of their buyers, and dates of commencement, completion and delivery. The second, tracing his dealings with galleries, was no less meticulous. Frantically, Holmes ransacked the drawer, and a look of disappointment passed over his face. He then opened the other drawers, one by one.

These held records of the lesser commercial transactions: with artists' suppliers, with carpenters and plumbers, with grocers and vintners, chandlers and coal-yards. All were painstakingly docketed and filed; none appeared to have been touched. Holmes groaned. 'You realise what has happened here, Watson?' he sighed.

'Only that they have made off with everything of value', I replied.

'If you refer to money, the fact is immaterial. It is hardly surprising that their lack of scruple over human life should extend to property also. No, the only item I should have regarded as of value has disappeared without trace. The third notebook is missing'.

'The third...?'

'Observe the documentary habits of Sir Leoline. It is unlikely that so much as a candle or a head of cabbage could have entered or left this house without being accounted for. He must have attached still greater importance to the financial dealings connected with his profession. We find the most meticulous records concerning galleries and clients. Where are those concerning his models?'

I was silent, and he continued. 'This, since it is likely to have identified them, was evidently the object of his murderers; and we must assume that they have made off with it. There is a fire smouldering in the grate yonder, but no sign of anything having been destroyed in it. Our only achievement so far, then, has been a negative one: we have seen nothing to link Miss Potter with the place, and must take care not to establish any. However, as there is a distinct chill in the air, and we have not breakfasted, a glass of sherry would not come amiss'. He made his way to the bookshelves, quickly located the volume marked *The Company of the Round Table*, pulled it towards him, and a whole row of false bindings fell forwards, revealing glasses and decanters inside.

He had just taken the stopper from one of these when a low whistle escaped his lips. 'Great heavens, Watson! Look at this!'

I crossed to where he stood, and saw that there had been a locked compartment behind the decanters. Its door, like the desk drawer, had been prised open. Holmes removed the decanters, and opened the compartment fully; but all it revealed was a row of liquor bottles. 'Aha', said Holmes. 'Our quest is not yet over. You see what this means?'

I shook my head. 'Why should they break open the cabinet when there was liquor in plenty in front of it?'

'Precisely, Watson. They were looking for something else. It appears that they did not locate the notebook after all. We must assume, therefore, that it is still here. We shall have to go over the ground again. Meanwhile, I think I will have that glass of sherry'.

He poured two glasses and we carried them to the fireplace. I raked up the embers, and we sipped meditatively: the late Sir Leoline's cellar was apparently an excellent one. Holmes' eyes began to dart over the painting above the mantel. It was, as Miss Potter had informed us, a self-portrait: the head was recognisably that which we had seen amongst the shambles below, but far younger, and with an ex- pression of vague eagerness. It was encased in a helmet with dragon-like wings, above which fluttered a banner inscribed 'Sir Galahad'. 'Hmph', muttered Holmes. He then turned his attention to a smaller frame below, which, like the first, had been let into the panelling. It enclosed some lines in manuscript. They were in the same hand as the documents we had discovered in the desk. Holmes studied them with an intent look, then turned to me with a frown. 'Curious', he remarked. 'Read, Watson'.

I did so. Beneath a heading which said *EPITAPH*, the lines ran:

If I should go
Discern me by
The running streams
That seek the sky.

'I suppose, Watson', said Holmes, 'we must regard you as the representative of literature. What do you make of the verses?'

'They are unexceptionable', said I, 'but no less unexceptional. One would be obliged to describe them as doggerel'.

'Exactly', said Holmes. 'And what, in your opinion, do they mean?'

'I expect', I suggested, 'since he has labelled them an epitaph, that they are an expression of Sir Leoline's religious beliefs. It sounds as if he was a pantheist: as if he expected to merge with the nature after death – something, perhaps, like Shelley in *Adonaïs*'.

Holmes shook his head decisively. 'Everything about Shelley', he said, 'from his skylark to his world-spirit, floated above the earth. Sir Leoline, on the other hand, as his critics have not hesitated to assert, and as we have observed for ourselves, was the most mundane of mortals. Why, again, should an artist forsake a medium in which he has gained some renown in order to express himself in one for which he has no ability?'

'I have no idea. Why should he?'

'For the same purpose as the rest of us who do not aspire to poetry, Watson: to communicate. To send a message. What can this message be? It directs us to a place where, in some fashion, he is to be found; and, knowing what we do of him, we must presume that it is a physical location. What are "running streams that seek the sky"? Where are they to be found?'

As Holmes spoke, he stood as if transfixed; the sherry-glass shattered on the hearthstone. Breathless, he ran to the hall; I followed at some distance. He took the spiral stairs in a series of leaps; and when I arrived, panting, in the Moorish room, he was running his hands gently and systematically over the tile-painting. At last his fingers seemed to engage something: he was pressing at the point where one of the fountains was outlined against a turquoise sky. Nothing happened. He reached out for the tip of the other fountain, pressed the two simultaneously, and the octagon in the centre hinged inward. Holmes took a candlestick from a side-table, lit the candle, and hurried inside. It was a large closet, subdivided into upright shelves holding paintings, all of which were neatly labelled by subject and date. The most recent read: 'Mordred/ Morgana'. Holmes pulled it out, and immediately I averted my eyes. The faces were those we had seen on the altarpiece; but the attitudes were such as Miss Potter had described to us. Holmes gave a cry of delight as, searching the lower part of the closet with the candle, he lit up a leather-bound volume on a stool. It matched the two we had seen upstairs; but the title stamped into its cover was 'Models'. Taking it outside, he leafed through the pages. There was the same exactitude as we had seen in the previous volumes: names, dates and payments were recorded with minute care. There was an entry for a man and a woman under the date of the evening before. 'This puts them at the scene', he said in a low voice, beneath which I sensed his elation.

'There is no record of Miss Potter', I pointed out.

'There was no payment', said Holmes. He turned to the back of the volume, where details were given under every name. Running his finger through them, he halted at an address in Soho. 'We have located our murderers'. Just then, we heard the door slam upstairs. 'Quick, Watson – the candle', said Holmes urgently. I ran to the closet and quenched it. Holmes took out the painting he had been looking at, laid it on the easel which stood above Sir Leoline's body, and pressed on the tilework again. The door swung to. Then, stuffing the notebook behind a divan, he drew me by the wrist into the dressing-room. There he fumbled with the panelling, found the catch, and pulled me after him, shutting the door behind me just as hob-nailed boots clattered on the stairs outside. 'Great Scott!' came the voice of Inspector Lestrade.

Holmes put his eye to the spyhole, then signalled me to look. The inspector, with a pair of uniformed officers and an elderly woman who looked as if she might have been the housekeeper, stood gazing in horror at the shambles. Lestrade fixed his eye on the painting, then walked slowly round the room, searching under cushions and behind furniture. In a moment he had found the book; and from his intent gaze at the latest entry, passing to the picture and back, I saw that he had made the connection. I beckoned to Holmes to look. After a glance, he nodded silently, then directed me towards the passageway, having first placed a finger to his lips. I tiptoed out, followed by Holmes, while the inspector barked orders to his subordinates. I made my way up the opposite stair to the one we had come down. To my relief, the door-handle at the top turned, and I stepped out into the hall. At that point, a cold metallic object was pressed into the back of my neck, and a harsh voice said: 'One move and you are dead'.

I stood against the column as directed, followed in a moment by Holmes. When we were allowed to turn around, we saw a hard-faced young detective who motioned us down the other stairs with his revolver. 'Found these lurking about above, sir', he said to Lestrade in a triumphant tone. 'Think they may be our murderers'. 'I am afraid not, constable', said Lestrade, with a hurried glance at the picture. 'These are Mr. Sherlock Holmes and Dr. Watson. But what *are* you doing here, Mr. Holmes?'

'The same as yourself, I suppose', shrugged Holmes. 'We received information that there might be something here worth looking into. But it is such a complicated building, and we seem to have lost our way'.

'Well, you need look no further', said Lestrade majestically, holding up the notebook. 'Do you know what this is?'

Holmes stared at him in blank puzzlement.

'I will show you, Mr. Holmes', said the officer. And he outlined, with great authority, the theory which Holmes had already expounded. 'So you see, Mr. Holmes, we shan't be needing you this time'.

'A very fine piece of work, Inspector', said Holmes with a look of pained innocence. 'In that case, we will take our leave'.

'There is only one thing that puzzles me', said Lestrade, gnawing at his moustache. 'The housekeeper, who summoned us here, does not remember the painting being on the easel when she found the body. Seemed to be seeing it with us for the first time: stood there with her mouth open, and said it was the work of a walking fiend'.

'Oh, that is easily explained', said Holmes airily. 'She *was* seeing it for the first time'.

'Beg pardon?'

'She was so horrified at finding her master killed that she had eyes for nothing else. You will find just such a case described by Professor Schirmer, of the University of Dantzig, in the Journal of Criminal Psychology for the year 1877'.

'That clears it up, I reckon', said Lestrade, scratching his head. 'Good day to you, Mr. Holmes. You too, Dr. Watson'. The young detective who had apprehended us whispered something in his ear. 'Oh, by the way, Mr. Holmes', he resumed, 'may I ask who was this informant of yours?'

'As you know', said Holmes equably, 'I am bound to respect the confidence of my clients. I need only say that it was someone who has every interest in seeing justice served in this case, and whose evidence, if needed, will be made available at the trial'.

But the case never came to trial. Following the indications in the notebook, a squad of police descended on the address in Soho. There they found a middle-aged woman stabbed through the heart, and beside her the body of a young man who had also received a knife-wound, in consequence of which he had bled to death. Nearby was found a large quantity of banknotes, over which, it was assumed, they had quarrelled. This was given out as the motive for Sir Leoline's murder, and the sensation, after rumours had floated about for a time, faded away.

After we had ascended into our cab at Liverpool Street, and were rattling back home under the pale sky of an autumn forenoon, Holmes asked me, with a touch of mischief: 'Now what would you prescribe for our patient, Watson?'

'She has had a great shock. She needs much rest'.

'Undoubtedly', agreed Holmes. 'But the greatest shock, it appears to me, has been to her faith in human nature. And for that I am inclined to think a different prescription is in order'. He rapped on the roof of the cab, and gave the driver instructions which soon had us turning off the crowded noonday streets into a quiet laneway in Holborn. Holmes got out and knocked loudly at a door which held the brass plate of a rising magazine. After he had been inside for a few minutes, he emerged in the company of a man in his mid-thirties, with pale hair and beard, eyes remote behind his spectacles, and a distraught look upon his face. When the two had seated themselves in the carriage, and Holmes, briefly, explained what had occurred, his expression turned to one of intense regret. 'I blame myself for this, Mr. Holmes', he said in a strained voice. 'I care greatly for Anna, but did not trust myself to speak to her. My previous unhappy marriage has made me circumspect; and I did not wish to presume upon our professional acquaintance'.

'On that point', said Holmes, 'you need have no fear. She shared your feelings, but, like you, did not know how to express them'.

'My God!' cried the young man. 'How blind I have been!'

'Tut', said Holmes. 'You showed the discretion of a considerate employer. But what she needs now is an understanding friend'.

When we arrived at Baker Street, Holmes waved Roger Clavinger ahead of us. Immediately he bounded up the stairs. 'Anna', we heard him call, 'thank heaven!' From her we heard an answering cry of relief; and when we had reached the head of the stairs, we saw her enfolded in his arms, her own clasped tightly about his neck. I felt Holmes' hand on my shoulder. 'Come, Watson', he whispered, 'I think we may leave the rest to nature'.

But when the wedding invitation arrived, he had reverted to his old misanthropy. 'Not for me, Watson', he snarled with contempt. 'There can be no place for a reasoner amid the inanities which festoon these occasions. I should be made positively ill by the mindless rejoicings over a relation as yet untested, the maunderings at the prospect of new bundles of unhappiness being precipitated into our long-suffering world. What? Yes, yes, Watson, of course. By all means, go if you please. And yes, you may carry my felicitations, if your humour runs to the fantastic'.

It was some years after this that Holmes, in the course of an investigation which had brought us to one of the larger cities of northern England, hurried me suddenly into a church on a side-street, which had been built in the Gothic style. Inside, the air was heavy with flowers and organ music; and I thought at first that he had come into this incongruous setting to escape some pursuer. Instead, he led me to the altar, over which stood the paintings I had last seen in Sir Leoline's studio, to which the smoke of candles had already given a patina of age. There were five panels, with the outer pair representing the patrons; while in the centre was the Holy Grail, emitting beams of light. On one side were its enemies, Morgana and Mordred, writhing in pain as they held up their hands to shut out its beams; on the other, a world-weary Arthur, turning as if in appeal to a radiant Guenevere. For the first time I saw all together the actors in the drama we had witnessed.

The evening service was just over; and a surpliced cleric, walking down the nave from the sanctuary, intercepted our gaze. 'That is the work of Sir Leoline Knightleigh, who died so tragically some years ago', he informed us in an undertone. 'The experts tell us it is his masterpiece. Indeed, it is my own opinion that in the countenance of the queen, transfigured by the vision of the Grail, he has captured the authentic spirituality of the ages of faith'.

As we left the church, I said to Holmes, 'We have seen his Arthur and his Guenevere; but who in fact were the other two?'

'That was never fully ascertained, Watson', he replied. 'Nor, under the circumstances, was it necessary that it should be. Both had an unsavoury reputation in the area in which they lived. The woman was said to have been of Italian extraction, and distantly related to the Rossettis. Of the young man nothing was known, save that he accompanied her everywhere. I expect that if one were to investigate the matter, it would be possible to arrive at the truth; but I do not wish to do so'.

'Not wish to know? Why not?'

'Because I fear what I might find'.

'Fear? How?'

'Remember the legend, Watson. Mordred was the evil son of Morgana, from her unholy union with Arthur. And Mordred was the murderer of his father'.

THREE

THE ORDER OF

CHARLEMAGNE

Our Paris adventure began with a visit to our rooms at Baker Street by Sir James Damery. Readers of 'The Illustrious Client' will recall how that veteran courtier, through the brilliance and persistence of Holmes, had saved a headstrong young woman from a marriage that must have ended in her death. On that occasion, Sir James had been the intermediary of an exalted personage who had insisted on anonymity; and, upon my recognising his armorial bearings, Holmes silenced me with the reflection that our client was 'a loyal friend and a chivalrous gentleman'. By the time these notes are read, it will no longer serve any purpose to deny that he was, in fact, Edward, Prince of Wales, who had since ascended the throne as King Edward the Seventh.

The masterful figure of Sir James, older now but still dapper, dominated our rooms. The years seemed only to have etched more deeply into his features the lineaments of a bluff and honest geniality. But his words struck a chill into my heart. 'I fear, Mr. Holmes, for the life of the King'.

Holmes' grave silence, punctuated only by the puffs of his pipe, invited him to continue.

'It is this visit of his to France', the courtier went on. 'As you know, His Majesty has always had a special place in his heart for France and the French; but since his accession has been unable to visit that country. The Fashoda crisis, in which we forced them to relinquish their claim to the Sudan, was a grave blow to French pride; and public opinion there has, accordingly, swung violently in favour of the Boers. Yet the King believes that an alliance between our two nations is vital as a counterpoise to Germany, whose ambitions, in the person of his nephew the Kaiser, he understands all too well. The idea of a visit, therefore, has been his own. The Cabinet, though in favour of an alliance, looks askance upon the visit, which they consider places him in personal danger. The French President, however, has warmly welcomed it, knowing that the King loves France, as it has been observed, both *gaiement et sérieusement*; and believing that his presence will create a climate in which the alliance can be realised'.

'All very reasonable', said Holmes. 'Why, then, do you entertain fears for his life?'

For answer, Sir James took an envelope from an inside pocket. From it he extracted a sheet of paper, of which he folded over the top and bottom, presenting the page to Holmes with its centre facing outward. 'I must ask you, Mr. Holmes, not to unfold the page, nor attempt to discover the person identified by the letterhead and signature'.

'I should not dream of doing so', replied Holmes, 'because it is perfectly unnecessary. The light-blue paper identifies the sex of the sender, while its scent' – he held the sheet for an instant to his nose – 'establishes her wealth. Her access to the highest circles in Paris, and her personal concern for the King, point to a lady whose name was once romantically linked with his. But you may assure her ladyship that her secret is personally safe with me'.

The courtier laughed heartily. 'I should not have attempted to keep you in the dark, Mr. Holmes. But I had promised to respect her confidence'.

'What I know of the lady vouches for the reliability of her message', said Holmes. 'And it could not possibly be a more serious one'. He handed the sheet to me. There, in a beautiful, but firm and urgent hand, was written: 'I have word of a plot to assassinate the King.   The Order of Charlemagne is said to be involved'.

'What can you tell me of this Order?', asked Holmes.

'Very little, I fear', replied Sir James.   'You will be aware, Mr. Holmes, that France at the present time is a nation deeply divided.   On the one hand, it has a republican government, which aims to establish irreversibly the principle of parliamentary rule; on the other, it retains a significant aristocratic and military element, which would dearly love to see the state reconstituted along the authoritarian lines of Germany.   Within this, the most extreme faction is represented by this shadowy Order, of which we know little more than the name.   Yet that in itself tells us a great deal. Charlemagne, you will recall, was crowned Emperor by the Pope, and dominated the Europe of his day.   The appeal to his memory is a clarion-call to French sentiments of empire and extreme Catholicism.   These are the most fanatical representatives of a class still powerful in France: those who believe that republicanism has betrayed the nation's glory to atheists, Freemasons and Jews.   They are smarting from their recent defeat in the events surrounding Captain Dreyfus: a mood which makes them the more dangerous, because more reckless and desperate, as they see public opinion harden against them.   Time is not on their side; what they need is some spectacular action which will weaken the present government: even if – perhaps I should say, especially if – it should lead to war.   We have had whisperings of this plot for some time; now, as you see, they are confirmed'.

'Surely the French police are aware of it?', queried Holmes.

'Certainly, Mr. Holmes, and they are a most efficient body. The difficulty is that we cannot establish the extent to which they may have been infiltrated by this fanatical Order.   Our embassy has its own system of informants; but, as it has no jurisdiction in France, it cannot act openly upon what we know.

Our only hope, therefore, lies in some such clandestine agent as yourself. If you have ever cared for your country, Mr. Holmes, now is the time to serve it. Rarely, in modern history, can events have hinged so upon a single life. It is not too much to say that the peace of Europe may depend upon our thwarting this plot. You must leave for Paris at once'.

So it was that, after an uneventful crossing, I stood amongst the alien cries and odours of the Gare du Nord. Holmes had gone to search for a porter, when I was approached by a shabbily-dressed man, asking if I wanted postcards. I had thought of sending one to Mrs. Hudson; but as I turned the man's wares over in my hands, I felt a growing horror. The majority were photographs of women without the slightest shred of...of modesty; but worst of all was a cartoon of Britannia lifting her skirts, revealing, on her posterior, the features of His Majesty. At that moment Holmes returned, and, seeing what I held, berated the vendor, in flawless French, for having insulted his English guest. Was it thus that one upheld the glory of France? The man slunk away, abashed. 'Thank you, Holmes', I breathed. 'You have extricated me from the most unpleasant experience of my life'.

'I hope it was an instructive one', replied Holmes imperturbably. 'The first rule of war is to know one's enemy. You see now the state of opinion with which the King will have to contend'.

I could not take the matter so coolly, and felt myself alienated from the wide, pale avenues that our *fiacre* drove through, already missing the warm red brick of the London streets. However, when we turned into an octagonal square with a triumphal column in the centre, and there alighted at an hotel in the lobby of which English could be heard mingling with all the languages of Europe, and which swam with brilliant and beautiful women and their escorts, I began to feel myself at home. I communicated as much to Holmes.

'That is why we must be on our way once our baggage has been seen to', he replied. 'It is not in such places as this, gilded and cosmopolitan, that one will hear the heartbeat of France'. And so, within a very few minutes, we were in another cab, and proceeding towards the Île de la Cité. Holmes explained that it was the germ of the great metropolis. 'It was here when there was nothing else', he said meditatively. 'Gibbon was bemused at how this glittering city has arisen from the wooded island which met the eyes of the Romans. Since then, it has witnessed the building of Notre-Dame and of the first royal residence: the Palais de Justice, with its Conciergerie. The prison of the unhappy Marie-Antoinette was the palace of her predecessors. The island is still the centre of ecclesiastical and judicial Paris. At the same time, you will still find here markets for birds and flowers: so that it has not altogether lost touch with its rustic origins. Its eating-places are no less comprehensive: we shall hear in them the conversation of policemen, priests and pickpockets – or any combination of those three'.

But in the event, the only topic that we heard of was ourselves. Holmes had paid off the cab at the entrance to a narrow lane behind the bulk of Notre-Dame, and led me to a cramped and unpretentious restaurant in what looked like an ordinary dwelling, but which, he assured me, served solid French fare in the provincial style. The conversation was animated as we entered, but all of a sudden died to an ominous murmur. I heard Holmes cough, and saw him stare at my hat. Immediately, I removed my bowler, and Holmes' fluent request for a table was the signal for a resumption of the babble. An unshaven fellow with the insolent air of a petty proprietor approached us with a cigarette dangling from his lip, and stood before us with questioning eyes. Holmes ordered the *plat du jour* in a careless tone, then excused himself and made for the back of the room. The proprietor returned from the kitchen and, to my horror, headed straight in my direction. His lips formed words which, after my first panic, I recalled from my school French as an enquiry about wine. I nodded, in imitation of Holmes, as authoritatively as I could. He then asked whether it was white we desired, or red. Remembering Holmes' preference when we dined at Goldini's, I plumped for the red. *'Rouge'*, I cried, with an air of great confidence. *'Rouge?!'* exclaimed the proprietor, with an initial consonant which sounded as if he were clearing his throat, and in a tone in which scorn and disbelief seemed equally mingled. Certainly, it brought all talk to a halt. In the midst of this silence, Holmes returned; and the proprietor, having scribbled exaggeratedly in his notebook, and wearing a sardonic smile, swaggered back to the kitchen. 'What on earth have you done now, Watson?', Holmes hissed in an urgent whisper.

'I have ordered our wine', I replied, with some pride.

'White, of course?', prompted Holmes.

'I thought you preferred red'.

'Red?' he exclaimed, with almost as much indignation as the proprietor. *'Red?'*

'For heaven's sake, Holmes', I said, exasperated by all this twaddle about a beverage, 'what the devil difference does it make?'

'To these people', Holmes replied, with a sidelong glance at the patrons, who were conferring with one another in subdued murmurs, 'it makes all the difference in the world. Did you not hear me order the *plat du jour?*'

'Distinctly', I replied.

'And you realise what is meant by *jour?*'

'It means "day"', I said, with satisfaction. '"Plate of the day"'.

'More or less', said Holmes. 'And what, pray, is the present day of the week?'

'Friday, Holmes, it is Friday', I answered, my patience at an end. 'And will you kindly now explain to me the point of this inquisition?'

'The point is this, Watson', said Holmes slowly. 'You have ordered red wine with a dish which requires white. France is a Catholic country, and the *plat du jour* for today will certainly contain fish. You can hardly wonder that these people are appalled. You have committed an offence against their religion'.

'You mean Roman Catholicism?'

'I mean food and drink. Catholicism, except for a fanatic few, is merely their denomination'.

'Then why, in heaven's name, do they not abolish these ridiculous survivals? Why not turn Protestant? It would simplify the matter'.

'It would not be interesting: it would end the debate. And now, Watson, I must try to undo the damage you have caused. Though I fear it will be to no avail'.

Holmes' fear was too well justified. The owner was evidently prepared for a scene. He recalled, with relish, every detail of what had occurred, revelling in his role as the entire establishment laid down knife and fork to savour the performance. He consulted his notebook thoughtfully, as if to refresh his memory. Monsieur had ordered the *plat du jour*? Two *plats du jour*. The other monsieur had ordered *vin rouge* as an accompaniment to these? These were the orders as given? There was no mistake? These had been conveyed to the kitchen. And now monsieur wished to re-order? The wine or the meal? Perhaps both? Monsieur perhaps imagined that an honest Frenchman had nothing to do but cater to insular insensibility? Holmes made a gesture of mollification; but the proprietor silenced him with clenched fists and fiery eyes, and a tirade that led up to a single explosive monosyllable.

'What was that final word, Holmes?' I asked, as, shaken, we emerged from the restaurant. 'I do not recall having heard it at school'.

'It signifies', said Holmes quietly, 'that he has wearied of our company'.

We crossed on foot to the Left Bank. Here Holmes led me along a quay on which stalls of second-hand books and prints lined the parapet, then plunged into a maze of small and crooked streets remarkable to me chiefly for their odour, but which Holmes hailed as the Paris of Dante and Duns Scotus. 'See', he remarked, pointing to a sign which read *Rue des anglais*. 'Here was the heart of scholastic Europe, in which the students of Bohemia gave their name to a way of life. And, as you may observe, little has changed'. The streets swarmed with youth of every description, from Nordic blonds to curly-haired Berbers, and with accents ranging from broad American to the singsong tones of Indo-China. They stood reading at the bookstalls, or sat at the pavement cafés. 'Here, at least', said Holmes, 'our Englishness will hardly attract attention'. He led me into a bare-walled room where some dozens of young folk were bent, hungrily, over pungent dishes. Almost immediately, we were served the same. It consisted of bright-red sausages in a liquid poured over some pulverised grain. '*Couscous*', said Holmes. I managed to consume some, out of sheer hunger. Never had I so missed a porterhouse steak and a pint of ale. 'I have a theory', I said to Holmes, 'that the reason the French make such a fuss about cookery is that they are still trying to work out how the thing is done'. Holmes smiled with his mouth full, chewing appreciatively. I saw that he was pretending to enjoy the foreign food. I have always held that in him the stage lost an actor of the first rank.

There was only one untoward incident. When I excused myself and went to the rear, I discovered that within what was labelled as a W.C., there was little but a hole in the floor. Around this was a shallow basin, with a pair of foot-shaped projections on which, apparently, one was expected to balance oneself. When I pulled the chain, I was still standing on them, and a cascade of water drenched my shoes and trouser-legs. There were no towels to be seen, and I went back to the restaurant sopping. As I entered, one of the students pointed at me, in a moment the rest had set up a roar, and the entire restaurant was rocking with laughter as Holmes led me out, mortified. 'Well, Holmes', I cried, bitterly humiliated, 'are you now quite satisfied about their feelings towards us?'

'Oh', said Holmes airily, 'they were not laughing at you as an Englishman. They laughed at you as an older man who has had a mishap. In the sparkling eyes of youth, nothing is more ridiculous than middle age. However', he went on, in a kinder tone, 'as we are returning to an ambience where the opposite holds true, we shall certainly have to find a disguise for you'.

He turned into a laneway in which an outfitter's stood, and soon I was encased in something dark, elegant and uncomfortable, my reassuring check suit bundled into a parcel. Holmes next led me to a hairdresser's. He thrust me into a chair and explained what he wanted, while he himself sat on a bench by the wall. As I studied him in the mirror, I realised that he needed no disguise. He had travelled in clothing which betrayed no hint of Englishness; while his high, beaked nose and intense manner suggested the Latin, a picture completed by the supercilious fashion in which he scanned the pages of *Le Figaro*. As the hairdresser tapped my shoulder, motioning to me to lie back, I recalled what he had told me of his French descent, and his kinship with the painter Vernet, and it came to me that what for me was a painful exile must for him be, in some fashion, a homecoming. It struck me, once again, how little I knew of my friend, and how much my regard for him was bound up with the enigmatic element in his personality. These thoughts revolved in my mind as, exhausted by the crossing and my subsequent trials, I nodded off. When I awoke, it was to another tap from the hairdresser. I started: a sinister Frenchman stared me in the face. He was the image of the villain in a love-triangle on stage: hair curling upward on either side, and a quivering, waxed moustache that put me in mind of the late Baron Adalbert Gruner. I did not think that I had ever seen so finished a scoundrel. As I rose to meet him, he rose too; and as I put out a hand to hold him at bay, his hand came forward to meet it. I realised, to my unspeakable horror, that the sinister Frenchman was myself!

Over my shoulder, the hairdresser smiled with satisfaction. I paid what he asked, and when his hand remained out, added a tip; and, when it still remained out, doubled it. He had done his work all too well. Whatever pomade he had rubbed into my hair enveloped me a sweet, sickly, alien scent. I became conscious, for the first time in my life, of the appalling experience it must be, not only to look like a foreigner, but actually to feel like one. In a burst of panic, I snatched at Holmes' newspaper, and flung it aside; but the startled face that looked up at me was not that of Holmes! '*Pardon*', I muttered, shame-faced, as the barber, smiling, handed me a note. It said: 'Will await you at hotel. Do not take cab. Holmes'.

All at once I was aware of danger. Holmes, with his usual acumen, had no doubt sensed it, and led our pursuer or pursuers away from me. These, clearly, expected me to return in a *fiacre*, and, in all probability, lay in wait at the nearest cab-stand. I made my way to the river, pausing to look back at every corner. To my great surprise, nobody seemed to be following me. In fact, not one of those who hurried past me on the pavement gave me a second glance. With a burst of exultation, I realised that I was invisible. Holmes' disguise had worked. But after I had crossed to the Right Bank, I soon lost my way. Once I began to ask for directions, I was met with suspicious or hostile stares. Some simply shrugged their shoulders, or held up the palms of their hands; others launched into a torrent of invective, out of which the only word I could distinguish consistently was *anglais*. I seemed to become entangled in an endless nightmare of broad, busy, thoroughfares or narrow, evil-smelling lanes, until at last, more by good fortune than judgement, I emerged onto the square in front of our hotel. Footsore, sick at heart and smouldering with resentment, I made my way upstairs. I found Holmes at the window, gazing out over the square, in which the buildings opposite glowed with a mellow sunset light. He had his violin to his shoulder, and was playing 'For He's a Jolly Good Fellow'.

'I appreciate your approval', I said shortly; 'but am in no humour to make merry over it. For all I know, I have barely escaped with my life. I assume that you have taken care of our pursuers'.

'There were no pursuers', said Holmes calmly, laying down the instrument.

'No pursuers!' I gaped in amazement, which quickly turned to rage. 'Then why, in the name of heaven, Holmes, have you sent me on this miserable wild-goose chase? It is utterly unworthy of you to play practical jokes on me at this juncture – as a fellow-countryman, as a gentleman and as a friend. I have wandered, exhausted, through the hateful streets of this hostile city. I have been rebuffed and reviled at every turn. I have been scorned as an alien and an enemy. I...'

'That will do very nicely, Watson', he interrupted coolly. 'I think you are beginning to get the idea'.

'What idea?' Holmes, as so often, had left me completely at a loss.

'The idea of how a Frenchman behaves. I only wish you could have seen yourself. You have shrugged, gesticulated, raised your eyebrows, turned down the corners of your mouth, and expressed such eloquence with your stick that I have feared some mischief to the chandelier'. He held up his hand before I could respond. 'Rest assured, Watson, that you would not have been subjected to this experience had I not considered it absolutely necessary. In the days to come, our freedom of movement may depend upon our ability not to call attention to ourselves; and on this, in turn, may depend the life of the King'.

The invocation of His Majesty immediately silenced my protests. What was my discomfort, even misery, if by it I could help Holmes or serve the King? I sank into the arm-chair matching Holmes', exhausted. 'I shouldn't get too comfortable there, Watson. I began to run a bath for you when I saw you through the window, and I expect our evening meal within half an hour'. I struggled to my feet, and felt immensely refreshed by the time the waiter wheeled his trolley through the door. Holmes had had the table set by the window, and we enjoyed a sunset view of the square as we sipped dry white wine to the taste of a lobster salad which recalled carefree days by the shingle of Southsea. This was followed by a steak Chateaubriand with excellent claret, every whit as good as what I was accustomed to at my club. I observed to Holmes, after the waiter had left, that the French were not half bad at cookery when they imitated the English. He nodded and smiled. We finished our wine while darkness closed over the square; and his last words of the evening were, as he gestured to it with his glass: 'There it is, Watson. There is our task, expressed with the most admirable Gallic brevity'.

I was too exhausted to question him; but when we were seated at the same spot the following morning, devouring coffee and fresh rolls, he returned to the theme. 'It is the most perfect space in Paris, Watson', he said, as he drank the pungent brew. 'To the English eye, the symmetry of the octagon suggests conformity, but to the French it is expressive of harmony and grace. And over it, in undisguised pre-eminence, stands the man who made France and Europe his own'.

I was aware that the tall column held a statue of Napoleon; but I failed to see what he had to do with our task, and said so. Holmes pushed back his chair and stood. 'Come, Watson. Our appointment at the embassy is for the afternoon. Meanwhile, there is no better way to explain than to illustrate'.

At the desk below, he ordered a *fiacre*; and after we had taken our seats, and he had given elaborate instructions to the driver, we clopped through the awakening streets at a leisurely pace. Having passed through the top of the square, we turned right, and travelled with the sun in our eyes until we came to a circus, in the centre of which was a large statue of a figure on horseback. 'Louis the Fourteenth', said Holmes. 'We have reached the Place des Victoires'. We took an avenue that angled left, and as we continued along it, Holmes sighed. 'You see our difficulty, Watson?'

'I have not the faintest idea', I said, my assurance restored by the morning air and the knowledge that I travelled incognito, 'what you are talking about'.

'The streets, Watson', said Holmes, gesturing with his stick. 'The streets'. And he gestured with his stick. I scrutinised the hurrying crowds as we passed, but could see nothing out of the ordinary. At the head of the avenue, I caught a glimpse of a triumphal archway, before we turned abruptly and headed towards the river. 'The streets', Holmes repeated; but again I could see nothing. We had passed from an area of banks and prosperous *boutiques* to one in which windows were broken and beggars stood at corners. We turned into a side-street, out of which opened noisome alleyways. Then we were back again in a broad avenue, and in a moment were approaching an archway which I recognised. 'Holmes', I said, 'we have passed this way before. We are being cheated by that villainous cabman'.

He uttered a few abrupt words, and this time, having turned in front of the arch, we continued to the river. Here the cabman turned again, and deposited us outside the Louvre. To my surprise, Holmes made no mention of his mistake, but treated him with the greatest friendliness, adding a large tip to the fare. The man raised his whip in salute, and drove away.

Inside, I had occasion, once again, to marvel at Holmes' omniscience. As we walked amongst the riches of gallery after gallery, he discoursed learnedly upon schools and styles of painting, until at last we stood before the masterpiece of Leonardo. I expected some reflections upon that most enigmatic of paintings, perhaps even Holmes' own solution of its mystery; but instead he remarked abruptly, 'I have a mind, Watson, to take a look at the Rosetta Stone'. And he turned away, with a resolute stride.

I was about to follow him when a thought struck me. 'But Holmes', I cried, 'the Rosetta Stone is in London! Don't you remember? We have seen it at the British Museum!'

A look of dawning recollection passed over Holmes' face. 'Why, so we have, Watson', he replied. 'And so it is. You scintillate this morning'. We passed out into the courtyard, and made our way upward through the gardens, in which nurses sat with children, poodles barked as if to establish that they were, in fact, dogs, and sparrows swept to the gravel for crumbs. We emerged into a square in which a large obelisk stood, flanked by fountains; and by the time we had crossed it, through a bedlam of traffic, and sat under the trees of a noble avenue, I was ready for the lunch which Holmes suggested. As he ordered, I reflected how unlike him it was to make a mistake. And he had made two this morning. Perhaps, living on nervous energy as he did, he was more exhausted than he seemed. I was wondering whether, as his physician, I should urge him to take greater care of his health. I coughed, and, to open the conversation, expressed my admiration for the view.

'In essentials', said Holmes, 'it is identical with that from our hotel window'.

I was now certain, not only that he was exhausted, but that his condition was acute. It had evidently affected his vision. 'Holmes', I began, 'we must return at once to our hotel. There you can lie down. You are not yourself'.

'On the contrary, my dear Watson', said Holmes, cheerfully, 'I have never been more truly myself. Do I strike you as a man suffering from delusions?'

I was silenced by his accurate reading of my thoughts.

'It is you, and not I, Watson', he went on, 'who fail to see what is before you. All this morning, we have been travelling through English history'.

'English?', said I, my mouth falling open.

'Yes, English, Watson', he repeated relentlessly.

I was distressed by this further evidence of mental disorder.

'You mean French, of course', I said, as calmly as I could.

'No, Watson, I mean English. I have taken you along the route we have followed this morning to imprint the realities of our situation on your mind. We started at the column of Napoleon, to which I called your attention, and with whom the French Empire may be said to have begun. There is no French schoolchild who does not recall his stirring address from the Pyramids. From here we passed through streets – to which, again, I directed your notice – named, in the flush of excitement which followed the great general's adventures, after *le Caire* and *Alexandrie*. Twice, at my instruction, the cabman drove us along the Rue d'*Aboukir* – best known to us for the Battle of the Nile, which brought these dreams to an end. Amongst the articles of capitulation which we imposed upon them was surrender of the Rosetta Stone, which, as you so rightly remarked, reposes in London. But it was Napoleon's soldiers who discovered it; upon which the general, fully realising its significance, generously sent copies to the scholars of all Europe. We demanded it meanly, and appropriated it gracelessly – though it was a French *savant*, in the end, who, by linking its language with the still-living Coptic, took the leading part in unlocking its secret. Do you wonder, now, that the French resent us? Such are the associations called up by our expulsion of their forces from Fashoda.

'Nor was Napoleon the only leader whose pride we have humbled. Two sovereigns stand pre-eminent in the annals of France. One brought her grandeur, the other glory; and it would be difficult to say whom they value more. Napoleon, as prince of upstarts, was supremely sensitive to the value of tradition; and so appropriated the symbols of Louis the Fourteenth. His column replaces a statue of that king, in a square which expresses to perfection the civilisation of his reign. In that limited space, glory and grandeur unite: it is an epitome of the pride of France, condensed into the perfection of an epigram.

'But when one reflects upon it in historical perspective – as the light lanced across it obliquely in last evening's setting sun – it is the expression of a double defeat. For as we dimmed the glory of Napoleon, so we tarnished the grandeur of his predecessor. The Place Vendôme is named for one of Louis' ablest generals, brought low by the Duke of

Marlborough. It was these reflections that passed through my mind as I played on my violin last night. Is it not significant that the tune which we have taken for a chorus of congratulation, assuring ourselves that somebody or other is a "jolly good fellow", should be the most melancholy of songs to the French, and bear the name of the feared *Malbrouck*?'

'But all of this took place', I protested, 'ages ago. It is water under the bridge. Can we not just forget it all, and be friends?'

'I am glad I brought you with me, Watson: you are so uncompromisingly English, our "jolly good fellow" to perfection. I, with the dash of France in my blood, can see the other side. The victor can forget, and, as he thinks, be friends; the vanquished, never. To the French, besides, the past is perpetually present, in a manner incomprehensible to the pragmatic Englishman. As Napoleon displaced Louis in the Place Vendôme, so he in turn was displaced when the Bourbons came back. He was restored by Napoleon the Third, and toppled again by the Commune. The French take a passionately personal attitude to the past. There is no more ghoulish example than when, at the Revolution, they tore Louis from his tomb. If they can be possessed by such violence of emotion where their own monarchs are concerned, how must they feel about us? We shattered their dreams at the outset of the eighteenth century, and again at the start of the nineteenth. Now, in the dawn of the twentieth, they see us poised to bring them down again'.

The food had lain untasted on Holmes' plate; and the waitress, with a frown of concern, asked if all was well. My friend, with his most winning smile, assured her that it was, and set to with appetite. When he had finished, and we were toying with our coffee-spoons, he said: 'I noticed your pained look, Watson, when I remarked that this vista was identical with that from our hotel. But it really is so, in essence. The

Champs-Élysées was an avenue laid down for Louis the Fourteenth. Being what he was, even his garden walk was monumental. But Napoleon pre-empted it with his Arc de Triomphe. It is a restatement of the problem expressed by the Place Vendôme: the problem of French pride, and our need to assuage it'.

He took out a well-worn pipe, and began to stuff it with shag tobacco. After the first few puffs, he pointed its mouthpiece up the avenue. 'In the problem, Watson', he stated, 'is implied the solution. In the question, precisely formulated, resides the answer. I have a theory – call it fanciful if you like – that within every Frenchman resides a Grand Monarch. Napoleon, as the Everyman of the Enlightenment, brought majesty within the ambience of the common man. That was the secret of his power: the revelation that in every soldier's knapsack was a marshal's baton. The French hunger above all for glory: it is a hunger that the Order of Charlemagne aims to satisfy. They labour, however, under one very considerable disadvantage. They have no great personage on whom to hang their dreams. The restored Bourbons were shadows; the last Napoleon, as Bismarck so accurately pointed out, was a sphinx without a mystery. Therein lies our opportunity. Behind our King lies the prestige of centuries of tradition, and the power of the greatest empire the world has known. The French, in their heart of hearts, cannot fail to be stirred. If the King can only persuade them that, in spirit, he is at one with them, his mission will be a success. I am convinced that he can: that no monarch in our history is better fitted, either by character or opportunity, for that role. And it is one that only he can play; no minister, no general, no ambassador, can simulate the presence of a king'.

Holmes checked his pocket-watch, and we took a cab for the British Embassy. Our appointment had been for three o'clock, and we had arrived precisely at the stroke of the hour; but at three-thirty were still cooling our heels in an ante-room. 'It is just as I expected, Watson', said Holmes. His voice was low, but under the controlled tone I sensed his irritation. 'The petty exercise of power is the known trademark – or coat of arms, if you will – of Lord Augustus Bland'.

'I have never heard of him'.

'He is a type still all too common in our ruling circles: the aristocrat whose arrogance is in inverse proportion to his ability. He belongs to one of the oldest families in the kingdom, whose ancestors fought at Agincourt, a fact of which he endlessly reminds the French. He has annoyed them still further by the fact that he resolutely refuses to speak their language. He says it reminds him of his schooldays, which he would prefer to forget. Considering his lordship's intellectual attainments, I have no doubt that this is true. But he added insult to injury when, in conversation with a *Times* correspondent the other day, he observed that the whole point of diplomacy was to get the other fellow to speak *your* language'.

I could not resist a chuckle. 'I must say I think it rather good'.

'The issue is not whether it *is* good, Watson, but whether it *does* good. And at this juncture it is highly inappropriate. It was all over *Le Figaro* the following day. The French feel that their language is the most elegant, the most expressive, the most exquisite in the world: in fact they consider that it *is* the language of the world, English a mongrel offshoot. Add Lord Augustus' dismissive remarks to the current mood in the country, and you will see the need for subtlety and restraint. Lord Augustus is in charge of arrangements for the King's visit: I should say his behaviour was reckless, did I not know it to be obtuse'.

Our interview proved Holmes in the right. When, eventually, we were shown in to Lord Augustus, he was standing by a window with his back to us, toying with a monocle, and humming a tune from an operetta. The faint scent of a woman's perfume hung upon the air. Holmes waited in an ominous silence which, it seemed to me, at length unnerved the noble lord. He turned around, surveyed us through the monocle, and then, as if finding what he saw of little interest, sat at his desk and began looking through some papers.

'I am here at the request of Sir James Damery', said Holmes with dignity. 'One moment', said the official, holding up his hand. After some moments of pretending to read a document, he gazed at Holmes with an absent smile. 'You were saying?', he prompted.

'I was speaking of Sir James Damery', Holmes began.

'My good man', exploded Lord Augustus, in a pretence of righteous anger, 'Sir James has long been superannuated. It would be a mercy to shoot him like an old dog, but His Majesty has retained some absurd attachment to him, which seems to make him think he knows one's business better than oneself. I am in charge here, and I answer directly to His Majesty'.

'We live in a constitutional monarchy', said Holmes suavely. 'It is to the public that you must answer if you fail to protect the King'.

The aristocrat resumed his monocle, and gazed at him as if with renewed interest.

'You know, Holmes', he said languidly, removing the glass and toying with it again, 'the ambassadress has just been here, and begged me to avail of what she called your "extraordinary powers". In what cause can these have been summoned? As far as I can ascertain, you are a last resort for lost lap-dogs'.

I was livid with fury. 'Mr. Sherlock Holmes...', I began; but Holmes took over with an icy sarcasm in which I recognised his deepest rage.

'I can assure you that the matter was of a considerably more intimate nature – as perhaps even your lordship can comprehend'.

The nobleman flushed deeply. He had been named in the society columns in connection with an actress, and it was rumoured that his wife planned to sue him for divorce. All of a sudden, he seemed to deflate before our eyes. 'I have been instructed', he began in a beaten voice, 'to offer you every facility – though why', he snapped, in an attempt to regain the initiative, 'I cannot imagine'.

'Quite', said Holmes.

'I have therefore', he went on, as if not having heard, and handing Holmes a sheet of paper, 'written a pass which will gain you access to the King's presence at all times. He will be kept under guard by the French police; as we do not know to what extent they can be trusted, the plan is to infiltrate our own men amongst them. We are expecting a division under Inspector Lestrade, of Scotland Yard, this evening. You may associate yourself with them or not, as you please'.

'How much do you know of this plot?' demanded Holmes.

'Only that the attempt is to be made at the theatre'.

'Which theatre? The King has two theatrical engagements'.

'Whichever, I suppose, is appropriate. That, at any rate, is the message I received'.

'From whom?'

'An agent who has since died. He tracked the conspirators to their meeting- place, overheard part of their conversation, was discovered, badly beaten, and left for dead. I was called to the hospital: his words to me were his last'.

'There was no clue as to which theatre they meant?'

'None', said the nobleman shortly.

'I think', said Holmes, as we emerged from the oppressive official atmosphere into the late spring afternoon, 'that a little dissipation would be appropriate'; and having returned to our hotel to change, had us driven to Montmartre.   I do not recall very clearly the events of that evening: it comes back to me in a kaleidoscope of whirling red skirts and an excess of *absinthe*. All I remember with certainty is that my head throbbed like a steam-hammer as I stood with Holmes the following day among the crowds that filled the Champs-Élysées.   The King's train was due to come in at the Bois de Boulogne. Here waited the President of France, who, upon the arrival of the King, set out with him in the first of six carriages, each drawn by four horses, and surrounded by a large escort of cavalry.   As the procession made its way down the Champs-Élysées, an uncanny silence prevailed.   A few scattered cheers could be heard for the President of the Republic; but above these came angry cries of '*Vive Fashoda!*' and '*Vivent les Boers!*'   The King sat straight-backed and smiling, refusing to be perturbed; but the President, it appeared, was gravely embarrassed, as he spoke in what seemed an apologetic manner.   The King's aides, meanwhile, looked gloomy and depressed.   'If this continues', muttered Holmes to me in an undertone, 'there will be no need for the assassins to make their attempt.   It will serve their purpose better to let the King alone'.

That evening, the King was due to visit the Comédie Française.   We were met in the lobby by an openly hostile Frenchman who, in heavily accented English, introduced himself as Inspector Laplanche, the responsible officer of the Paris police.   He took us to a dressing-room, where we were fitted out in the livery of the theatre, and then upstairs.   As we rounded the corner of a corridor, an oafish fellow in similar uniform collided with me, and we both fell to the floor.   As I picked myself up and dusted myself, I looked at him in amazement.

'Lestrade!'

He blinked at me in puzzlement.

'Don't you recognise me? Watson. And this is Mr. Holmes'.

He gave an astonished laugh. 'Mr. Holmes I know; but as for you, Dr. Watson, I shouldn't have recognised you in a month of Sundays. Gone native good and proper, by the look of things'.

'Only in externals, Lestrade', I replied. 'Like yourself'.

'Between you and me, Doctor', muttered Lestrade, as Holmes beckoned me from up the corridor, 'I'll be glad when we're out of all this. Never seen such people in my life. Talk gibberish and eat vermin. And can't even carry out a murder like honest men. Be happy to be back among criminals of my own kind, if you see what I mean'.

We stood at the rear of the royal box as the King entered. His reception was, if any- thing, worse than that of the morning. Far from that warm and encouraging hum which generally precedes a performance, the air of the auditorium was cold and hostile. As the King took his seat, hisses were heard.

When the performance began, I realised that what remained of my school French was far from adequate to the occasion. My thoughts gradually turned to the danger that beset us while, surrounded by foreigners and traitors, the King risked his life for the sake of his people. Tears had formed in my eyes, when a sudden murmur and movement told me that we had reached the entr'acte. Suddenly, the face of my beloved King was in front of me as in a nightmare, his eyes bulbous and staring as he shouted a brief command that seemed to end in the word '*fou!*' – a word I had heard all too often from my French master at public school. It seemed to me that he had seen through my disguise, and that he took me for a fool, if not an outright lunatic. The King's tantrums were rare but volcanic, and I thought, with sadness, of how the strain of his inhospitable reception had worked upon his normally affable nature. But Holmes immediately leaped forward, offering the King a light, and, as the monarch smiled his thanks, I realised that what I had heard was '*du feu*'. Holmes took advantage of his good humour to express, in fluent and voluble French, effusive gratitude for His Majesty's condescension in paying a visit to his so-beautiful France. The King softened visibly as he listened, then stubbed out his cigar with decision. 'I will walk in the foyer', he said, in a voice that did not brook contradiction.

The disguised policemen looked at one another in consternation. Laplanche rolled his eyes. But Holmes, in a moment, was at my side. 'Quick, Watson!' he hissed. 'We must follow him. Keep close; place yourself in the way of any assailant'.

I thrilled at the notion of being of service to the King; but, as it happened, it was unnecessary. As His Majesty strolled in the foyer, wearing on his shirt-front the Grand Cordon of the Legion of Honour, he caught sight of a lady who, as Holmes later informed me, was a noted French actress. Taking her hand, the King recalled how he had seen her on the London stage, where, he said, in a French so clear that even I could understand it, and so loud that all around could hear it, 'you represented all the grace and spirit of France'.

These were the words that turned the tide; and it gives me great pleasure to recall that it was my friend Sherlock Holmes who was the occasion of the King's uttering them. By the following morning, they had been repeated all over Paris; and, as the King drove out to a military review under the grey tower of Vincennes, the crowds were noticeably warmer than on the previous day. Gravely, the His Majesty saluted the French tricolour; and, as his own royal standard was unfurled, there was an outburst of cheers. When he spoke of his feelings on his return to their charming city – always, he said, like a homecoming to him – a tremendous ovation thundered forth. Veteran diplomats later declared that so total a change in the attitude of a people was beyond their experience. In the afternoon, the King journeyed to Longchamp, where a race-meeting provided opportunities for his known love of betting. I myself could not resist a flutter; and my halting French, and evident English accent, were as much matters of congratulation and conviviality as on the day before they had drawn forth reproach and execration. I was about to join some excellent fellows in a glass of wine when Holmes whispered, 'Let us go, Watson, or we shall fail to catch up with the King'.

'But the King is in his box'.

'Someone is in his box, and is wearing identical costume. But you will notice how the hat has been pulled down over the eyes since the last race, and the scarf pulled up about the neck. The man is an actor, who has more than once been called upon to impersonate the King'.

'Where, then, has His Majesty gone?' I asked, a sense of dread forming in my stomach, as our carriage moved out of the enclosure.

'There', replied Holmes, 'we enter upon a somewhat delicate subject. The royal pleasure in the company of the fair sex is known, I presume, to everybody in the Empire. His Majesty has betaken himself to a place where he can indulge it'.

'You do not, I hope, Holmes, refer to a house of prostitution?'

'I do, Watson; I do indeed'.

'But...but...' I felt altogether at a loss as I attempted to put into words my sense of horror at the thought of the King of

England in a common brothel. 'But what', I stammered, aghast, 'what will the French think?'

For answer, Holmes burst into a peal of laughter. He rolled helplessly on the carriage seat until he was breathless, and tears of amusement streamed from his eyes. 'Ah, Watson', he said, when he had got back his breath, 'You are a veritable compendium of conventional English opinion. The French' – and he laughed again – 'the French have a house – you know what I mean, I hope – in which the chair on which His Majesty sat is on display as their proudest advertisement. *That* is what the French think'. And he burst into another round of helpless laughter. I looked out the window.

'You will be pleased to hear, however, friend Watson', spluttered Holmes, 'that His Majesty has taken some pains over his reputation. On previous visits to Paris, he has had himself announced as the Duke of Lancaster, or the Earl of Chester. One must admit, however, that these attempts are superficial. When the Earl, or Duke, flirts with his Suzettes, or presses champagne on his *danseuses*, he can be seen to carry a stick imprinted with the royal monogram. Our sovereign's notion of anonymity, Watson – there is no gainsaying it – is a schoolboy's. It is not a disguise; it is a dressing up. Beneath the mask, he longs to be seen for what he is, and applauded for his cleverness. And for this the French love him still more. For he possesses that last and rarest mark of the born monarch: the gift, truly regal, of the common touch'.

We had by now reached a street of tall and dignified houses on the Left Bank. They were masterpieces of cut white stone and elaborate wrought iron; but in front of them a great deal of road-work was taking place. Holmes glanced at the labourers and remarked: 'Yes, Watson, I think that we may safely leave the King in their hands'.

'What on earth are you talking about, Holmes?'

'Surely you realise who they are?'

'They look like road-workers to me'.

'They are meant to. They are members of the French police. Observe the man with the whistle. Remove the villainous beard, and you have Laplanche. When the King makes a private visit in Paris, it is their practice to take over the nearest café, where they pose as customers: a welcome duty, you may be sure. Here, where there is no such establishment, they are reduced to digging up the road'.

We returned to the Embassy, where a meeting was taking place to co-ordinate plans for the following night, when the King was due to run the gauntlet of the theatre a second time. On a table was a scale model of the grandiose Opéra, which opened to show details of the seating arrangements, as well as every entrance and exit. Blue counters showed where members of the French police were to be stationed, while red stood for the British. Lord Augustus ran over the details, pointing out that the structure had been specially designed to foil assassination attempts upon Napoleon the Third, with an entrance that enabled a coach to pass directly to the dress circle. Guarded as it was, the aristocrat pronounced the building impregnable.

'I trust, Mr. Holmes', he said with heavy sarcasm, 'that you find our arrangements satisfactory'.

'Perfectly so', replied Holmes with courtesy, 'insofar as any arrangements can be. What we cannot know is what is going on inside each of those small blue counters'. And he pointed to the board. 'The conspirators are as well aware of the difficulties as are we, and will have planned accordingly. If they have said that they will strike at the theatre, that is what they will do. You are certain that that is what they intend?'

'Yes, of course', said the aristocrat languidly. 'More or less'.

'"More or less"!' cried Holmes in disbelief. 'A king's life hangs in the balance – the peace of Europe depends upon it –

and you speak to me of "more or less"! What were the exact words you heard from your agent?'

'I do not know that that concerns you, Mr. Holmes'.

'I will show you how much it concerns me. Does the name Mycroft Holmes mean anything to you?'

I could see from Bland's cornered look that it did. I have had occasion in the course of these narratives to refer to Holmes' brother, a reasoner of even greater force than my friend, but hindered, by his immense and uncouth physical inertia, from applying his powers in action. Instead, he sat in Whitehall, where his incisive intellect had more than once made him arbiter of national policy. There were occasions, Holmes had revealed to my astonishment, when he might indeed be said to *be* the British Government. The mere mention of his name was enough to make the flippant aristocrat quail.

'Mycroft', Holmes went on, in a tone of menace that I had never heard him use before, 'is my brother; and I assure you, Lord Augustus, that if any harm should come to the King through your obstruction, you will not only, personally, never hold public office again, but the ensuing scandal will shake the very foundations of the order to which you belong. You great nobles hold command over us as if by right of birth; but in the minds of many, your day is long done. Defy me, and I will see to it that a system which perpetuates aristocratic incompetence is forever discredited. The name of Augustus Bland will become a byword, and you will enter history to be pointed at in loathing and scorn. Now what was the message?'

I had never seen my friend in such a passion. The nobleman looked pale. 'I will tell you everything, Mr. Holmes', he said in a shaking voice. 'But you must realise that I had what I considered very good reasons for not confiding fully in you. The message, as it stood, was so disrespectful to the King that I felt it unbecoming to repeat it'.

'The message', demanded Holmes, implacable.

Lord Augustus brought out a pocketbook, which he opened and handed to Holmes. 'Here is what the agent overheard', he said. 'I took it down at his bedside'. Holmes read it aloud, frowning. 'The old lecher is a heretic and a freemason. We shall dispose of him at the appropriate – theatre'.

'This agent of yours: was he English or French?'

'French', answered Lord Augustus. 'But he was the most loyal...'

Holmes, with an urgent gesture, cut through his protestation. 'And this word "theatre"', he went on, stabbing at the paper, 'did he pronounce it as English or French?'

The aristocrat stared at Holmes as if he had been the very devil. 'As it happens, he lapsed into French for that one word. He was struggling for breath; it was the last word he spoke; I took it that he was already delirious. But he had given us the one piece of certain information we know: that an attempt is to be made upon the King's life at the theatre'.

'We know no such thing', said Holmes, with furrowed brow. 'The French employ that word with great freedom. As we speak of a theatre of war, meaning a site or location, so do they of a *théâtre d'un crime*, or scene of a crime. If they were to say that a quiet village had been a *théâtre d'événements peu habituels*, they would simply mean that it had witnessed unusual happenings. It denotes little more than a setting. He was struggling for some such word as he died; and all he could bring to mind was his native French. And, thanks to your incompetence, the King has been in mortal danger all this time. Our thoughts, however, must now be for the present. What setting, or scene, would these people deem appropriate?' His brow remained furrowed, concentrated in thought.

Just then, Inspector Laplanche arrived. Lord Augustus, now thoroughly cowed, asked if he had returned with the King.

'By no means', replied the inspector, with what seemed to me a pinpoint of triumph in his eyes. 'His Majesty desired some refreshment, and we left him in a nearby café'.

'Alone?' asked Holmes in alarm.

'Of course not, M'sieu', said the Frenchman, with expansive hands. 'When I informed him that my men were exhausted by their labours, he showed the greatest understanding. I have therefore sent them home, with the exception of four who will follow his carriage at a respectful distance'.

'Along which route?', demanded Holmes.

Laplanche walked to a large-scale map of Paris which hung on the wall. His finger traced a route from the Left Bank to the Right, passing over the head of the island between. I saw Holmes' eyes narrow. Then, electrified, he grasped me by the arm. 'Come, Watson! We have not an instant to lose! Pray God we are not too late!'

Holmes raced down the stairs, commandeered a passing cab, and, waving a sheaf of banknotes, urged the cabman to make for the river with the utmost speed. I jumped in after him as the vehicle began to move. 'Have you got your revolver, Watson?', he asked in a breathless tone.

'Yes', I replied. 'It is here in my pocket. But what...?'

'There is no time for explanations. Take it out and see that it is ready. It is little, but it may be of some use. If only I had known!' And he shook his head in a paroxysm of despair.

As our cab raced down the Rue Saint-Honoré, I leaned out, and saw pedestrians scatter in our path. At the bottom of the street, we swung right, and the bridge over the Seine hove into view.

We arrived at the Pont-Neuf just as the King's carriage started onto it at the other end. Holmes shouted to the coachman to whip up his horses. As we neared the centre, and arrived on the island, I saw a shadowy figure emerge from behind a statue to the right, holding something in its hands, which it was preparing to throw. Some flash of memory came back to me from an ambush in Afghanistan; and, unthinkingly, I raised my pistol and fired. The figure crumpled over, and as we drove on at high speed, the royal carriage passing us on the other side, a brilliant flash became visible through our back window. It was followed by the sound of an explosion. Holmes called to the driver; we slowed and turned. When we arrived again at the centre of the bridge, we were met by a horrible sight. There was no body to speak of: the pavement was a bloodied mess. Even I, who had witnessed so many dreadful sights in the course of my military career, turned away, sickened. A clatter of hooves and wheels approached from the Left Bank, as the French police escort belatedly reached the scene. From the Right Bank, simultaneously, came Bland and Laplanche. The royal carriage had by now disappeared.

Later that evening, when we had returned to our hotel room, Holmes held a glass of fine cognac against the light, then gestured with it to the figure on its column outside the window. 'We must be grateful to Napoleon, Watson', he remarked, 'for establishing the continental practice of driving on the right. Had the positions of the carriages been reversed, no human agency could have saved the King. As it was, we were close enough to his assailant for you to get in that shot'.

'I still do not understand how you knew he would be waiting there'.

'Not knew; suspected. But by the time I hurried you from that room, it was a suspicion close to certainty. Once I saw Laplanche's finger point to the bridge, I felt that we had found our location. It was the perfect spot for an ambush: narrow, concentrated, and, at the point where it crossed the island, with its quiet park, providing the ideal hiding-place'.

'So that is how you knew he would be there?'

'No, Watson, not at all. These reflections came to me afterwards – if one can speak of before and after in a chain of reasoning which was compressed into a single moment. You see, that little patch of grass and trees is known as the Square du Vert-Galant. This immediately chimed with Lord Augustus' message. *Vert-galant* has very much the same meaning as "old lecher" except that it is admiring where the other is derogatory: a perennially youthful lover, rather than an elderly rake. It refers to another king, who died at the hands of an assassin on this spot, and who was, in the eyes of the majority of his subjects, a heretic.

'This was the first thought that flashed into my mind. Then, suddenly, with a dreadful sinking in the stomach, I realised the full significance of the site.

'I have spoken to you, Watson, of the capacity of these people for remembrance. And on that spot there took place an event which, more than any other, has re-echoed in the memory of France. There, on the 24th of March, 1314, was burnt Jacques Molay, last Grand Master of the Order of the Temple, while the King of France watched from the window of his palace.

'To this day, the true meaning of the event is unknown. But what is more certain is that when Louis the Sixteenth was led to execution, near that place on the Champs-Élysées where we sat the other day, the whole vast arena was crowded with sombre French men and women, who watched silently as the King was dragged, struggling, to the guillotine and held down under the blade. When it had descended, and the severed head was held aloft, the sight was met, still, with silence. Then, above it, there rang out a voice of triumph.

"Vengeance!" it cried. "Vengeance on the murderers of Jacques Molay!"'. So, to one side of the French conscience, justice at last had been meted out, after the space of almost five hundred years.

'The speaker was never identified. But the Revolution was prepared in the Masonic lodges of Europe; and French Masonry traces its lineage to the Order of the Temple. The most distinguished Freemason of today is, as Bland reminded us, our own King. To the conspirators of the Order of Charlemagne, he is the other side of a debate which has raged for centuries in France, and which vexes it still. By assassinating him, at a site of the most perfect historical significance, they hoped to resolve it in favour of themselves: to undo the Revolution, both in sign and in reality. Nothing could be more "appropriate"'.

'It is masterly', I said.

'Tut', replied Holmes. 'It was the work of a moment. All the information was available to me; I had only to find the thread'.

Next day, the King drove to the Opéra through a cheering throng; and when, on the day following, he boarded the train for London at the Invalides, the Paris newspapers described it as *fervent, passionné*, even *délirant*. As the air resounded with cries of *Vive Edouard!*, and *Vive notre roi!*, Holmes turned to me with a smile and a lifted eyebrow. His reading of French feeling had been triumphantly vindicated.

What happened next is history. The French and English Governments met to negotiate the Entente Cordiale; and even his bitterest critics have not denied that it was the King who made it possible.

That Laplanche had colluded with the conspirators could not be proved; but he thought it prudent to resign, soon after, from the force. At about the same time, Lord Augustus Bland discovered that family matters required all his concentration, and retreated both from public life and from his liaison. Holmes and I had meanwhile been summoned to Buckingham Palace to receive the royal thanks. Holmes, characteristically, refused the credit. 'Your Majesty', he said, 'owes his life to the quickness of eye and steadiness of hand of my friend, Dr. Watson'.

'In that case', said the King, in his guttural voice, 'Watson has saved Europe'.

It was the proudest moment of my life. There was talk of a knighthood; but, knowing that Holmes had declined a similar honour, I asked instead for some memento of the occasion: some slight personal possession, perhaps, for which the King had no longer any use. Looking about him, his eye lighted on an ebony stick, set with diamonds, in a stand behind the door. 'Here', he said, 'friend Watson, this has been of support to me, even as you have. A king's only power is the place he holds in the hearts of his people'.

The diamonds form the royal initial. Holmes informs me it was a well-known sight in Paris when the King walked its streets, as he liked to think, incognito.

FOUR
THE MASS OF THE
PRESANCTIFIED

There are stories that cannot be told, even to so tried and true a friend as Watson. It is of one such that I am now about to disburden myself, in these papers designed for no eyes but my own. You, who may stumble across them in some unimaginable future, will find here no gruesome murders, no financial misdemeanours, no political intrigues. If I call what follows a mystery, it is in the original sense of that word: an initiation into secret knowledge, into what has hitherto been kept mute, and the change in your awareness that will ensue. At the end of this tale, you will have a very different perception of me from that which you now hold. And yet, as with every genuine revelation, you will realise that it is something you have always known, or sensed. In the narrations of Watson, clues to it abound. Like them, this tale involves two kinds of mystery: that of the unknown, to which I have already referred, and that of the path by which it is reached. This latter is a mystery in the sense of a calling or a craft: it is the tale of what has made me what I am. You could call it, therefore, in both senses of the word, the Mystery of Sherlock Holmes.

You saw my mistake with Bland. There was nothing wrong with him except inadequacy. He could not help being what he was; but I should have known better. It was I, and not he, who was the failure. I ought never to have allowed him to anger me. Had I kept my temper, instead of taunting him, I might have extracted his information, in a lucid and orderly progression, from the start.

Or take, again, my diatribe against aristocracy. That was hardly necessary. Mere mention of Mycroft, with a lift of the eyebrow, would have sufficed. But once again my anger prevailed.

All this will show you how far I am from the perfect reasoner that Watson portrays. But the fact is, in this instance my reason was overwhelmed. I never should have acted as I did, had it not been for that whiff of scent upon the air. Of the 75 separate fragrances that I have alluded to in *The Hound of the Baskervilles*, this was far and away the most evocative. It brought me back more years than I cared to remember, to where the memories thronged about me, as once around Odysseus the spirits of the dead. I kept them at bay by burying myself in my task: having found that work, as I once remarked to Watson, is the best antidote to sorrow. I left no moment unoccupied. I invented an obstacle- course for my friend, when I could as easily have explained to him what I meant. When all else failed, I took to my violin. But there, too, in the ballad of *Malbrouck*, strange and unwelcome thoughts welled to the surface.

> *Madame à sa tour monte,*
> *Mironton, mironton, mirontaine;*
> *Madame à sa tour monte,*
> *Si haut qu'elle peut monter.*

In the tale of the lady who mounted the tower of her castle, ascending as high as she could, the ancient grief returned. I tried to put it away. This was something that had happened a long time ago. It was an old song, old perhaps even when Marlborough went to the wars. There is a tale that the Crusaders sang it before the walls of Jerusalem. Far away, I told myself: far away and long ago. But again, with relentless insistence, the words burned themselves into my brain.

Monsieur Malbrouck est mort,
Mironton, mironton, mirontaine;
Monsieur Malbrouck est mort,
Est mort et enterré.

Yes: the lady's lover was dead: dead and buried. Let him remain interred: it was better so. But on the last evening of the King's visit, a note was handed in to our hotel. It read:

Sherlock – I must see you. I know I deserve no consideration at your hands. But if ever you have cared for me, meet me tomorrow, at any hour or place you will. A note to my residence will confirm the appointment. Yours ever, Caroline.

It was as Caroline Musgrave that I first had made her acquaintance. Readers of Watson's memoirs will recall the bizarre episode of the Musgrave Ritual, which involved an acquaintance of my university days. Reginald Musgrave was a man of old family but retiring disposition and few friends. I was greatly surprised, therefore, when, one morning early in Hilary term, on visiting his rooms, I found him closeted with a lively young woman. As I entered, she was laughing, and was still laughing as she turned to me. 'You must be Sherlock'. I bowed, a little uneasily, not knowing what to make of such ready informality. 'Reginald has been telling me the most extraordinary things. He makes you a worker of miracles. It is as if you could see through walls – not to speak of people'. I demurred, smilingly. 'Let me test you', she went on. 'Tell me, what do you see in me?'
'Very little', I replied. 'Only that you are a relative, that you come from Hampshire, and that you are a Roman Catholic'.

107

'This is unfair, Mr. Holmes', she exclaimed, though she seemed a little taken aback. 'Reginald has been telling you about me'.

'By no means', said I. 'He is most punctilious in such matters. That you are a relative is plain from your features – a suggestion about the eyes – and is confirmed by the genealogical table which is open on the table between you. The small gold crucifix around your neck proclaims your faith. The only real difficulty is Hampshire; but I deduced that from the traces of mud on your left boot. As Reginald will tell you, geology is one of my hobbies'.

A thin smile crossed the languid and aristocratic countenance of Musgrave; while it seemed to me that a wary look had crept into his kinswoman's large and expressive eyes. 'You are correct on every point, Mr. Holmes. An ancestor of my father's served under Wellington at Waterloo; and it was on a tour of the battlefield that he met my mother, an ancestor of whose had fought on the opposite side. As you can well imagine, some of Napoleon's officers were not anxious to return to France under the Bourbons; and so he took service in the new kingdom of Belgium. My mother's family made it a condition of her marriage to my father that any children should be brought up as Catholics. Were Reginald less reticent than he is, you would know that his side of the family has never quite accepted her'.

I had indeed seemed to feel a sense of disapproval emanating from Musgrave, which I had put down to her freedom of manner; and when she suggested they lunch together, he excused himself coldly. I could see that she was hurt; and, not wishing her to think badly of our college, offered to accompany her. She accepted with alacrity; and Musgrave, I could see, was relieved. His attitude to her was that of the Englishman of the upper classes to the incomprehensible foreigner; and that she was a relative only made the matter more difficult.

I brought her to a tea-shop popular amongst the students, as she wished to see something of university life. We sat at a window table, with the vista of Oxford in motion outside: abstracted dons and animated students, strolling amid the medieval walls, or making way for the occasional carriage. With her ash-blonde hair and black velvet dress, relieved only by the glitter of the thin gold chain and its ornament, she made a striking figure; and, in the course of the afternoon, acquaintances seemed to look upon me in a new, and apparently startling, light. I later heard that the word had spread like wildfire, from the boathouses on the Isis to the inmost recesses of the library, that the college hermit had been seen with a stunner. I hardly remember what we talked about; only a growing sense that we had always known each other. When the time came for her to go, it seemed to me she did so with reluctance; while, as I watched her train gather speed as it drew away from the platform, I knew that I had fallen in love. It was an unaccustomed sensation, but I analysed it with my usual care. It was, I decided, a cross between high fever and vertigo before an unusually perilous precipice. There was nothing for it, I thought, but to stand back from the latter, and wait for the former to subside. I did not expect to hear from her again.

But some days later there came a note from her, thanking me for my hospitality, and adding, in the form of a P.S., that she planned to be in the vicinity over the succeeding weekend, and would be pleased if I could find time to see her. She named an inn that overlooked the placid lake of Blenheim, with the great Roman bridge that rides across it to the palace of Marlborough. It was here, in that magnificent park, that we wandered together that Saturday afternoon. The vast and antique setting seemed both to transport us to another time, and to make our youth more immediate and intimate. As I took my leave of her in the gathering dark, she kissed me on the lips and said: 'I think you had better go'. I was still unschooled enough not to realise that she meant the opposite.

Love was no longer fever; it was delirium and a dream. Next day she hired a carriage, and we drove to Rousham, where, beyond the fallow fields, a classical arcade glimmered across the river. It was there, in a strange old garden with a stream that runs serpentine between stone runnels, that we became lovers. Why this was happening to me was something I could not understand; but she told me afterwards that I had the look of a doomed poet. There is a photograph from that time which might lend some support to the suggestion: in which the ascetic features which have been described to you are softened by youth and a wistful melancholy. As to poetry, it will no doubt also surprise you, who have known me only as I have seemed to Watson, that I perpetrated some at this time. And for the doom, you will hear of it in due course.

Before me, as I write, is the letter which brought me for the first time to Paris. Here she suggests that, since the Easter vacation is approaching, we spend it there together. She knows that for a student this will be a great extravagance; but as her family has made her a generous allowance, she wonders if I will permit her to bestow on herself a gift she would treasure above all else.

It was not possible to refuse an invitation couched with such tact; nor did I need any but the flimsiest cover for my pride. I am not sure, on reflection, that it was not the waiting that was most wonderful. I wrote to her every day, and sometimes several times a day: every triviality of college life seemed significant as I stored it up to tell her, and subject to the alchemy of our relation. It was a showery spring; and it was then I noticed that, under rain, the stone of the Oxford colleges turns to gold. It seemed to me an image of the transformation that had occurred in my ancient, ascetic and unvarying way of life.

Another image: there was a late fall of snow one Sunday; and the lights behind the diamond-paned windows of the quadrangle on which I lived burned with a more intense glow as they made a path across it. So, too, our voyage beckoned to me as I marked a cross each evening on my calendar.

Like all that is looked forward to too intensely, our reunion was not at first a success. Petty annoyances – a surly porter, someone else in our seats – made her petulant; the crossing was rough, and she was ill. By the time we arrived in Paris, I was convinced that the venture had been a mistake. My glimpses of the city seemed remote as picture postcards as we drove to our hotel, a rambling seventeenth-century house in the Rue Serpente. Though it was part of the medieval district, and not very far from Notre-Dame, I did not stir from it, but remained reading at her bedside as she slept through the rest of the day.

I dozed off where I sat. It was still dark when I was awoken by an urgent shaking. As I came awake, I saw the sheets thrown back to reveal the paleness of her body. Only a very few moments, it seemed, after we had clung to each other in exhaustion, we had resumed. All that day we drowsed or reached for each other, until, after dark, hunger of another kind drove us out. So it was throughout our time there. Some evenings, we sat quietly in some café along the Boulevard St.-Michel, content as some old couple with each other's company, as if we had already used up our lives. Others, we sought out the noisier haunts of the workers, as in the Place Contrescarpe, where beer was imbibed instead of wine and the people seemed more interested in one another than in their effect on passers-by. There were days when we went out in the early dawn, when the white stone of Paris looks newly minted, and wandered through streets where the smell of the day's fresh-baked bread arose from the gratings, until the café chairs were taken down from the tables where, inverted, they had lain stacked overnight.

There was a park where we sat under trees in the warmest hours of the day, the river lapping at our feet as it urged its journey seaward through the heart of the city, on the prow of the ship that is the Île de la Cité. It was when we were coming back from here up the steps to the Pont Neuf that my eye caught the word *Templiers* in an inscription, and acquired the information which, so many years later, was to save a king's life and astonish Watson. At the time, my reflections were more sombre. The destruction of the Order of the Temple, I thought, was the victory of power over mystery.

The city was not a place for me, but a state of mind: everything I saw was part of her novelty and strangeness. Once, as we lay by the river, while a willow rustled overhead and the shadows of its leaves flickered over her face, I asked her to tell me of her first lover.

'I do not know if you could call him a lover', she said. 'I never discovered his name'.

This piqued my curiosity still further, and she told me. It had been in the previous springtime, during her final year at school. Her family had sent her to be educated at a convent in Bruges. She had never felt completely at home in England: her faith, and her mother's foreignness, had brushed her with a tinge of the unacceptable; and the old and beautiful city, on its medieval waterways, seemed now to stir some ancestral memory. In place of confusion, she found peace. There was a death-like perfection about the setting that seemed to her an image of the absolute. The walls of the convent, with the water lapping around them – 'it was like here', she said to me, 'only there the water is still; and the city, too, seems frozen in time' – seemed to offer a quiet beyond all questioning.

She had begun to think she might make it her life. There had been gentle nudgings and pressures from the sisters, who, with their high white coifs, reminded her of the swans reflected on the surface of the city's canals. But, as the time approached for her to make a decision, she became increasingly uncertain about the drastic step that was required of her, and began to feel hemmed in.

One day, when out on a walk in the surrounding countryside, the girls marching two by two in a long crocodile, she was oppressed by the sense of conformity, the lack of individual will. Then it started to rain. On impulse, she had broken away from the group and, their cries following her, made away across the fields, flat and sodden between desolate alders. She ran a long way until her companions could no longer be heard. The downpour, meanwhile, that drove across Flanders on the wind from the North Sea, had soaked her to the skin. When she found a barn, she entered it. The interior was in semi-darkness, like a church; the wooden pillars that held up the high, slanted roof intensified the resemblance. But the smell was different. It was warm there, and the moisture in the air brought out the odours of the earthen floor and the baled straw. She took off her clothes, wrung them out, and spread them to dry over one bale of straw while she sat on another.

As her eyes became used to the gloom, she was aware of being watched. Then she saw him. He was a young man, scarcely more than a boy – a peasant with tow-coloured hair – who stood against one of the pillars. Her gaze in return did not seem to disconcert, rather to invite him: perhaps, she thought later, it had. Gradually he approached, still gazing at her, and walking as if in a trance. His eyes held hers until, as she had somehow realised he would, he dropped to his knees before her. Scarcely knowing what she did, she placed her hands on his head, as if in blessing. Perhaps he took it as a signal; because he sank his head, and she felt his tongue rustle gently over her pubic hair.   She sank back, opening herself, while with the same gentleness he brought her into a trance of her own.   When she started up again, he was gone.

She was punished when she returned to the convent; but she no longer cared.   She knew, now, that her vocation did not lie within those hallowed walls.   In a ritual still more ancient, in a sanctuary far more primitive, she had served in a worship of which she was the idol.   It was a ritual of which instantaneously, as if along the pathways of a memory older than her own, she had understood the meaning.

A cloud covered the sun as she concluded this story, and I felt a sense of foreboding.   There was something in the tale which disturbed me, which seemed to presage the end of our love, but I could not tell what it was.   Sensing my mood, she touched my cheek with the back of her hand.   'I never saw him again', she said soothingly.   'You have no cause to be jealous'.

Yes, that no doubt was what it was.   I shook away the thought.   'So that', I observed, 'was how you lost your religious faith'.

'Oh, no', she replied, 'I have not'.   And I knew immediately she spoke the truth.   She had never taken off the crucifix, even when she wore nothing else.   While her body glistened with perspiration, it continued to glitter there.   As we returned to our hotel, I realised that it was this that had disturbed me.   I decided it had to do with her being Catholic.   There is a puritan strain in Protestantism, for which things must be what they seem: in which sinner and saint are distinct.   She could move between one and the other: could sin and confess, and clear her conscience.   What for me was a matter of choice, of weight and counter-weight, of computation and conclusion, required no such effort from her.   She could fall

114

and repent and, like a naughty child, be sure of her parents' pardon.

One world of hers was as strange to me as the other. It was also as beautiful. That day she took me to the Sainte-Chapelle. The sunlight, shining warmly through the coloured glass, made that lucent space like a jewelled chalice, while about it was entwined, in piercing beauty, the song of an antique service. It was Thursday; and on the opening notes of *In monte Oliveti*, I felt myself enter her earlier world. It was a world at once more civilised and more spiritual than our own. In a few sounds, sprinkled like shooting-stars over the dimmest recesses of the mind, I found all the vaunted progress of our century set at naught. The disciplined dance of the polyphony, the soaring of the upper registers over the repeated waves of the lower, brought me into a place where multiplicity and singularity, discipline and passion, were one. In that strange combination of immobility and motion, I seemed to be taken to a place outside time: a world of suspended animation, in which death seemed but a finer form of life, and life an elaboration of death. In that moment of the intersection of worlds, I felt, the artist had attained the stillness which is at the heart of the interweavings of love. Within that jewelled chalice, borne on its ship-like island, I felt desire and death intermingle, as in the poisonous potion on the craft that carried Tristan. I cared as little as he, in the ecstasy of the moment. But as twilight fell, and the windows blackened, I was chilled at the passing of all things mortal. Friday was our last full day in Paris: she had arranged that we were to return on the Saturday. After a morning's lovemaking, over which, already, there hung the shadow of the morrow, she took me to Notre-Dame. It was an overcast day, and the spaces between the columns were shrouded in gloom. Gloom, too, visibly covered the pictures and statuary in the form of purple draperies. An icy rain had begun to fall outside, and the

115

worshippers, as they came in, added to the sensation of odoriferous damp. On the bare altar the box was open, like a rifled safe. The priest carried the golden cup from an altar at the side, in front of which a red lamp burned, and from it fed the faithful, muttering. It was incomprehensible to me. I remarked, as we came out on the steps: 'I have never seen a Mass before'.

'It is not a Mass, properly speaking. There is no consecration'.

'Consecration?'

'Yes. The changing of the bread and wine. Today is a day of death, on which nothing can be transformed. All that was done yesterday evening. Those who communicate today do so on the basis of yesterday. What you saw is called the Mass of the Presanctified'.

Again, I was seized by a dread I could not name. These ancient, indecipherable rituals moved with a strange and ambivalent force of their own. In speaking of a life beyond death, they brought death into the heart of life. That night, our lovemaking was overshadowed: I was chilled by the desolate ritual we had witnessed. It was not only the joy that had gone out of it, but the sense of meeting and completing each other.

Next morning, before taking the boat-train, we visited the Sainte-Chapelle for the last time. It glowed again in the early-morning light; but its chalice seemed empty, drained by a chant of ruin and dispossession. 'The stones of the Temple', it sang, 'are scattered, at the entrance to all the ways'.

Dispersi sunt lapides sanctuarii
in caput omnium platearum.

It was on the boat that my worst imaginings came true. She would not see me after this, she said: she was going home to be married. 'To whom?' I gasped irrelevantly, my brain numbed by her words. To the young Duke of Axbury, she replied. It was a brilliant match.

'You love him, then?', I faltered.

'No. But he fancies himself in love with me'.

The hope aroused by her words quickly faded, as she explained to me what it meant to her. At one step it would bring her position and power, wipe out every humiliation she had suffered from Reginald's family, and make her free. She would fulfil the obligations expected of her; after that, her life would be her own.

At first I could find no words to answer her. I was so bereft of feeling that it drove out all speech. Loss, protestation, anger came slowly to take its place. But, for every protest of mine, she had an unassailable answer.

'How could you have done this to me?'

'Done? Do you resent what I have given?'

It was my turn to be astonished. 'Given? But you never gave. You only seemed to. It was a sham, a charade...'

'I gave what I could. I held nothing back from you'.

It was true: I remembered the abandon of her lovemaking. Then another memory returned to me, of the three words she had whispered at the height of her ecstasy. 'But you said that you...'

'I did. I do. But this is not a question of love. This was determined long ago. It has nothing to do with you. Or, in a very real sense, with me. This is what must be done. It is the opportunity of a lifetime, and a lifetime such as most women can only dream of. You would not deprive me of that?'

I could not say that I did: I loved her far too much. Into my dejected silence came another question.

'Do you regret what I have given you?'

Again, I could not say that I did.   But it seemed to me that such giving implied continuance.   I tried to say so.

'You speak as if we had a contract.   What promises did I make?   Did you think we were engaged in *trade*?'

She spoke the last word so offensively that I was silenced. I realised exactly what she meant.   She belonged to a caste that thought itself beyond obligation, save to itself; that expected what it gave to be received as largesse.   It was a world in which I had no place.   She had taken me up; she could drop me.   She had been hungry for experience; I was one of her experiments.   She had sensed, in me, a worshipper; I had obliged with idolatry.   If she chose to shatter the icon, that, in her own view, was her right.   I had no claim upon her whatever.

This was what I learned on the crossing, as we moved steadily homeward across a glassy sea.   It was there, on the ship, between two worlds, that I drained her poisoned chalice. All too quickly, the coast of Britain hove into view: I had never thought a land- fall there could be so bitter.

I was lost for words at the harbour.   Then I had one last, desperate idea.   A final night together, and I would resign her. One more meeting, to prepare my heart to let her go.   There appeared in her eyes a look of panic such as I had never seen before, and I knew her reply even before she shook her head and hurried away.   In that look I saw everything: my persistence was a threat to her real life: that glittering life in which I could have no part.   I had nothing to offer her; and the only emotion she retained towards me was fear.   She was afraid that I would make a scandal.

The whistle blew for the London train; I boarded it like an automaton.   As it began to move, I almost jumped out again to follow her; but the memory of that look restrained me. In London, the streets were prim and sanctimonious in their Sunday silence, broken by the pealing of bells.   Without thinking, I had looked up the connection for Oxford; but immediately realised that I could not return there. Every corner of the city was steeped in her memory: here we had walked together, there I had torn open a letter from her. To have gone back would have been to inhabit a house of the dead. There was only one solution: Mycroft.

It was my brother who, in teaching me to apply my reason, saved it. For him my disaster was a problem in logic, nothing more. Himself immune to the unreason of passion, he was severe upon my failure to grasp the essential clue: the visit to Musgrave. Why else should she, who set no store by abstract matters, for whom – as I must quickly have realised – immediacy of interest was everything; why should she wish to explore her genealogy? Surely it must mean that it fulfilled some immediate need? What could this have been, except a prospective marriage – and a marriage in which ancestry was of supreme importance? A marriage which displeased cousin Reginald, whom she would now outrank: a displeasure I had misread as personal disapproval. A marriage, then, by implication, to a social superior. To Mycroft, the aristocratic match was plain from the outset.

The question, indeed, had occurred to me. On that first afternoon, I had asked indirectly about the cause of her visit. She answered me with equal indirection. The taciturn Reginald was the head of the family, she explained; but she had found that – as I myself was to discover later – he took little interest in the family past.

At that time, the question could not possibly be of any concern to me. By the time it was, I was too deeply involved with her to frame it. 'Precisely!', growled Mycroft. I had shied away from knowledge, because I did not wish to know. For him, the fault was mine. I had failed in reason, because I had allowed something other than reason to skew my judgement.   Reason must be immovable, impersonal, absolute.

I strove, in order to regain control over my own mind, to apply his principles.   It was then that I acquired those powers of logic, so simple in themselves, but so rarely cultivated that the person who possesses them passes for a prodigy.   It was then that I became Sherlock Holmes.

It was not attained without a struggle.   I roamed the streets of London in a daze.   I did not dare to think of what had befallen in Paris.   Our island had become an isle of death to me.   From it, there came words that repeated themselves over and over, hammering their way into my brain.   They came from that last church service of the Saturday morning, and they seemed to express my innermost thought.   They were those words of lamentation for the fall of the sanctuary.

Quomodo obscuratum est aurum;
mutatus est color optimus.

'How has the gold been dimmed; its incomparable glow degraded'.   The words, unbidden, came to mind by the fountains of Trafalgar Square, or on the crowded pavements of Fleet Street.   They came to me with their music; and to you, who have read the narrations of Watson, it will come as no surprise to learn what that music was.   He has written in awe, in his account of 'The Bruce-Partington Plans', of my ability to lose myself, in the midst of an issue of the utmost national importance, in a monograph upon the polyphonic compositions of Lassus.   In this he was correct; but he little guessed what pains that detachment had cost me.   I had set myself upon that monograph to expunge from my mind, through the rationalisation of scholarship, the power of the music over my emotions.   I do not know that I succeeded: to this day, I have not finished it.   When, again, in 'The

Dying Detective', he represented me as chanting strangely, in a fashion that appalled him, and left Mrs. Hudson trembling and weeping, while I lay, as he thought, in the last stages of some tropical fever, these were the words that he heard. What more appropriate lines to suggest the impression of delirium? How better to chill the blood of those who loved me than to intone again the phrases which had chilled my own?

There is much else in the narratives of Watson which the present story will now make plain. He has noted how reluctantly, and slowly, I spoke to him of my early life. In his account of 'The Gloria Scott', he has spoken of my very first case, worked upon 'during the two years that I spent at college'. This is true: after that Easter, I never went back. But in the immediately succeeding story, I refer to acquaintances made during my 'last years' there. The acquaintance of whom I went on to speak was Reginald Musgrave; the case was 'The Musgrave Ritual'; do you wonder, in that context, why I should evade any suggestion that might raise the question of why I left?

I could go on; but to what avail? You now know why I almost fainted at that whiff of perfume, and how I felt when, once again, I held in my hands a specimen of Caroline Musgrave's handwriting.

Why I agreed to see her was not quite clear to me at the time. What I was most aware of was a sense of pride. I had become the famed reasoner whose name Watson has blazoned to the ends of the earth. This nature of mine had been shaped in a forge of no ordinary calibre: Mycroft Holmes was the hammer, Caroline Musgrave the anvil. I wished to prove myself worthy of my tutelage: that, at any rate, is what I told myself. I replied, accordingly, that I should be pleased to meet her inside the Musée de Cluny, at three o'clock the following afternoon. Watson was easily put off. I represented to him, with perfect truth, that I was engaged upon matters connected with my treatise on polyphony. He was all consideration and tact, and proposed to himself to make a tour of those sights of Paris which he had not yet had the opportunity to see. Taking advantage of the change of mood of its inhabitants, he washed out his moustache, resumed his bowler, and once again became that solid and reassuring English presence upon whom I have so often relied. I later heard that he began with Notre-Dame, around which, of course, he succeeded in getting himself lost. Suddenly, he found himself walking down the alley in which stood the restaurant we had so unluckily entered on our first morning. Before he could retreat, he had been noticed by the proprietor, who, to the joy of his regular customers, insisted upon treating his English friend to both red wine and white. Watson was a little awkward in the telling of this; and it was only after a great deal of persistence that I succeeded in establishing that the proprietor, in the middle of the street, had greeted him with resounding kisses on both cheeks.

The museum was quiet when I entered. As I came through the courtyard, with its turrets and its decorated well, I marvelled once again at the presence of this medieval residence in the heart of the modern city. I walked through room after room, each piled with the treasures of that age. Sculpture, enamels, vestments, jewellery: the fragmentary records of a once-teeming life. Each had its place in the puzzle of history; but my thoughts were on the room where hang the Brussels tapestries of lady and unicorn. In five of the pieces, she tastes the attractions of the senses; the sixth is inscribed *à mon seul désir*. All this is rendered in the style known as *millefleurs*: the background of flowering meadows, made present in the most exquisite detail. It always came to me in front of it, with overwhelming force, that however significant, even fascinating, the records of the past, it is in its art alone that it meets our eyes on its own terms.

I was musing in this fashion as I entered the chamber. As I looked up, I saw a female form silhouetted against the tapestry. I knew that auburn head; but, as I made to retreat, she turned and smiled. 'Good afternoon, Mr. Holmes'. It was the young woman I had known as Anna Ponderby. The smile was radiant as ever; but there was a calm at its core, and a fullness about the body, that bespoke content. She informed me that she and her husband had visited the city, as he had wished to record the King's visit, and French opinion concerning England, for his journal. Today he had gone to the Parc Zoölogique with their son...

'Your son?'

'Yes, he wants to see whether French elephants and tigers are the same as English. As we wish him to discover the world for himself, Roger has taken him there'. She said this with an archness in which, however, there was no trace of mockery.

She evinced no surprise at seeing me. It transpired that she was staying at my hotel, had seen my name in the register, and, assuming that my visit was connected with that of the King, had tactfully refrained from making herself known to me. She was too well-bred to ask what I was doing in the museum, and a brief silence followed. To break it, I indicated the tapestries. 'It may interest you to recall', I remarked, 'that, having hung for centuries in a provincial château, they were brought to public attention by George Sand'.

Her response astonished me. '*L'homme c'est rien*', she murmured; '*l'oeuvre c'est tout*'.

I, who have so frequently caused others to stare, was reduced to the same condition myself. She had uttered the very words that were running through my mind as I entered the room.

'Where on earth', I asked, 'did you pick up that quotation?'

'From you: at least Watson attributes it to you at the conclusion of "The Red-Headed League"'.

'So he does; so he does', I repeated nervously, my brain in a whirl.

'But what I wonder, Mr. Holmes, is this', she went on, with that calm imperturbability of gaze, that quality compounded equally of innocence and intelligence, which had struck me at our first meeting with her.   She paused momentarily, while the question I dreaded hung in the air.   'Is it true?'

Indeed.   It was the question that had vexed myself ever since I had inhaled that whiff of perfume, which took me back across the lifetime of this beautiful young woman, now so serene and fulfilled.   What, compared to her, had I?   Work might well be an antidote to sorrow.   But was it any substitute for the fulness of life?   I should know in a very few moments.

'I have to tell you', I said, emboldened by that wide-eyed innocence to confide in her as I should not have done in any other, 'that I am here to meet a woman, and that she is not a client, nor connected in any way with the case that I have been working on.   This will no doubt surprise you.   Since you have spoken of Watson, and evidently perused his narratives with some attention, you will have come to regard me as the rest of the world does: as a mere thinking machine'.

The calm gaze of those wonderful eyes did not flicker, as her lips relaxed into an indescribable smile.   It was not knowing, or superior, but understanding.

'I have never done so, Mr. Holmes'.

In a riot of emotion, I took my leave of her, continuing through the galleries.   Descending, I found myself in the large bare room which survives from the Roman foundations, and in which grows a forest of sculpture.   Here were the oldest artefacts of historic Paris: the columns with their boat-shaped capitals, the Gallo-Roman gods.   Unliving they stood, yet eerily alive. There came to me the lines of Goethe, in which the perfected tranquillity of sculptured forms is juxtaposed with the still-vivid disquiet of human suffering. They are bloodless: born of our passions, but beyond them. And yet, in the words of that great master, they seem to gaze upon them with a world of pity.

> *Und Marmorbilder stehn und sehn mich an:*
> *Was hat man dir, du armes Kind, getan?*

I stood at the foot of the horned god Cernunnus, antlered spirit of the forest that once covered the site, its wildness banished to this vestige under the ground, Dionysus to the city's Apollo. Was it this which was the reality, or the world above? Life tamed into form, or the urges that created it, and in the course of which, ever and again, it is reduced to chaos?

A hesitant step behind made me turn my head. Watson has spoken, in 'The Sussex Vampire', of the feelings with which we greet again those we have known in youth; I shall not attempt to do so. Suffice it to say that we were soon after seated in a small park near the museum – a handful of old trees, with benches underneath, and sparrows pecking for crumbs in the gravel. I was guarded, she perceptibly nervous. She spoke briefly of her married life.

'I had two children, a son and a daughter. I did not love them as I should have, because I did not love their father; and, as children will, they sensed it. In the case of my son, the indifference I felt for him turned into self-hatred: he took a commission in the Army, and perished in South Africa'.

I murmured my sympathy. She dismissed it with a toss of the head, and went on: 'My daughter was even more difficult. She is equally conscious of my having let down her father; but she has identified herself powerfully with his sufferings, and so hates me with an intimate, burning animosity.

Her revenge has taken the form of moral superiority: she is about to take the veil in the order which gave me my schooling'.

'In Belgium?'

'No; in England. A few years ago, they determined to establish a convent near London. Quite unexpectedly, they found the perfect building waiting for them. It was a house in the style of the middle ages – complete with stained glass – in Epping Forest. It had belonged to a painter, who was murdered, it seems, by two of his models. Nobody ever knew exactly what had happened'.

'"Nobody" is an exaggeration. "Almost nobody" is correct'.

'You mean that you...'

'Naturally. It is, as you might say, my trade'.

I put into the last word all the heavy irony with which she had invested it at our last meeting, twenty-five years before. She looked humiliated and tired. 'Your profession', she said, 'has brought you fame, and a life of such public and private usefulness as a prince might envy. I am left with nothing. I have lost children, husband, position, caste.

'There is only one rule to be observed amongst the people with whom I lived. One may do what one will, so long as one is discreet. At the country-house weekend, one may engage one's hostess to arrange assignations, send one's servants with messages, leave signals at one's door. But one must never betray, by as much as a flicker of the eyelids, with whom one has passed the night – even when this is already known. There are forms to be observed; I failed to do so. I was infatuated with a younger man, to whom I was nothing but a society conquest. I tried not to resent his other women, but when he tired of me, I created a scene. It was in public, at Covent Garden. I made myself ridiculous.

'My husband has been very good about it. His concern is for his family, and he will grant me a generous allowance if I accept a separation without fuss. I return tomorrow to the convent at Bruges, for an extended religious retreat. My life heretofore seems nothing but vanity and vexation of spirit'.

Clouds tumbled over one another, deeply shadowed by the brilliant sky. They passed in front of the sun; she shivered. I suggested we go indoors.

After we had moved into the darkest alcove of a nearby restaurant, and the waiter had lit a candle and provided us with some wine, I began as I should have done with one of my clients. 'Why have you come to me? Tell me clearly and without equivocation. Attempt no games, or I walk out that door' – I gestured to where horses drew their cabs in the fading light of the afternoon – 'and you will never see me again'.

I spoke with all the severity I felt, and she cast her eyes down for a moment. But when she looked at me again, it was with a directness which brought me back twenty-five years in this city, and made my heart turn over.

'You ask why I have come', she replied. 'To ask forgiveness. Is that so strange?'

'What is there to forgive?', I asked with the same severity, though perhaps with a greater edge as I strove to contain my emotion. 'I have not thought of you in years'.

She paused. 'At the risk of provoking the execution of your threat', she began at last, 'I must venture to tell you what I think. It seems to me you have thought of little else'.

I seemed to disintegrate inside. But I shot her my coldest look, and steepled my fingers. 'Your evidence, pray'.

She took a sip of her wine, and again was silent. When she spoke once more, it was to offer me a reprieve. 'Are you certain you wish to know the truth?'

'I have said so'.

'Very well, then'. After another quick, nervous sip, she composed herself, clasping her hands before her on the table. 'I will tell you what I have deduced'.

Her choice of language was not lost upon me. I was to be the client, and she the consultant. What followed offered confirmation.

'I have read', she began, 'every one of Watson's tales. I have seen how you have impressed – I am tempted to say, imposed upon – that good and kind friend of yours. To him, who wears his feelings on his sleeve, you are the epitome of reason and restraint. You are, in his view, everything he is not; and he fails, therefore, to see where you are alike. There have, indeed, been moments when he has been aware of a lifting of the mask, and a glimpse of the passionate man who hides behind it. Yes, hides', she said, for I had drawn back instinctively. 'You asked for the truth, and you shall have it.

'That man has been made clear in a hundred details. Watson has written them down; but, as you have remarked to him, he has seen but not observed. He is deceived by the first and insuperable illusion: that you are of a different species from himself. And yet, had he been capable of it, he might have guessed, not alone at what in general has made you what you are, but every detail of our story'.

I found myself echoing Watson. 'This is preposterous!', I cried.

'It is indisputable', she responded, unshakable. 'Consider the nature of your work. It is done, as you have so frequently remarked, for its own sake. It is more to you than a career; it is a vocation. You expose evil; you punish the evildoer; you take upon yourself the prerogatives of judge and jury; you have considered assuming those of the executioner. You are possessed of a sense of justice so intense that it indicates that you yourself have been cruelly wronged. And who are those who call forth your reprimands? Those who have hurt the feelings of others. You were ready to horsewhip that man who toyed with the affections of his stepdaughter; but your severest strictures are reserved for those who, possessed of wealth or position, use it to the disadvantage of those beneath them. It was thus that you reproved the millionaire Gibson, for daring to attempt the virtue of one who was under his protection. You were willing to break the law, and risk standing in the dock, to expose the seducer Gruner. *Baron* Gruner; for it is power connected with aristocracy that calls forth your deepest hostility. Watson, no doubt echoing his mentor, has written of "that not too common type, a nobleman who is in truth noble"; while you yourself have reflected sardonically to my cousin Reginald that his butler was possessed of more intelligence than ten generations of his masters. Do you deny it?'

'I deny none of these things. But they are such actions, or reflections, as were natural under the circumstances. What leads you to imagine they are connected with you?'

'You have never married. Watson has; and you defer to him, with some irony, as the expert on our sex. But even Watson has noticed that, while you behave towards us with impeccable chivalry, it is from within a fortress of deep suspicion. Oh, you have put him off with your talk of Irene Adler; your referring to her as *the* woman. But I am not deceived'.

'You make no sense', I said, with a feeling akin to that with which one might hear one bulkhead after another collapse in a sinking ship.

'I make perfect sense, and you cannot deny it. Irene Adler was a screen for me. She associated with ancient nobility, and she possessed all the arts and talents of the actress, as you no doubt thought that I did. Above all, she outwitted you. She was your superior in skill and knowledge, and she left you standing. She was such a mate as you might have respected; but, like me, she gave herself to another'.

I made no further protest. She had silenced me. The domino under which I had imposed upon Watson, and, through him, upon the world, had fallen from my eyes. I must have looked my bafflement; for she reached out and took my hand.

'I am about to tell you something you must know, and which I fervently pray you can believe', she said urgently, holding my gaze. 'It has been my secret for a quarter of a century. I have never told it to a living soul. I hoped that, in time, it would fade, and I be able to forget it. But it has tormented me, even as your secret has tormented you.

'None of what we shared with each other was pretence. Oh, it began as a fling, as you must have suspected: a last indulgence of freedom before I entered on a more circumscribed life. But as we passed our days here, and grew to know each other, I began to feel myself fall in love. What I cried out to you that night, as we reached ecstasy together, was true. It frightened me when I thought about it the following day. For it threatened everything which the world seemed to offer me.

'For you, there can have been nothing more cruel than my turning away from you at the last. Not to give you that final consolation: that must have been bitter indeed. And I can understand how necessary it has been for you, since, to build a new life – indeed, a new self – out of the ruins that I left behind. But I beg of you, by all that I once meant for you, to trust me in what I am about to tell you now. One more night with you, and I could never have returned. For you, I would have thrown away the world. It was not indifference that made me act as I did; it was terror. And that terror grew out of my love'.

The rectangle of light from the street had now become dim. The glow of the candle between us had grown in intensity as the room darkened. What I had heard – and I could not doubt it – made what had happened all the more horrible. It was not the suffering of one being from unrequited love, but the parting of two, each from its natural mate. It was not injustice, but waste. I felt I had wandered in a desert through the intervening years.

'I know how you must loathe me', she went on. 'But it is nothing to my loathing for myself. When I was overwhelmed by that hideous scandal, I thought of how you must have suffered, and felt myself justly punished. When I spoke to Bland, and heard that you were here, my heart leaped. All my life, I have been tormented by what I have done. I wished, if I could, to make amends'.

She took out a key, and laid it on the table between us. 'It is little', she said; 'but at this late stage, it is the best I can do. I have engaged rooms at our old hotel, in the Rue Serpente. If you still desire it, you may have your night with me. I can never make up for the past. But this is all, any more, I have to give'.

Perhaps it was the wine; or perhaps the pleading look in her face. Whether she was pleading for me or for herself, I did not know. I picked up the key unthinkingly: I told myself it was to spare her further humiliation.

But when, having removed her outer garments, she approached me in the bedroom, something glittered in the light from the street. I saw that the crucifix still hung about her neck. Immediately, I was repelled. So she had come to me for her forgiveness, her easy absolution. One automatic ritual, and she was free, in conscience, from all she had subjected me to: from the accumulated pain, which she had understood as nobody else could, of twenty-five years. It was her last and greatest illusion; her masterpiece of theatre; her final deception, and her most brilliant achievement: the duping of Sherlock Holmes.

I pushed her away, with a murmur of being no longer young, and having been exhausted by the events of recent days. She disengaged herself silently; but I knew from her posture that she was bitterly hurt, and a wave of exultation swept through me. So this was how it felt, to find justice at last: to make her know the humiliation she had once imposed upon me, suffer rejection as I had done; realise that there was a price to be paid for all evil. It was with a light heart that I prepared for sleep.

There was one large bed in the room, and we lay down on opposite sides of it. I was in truth exhausted, though less from my adventures with Watson than from the emotions I had had to relive, and I quickly drifted off. When I awoke, the light had changed. The moon had risen, throwing long slanted lines through the mullions of the dormer window. I realised, from the silhouette of the rooftops across the way, that she had taken the room in which we had passed those earlier, delirious nights together.

I turned to look at her; and for a moment my heart stood still. She lay like an effigy under the bedclothes, her face alabaster, the eyes staring open; and my first thought was that she was dead. I reached out a hand to touch her cheek; it came away wet. I realised that the reason her face glistened in the moonlight was that she had been weeping.

I have sometimes considered a monograph upon the varieties of tears. On the English male, however, I have suffered from a dearth of material. Tears of joy in victory or sorrow in defeat, or even in deepest grief, are thought to be in poor taste. Our women, on the other hand, have greater latitude; and the very fact of our discomfort with their weeping lends it enormous power. As we feel it unmanly in ourselves, so we suspect that the behaviour which has elicited it in others must have been lacking in consideration, if not downright brutal. We are at our weakest when we wish to halt it; and I have learnt to be on my guard against the tell-tale signals that it is being deployed as a weapon: the batting of the eyelashes, the sidelong glance to judge of the effect.

This was different. These were spontaneous tears, the tears of a child for whom the world has suddenly become both awful and incomprehensible. She was weeping to herself; and, when she felt the touch of my hand, turned away. I reached out to draw her to me; and she turned and cradled her head against my shoulder. 'I never thought it possible', she whispered, 'to be so completely alone'.

I remembered my own feelings when she had left me. But I no longer resented her. Where her face had been clammy, her body was warm. Was I falling into a trap? I no longer cared. Had I never ceased to love her, under all the resentment and hate? Had I forgiven her? Or was I forgiving myself: surrendering the righteous indignation which was but another form of torment? It did not matter. I put away these questions, and I have not asked them since. They are not amenable to reason, and in that moment I ceased to reason. I surrendered to instinct; so did she; and I like to think that, though no longer capable of the frenzy of youth, our suffering had brought to our lovemaking an understanding such as we had never known in that earlier season. I felt as if, at last and for the first time, we met in perfect communion.

When I awoke, the light in the room was grey. She was coming back from the door, a wrap of Japanese silk flung about her, a tray fragrant with coffee in her hands. She explained that she had rung down for it. 'At this hour?' I asked, rubbing my eyes.

She smiled, a familiar smile, but grown mellow with the years; and her answer then assured me that we had indeed shared the understanding I had hoped. 'Watson', she said, 'Watson must never know'.

Of course: she was absolutely right. Holmes in love was not a subject of which Watson could treat. If I were to become human to him, I should cease to be that enigma which was the source of his inspiration. How was it that he had put it? Yes; 'A Scandal in Bohemia':

> It was not that he felt any emotion akin to love... All emotions, and that one particularly, were abhorrent to his cold, precise, but admirably balanced mind.

It was the 'perfect reasoning and observing machine' that was the object of his adulation, and that his public demanded. And Caroline understood. She understood because she had brought it into being, and also because she loved me. As I did her. I drew her towards me, for a final embrace. Yes: Watson must never know.

FIVE

THE KISS OF JUDAS

It was a damp, overcast day when Mr. Bernard Shaw appeared in our Baker Street rooms. All I knew of him was that he was one of those who urge the penalisation of the industrious and the fortunate on behalf of those who are neither; and what made the matter worse was that he was prepared to abandon all morality in the name of his mania. He had written a play, Holmes had given me to understand, which portrayed prostitution as the only profession open to the poor in what it pleased him to describe as the decadent state of our society. This burlesque was considered unplayable in any reputable theatre: very properly, in my opinion. I was, I freely admit, prepared to dislike Mr. Shaw; and his appearance amply confirmed my preconceptions. My medical eye immediately detected an unhealthy pallor that, set against the flaming red of his hair and beard, made his face look positively green. I asked if he were anaemic, and he replied:

'In the literal sense, yes. I do not consume blood. I am a vegetarian'.

He said this with a twinkling smile, and a crinkling of the whiskers, as if revelling in the prospect of debate; but at that moment an extraordinary odour, oily and fetid, assailed my nostrils. I had opened a window on the announcement of our visitor in order to dissipate the accumulated fumes of Holmes' day-long smoking; I now made to close it again. 'Someone', I murmured, 'seems to be driving a flock of sheep through the street outside'.

'That must be me', said Shaw, imperturbably.

'I beg your pardon?'

'It is this suit I am wearing – untreated wool, you see. It allows the body to breathe naturally...'

'I fear', I replied with some asperity, 'it does not allow other people to breathe naturally'.

'Well, Dr. Watson, I see I shall not convert you', said Shaw, shaking his head with the air of a disillusioned schoolmaster. 'But the fact is, I have come here on a different errand. It concerns my fr... my fellow-countryman, Oscar Wilde'.

'You hesitate to call him friend', observed Holmes sharply, taking the pipe from his mouth. 'Why?'

'Because he is not', said Shaw simply. 'In Dublin, our families moved in different circles, or perhaps I should say different squares. Wilde's people were society; mine were not. The difference has carried over to London. Yet Wilde showed me kindness when I was unknown; that is why I would help him now, when he is on the verge of ruin'.

'Ruin?' queried Holmes. 'You do not mean financial ruin, surely?'

'I do not. Financially, no man could be better placed. He has two plays running in the West End, and the second of them promises to be the greatest success of his career. No, I was thinking of the rumours which have hovered about him for some time, and which have now gained an ugly permanence. Names, dates, personages are being spoken of. It is said that he is being heavily blackmailed'.

'Over what?'

'Over his...his friendship with Lord Alfred Douglas'. Shaw looked put out.

'I take it that in this case you consider there is more, rather than less, than friendship involved'.

'I do. I have seen them together'.

'My God!', I exclaimed passionately. 'Am I to understand that you have come here to ask Mr. Sherlock Holmes to undertake the protection of a pervert?'

'I ask him to undertake the protection of what there is of English thought. If Wilde is brought down, philistinism will feast on his carcase. Originality and brilliance, which he has brought back into fashion after a century dull as ditchwater, will once again be suspect, and the world made safe for mediocrity. And the worst of it is, Wilde's downfall will favour none of the moral values that will undoubtedly be invoked. Everyone knows that what Wilde and Douglas practise is carried on more or less openly at your public schools, and more or less furtively at the highest levels of your society. His condemnation will serve no cause other than that of hypocrisy'.

'I do not doubt that there is some justice in what you assert', Holmes replied calmly to this tirade. 'But what you describe as hypocrisy has one unquestionable advantage: it enables us to look the other way. If he behaves discreetly, he will not be prosecuted'.

'Oh yes, he will', Shaw rejoined. 'Lord Alfred's father will see to that'.

'The Marquess of Queensberry', said Holmes thoughtfully.

'Precisely, Mr. Holmes', said Shaw. 'The man who has codified the rules of boxing. Thanks to Dr. Watson's accounts of your cases, you are the most celebrated exponent of those rules; and if he listens to anyone, it will be you. For the sake of a great artist and the society which – on the deepest level – he serves, persuade his lordship to call off the prosecution it is known he is intent upon'.

'I will certainly give the matter careful thought', said Holmes. Then, mischievously, he added: 'Allow me to offer you some refreshment before you go: a glass of brandy and soda, perhaps?'

Shaw's verdigris face turned greener still. Then he returned to his strutting pose. 'I am a teetotaller', he stated, twirling his moustaches. He spoke with the exalted face of the fanatic, which made me dislike him even more than I had.

'Well', said Holmes when he had taken his departure, 'what do you make of our visitor, Watson?'

'I do not know which I detest more', I replied vehemently, 'his pretence of moral superiority, or his defence of moral depravity'.

'Stoutly put, Watson', said Holmes, stretching out his long legs in front of him. 'But have you not noticed how it is invariably the most insignificant dogs that bark loudest? Or the little men who are most anxious not to be overlooked?'

'Elementary, my dear Holmes'.

'Quite so', said Holmes, with a smile. 'And Shaw is simply a more complex instance of the phenomenon. If he seems, on the surface, the embodiment of overweening ego, what are we to make of him deep down?'

'Am I expected to believe', I demanded, 'that that appalling display of vanity and presumption is the sign of some inner weakness?'

'You know me', said Holmes. 'You are aware that, as you can tell the slightest deviation from regularity in the pulse of a patient, I keep my finger on the throbbing life of this metropolis. You know that all rumours, all whispers, all suggestions of unsavoury truth, make their way to me sooner or later. For a long time, I have known something of the not-so-secret life of Oscar Wilde. I have also heard a most peculiar story concerning Mr. Bernard Shaw'.

'You mean that he is another of this unholy persuasion?', I breathed.

'By no means', replied Holmes. 'His vice is that he has no vices. He is the passionate perfectionist he appears to be. Like all perfectionists, he is striving for an ideal. And his ideal is – to exist'.

'I fail to follow you'.

'It is simplicity itself. His avoidance of vices – even to the mildest degree – is an indication that he has witnessed their appalling results. And that is what my sources tell me. Shaw's father was a hopeless drunkard, and his children suffered the attendant ills of poverty and degradation. You can understand why he holds himself aloof from that particular weakness'.

'That does indeed offer some palliation of his unsociable behaviour', I conceded.

'But there is more. The father was married to a woman of character. What would a person of this kind do in such circumstances?'

'Leave him. Bring up her children alone'.

'Precisely. Leave him she did, and came to London. But she did not do so alone. She made the move with a gentleman who was not her husband'.

'So that is why he defends immorality!'

'My dear Watson, Mr. Bernard Shaw makes no attempt to conceal the facts of his upbringing. He is mercilessly funny on the weakness and inebriation of the father, and the strength and independence of the mother. His explanation is that one can take the intolerable as tragedy or comedy, and that he prefers the latter'.

'A very healthy attitude, if I may say so'.

'Yes, but why proclaim it at all? Wilde's family life was no less disreputable. The father was grossly and publicly unfaithful to the mother. There were mistresses, illegitimate children – even a highly-publicised action for rape. But Wilde shies away from all reference to these matters: surely the natural reaction'.

'What are you driving at?'

'Simply this: that by making public holiday out of his obvious humiliations, he wishes to screen a more private and devastating one. And here, again, my sources have not failed me.   Dublin rumour has followed the Shaws to London, and provides a significantly different picture of their ménage to that put forward by Mr. Bernard Shaw'.

'I do not see how it could be worse'.

'What Mr. Shaw asserts in the course of his comic turn is that his mother's presumed lover came to know her some time after he was born.   If what I hear is true, this happened some time *before*.   You see how this alters the case?'

I sat dumbfounded.   'You mean that Shaw believes he may be the son of his mother's lover; that he has no real right to his family name?'

'Exactly, Watson', said Holmes, 'and a matter for which there is independent evidence. His first name is George; but this is also the name of both his legal and his putative father. It is a constant reminder of his uncertainty.   So at least we must presume: because he has dropped it, and goes under his second name of Bernard.   That at least is his own'.

I felt a twinge of pity for the man.   I said as much to Holmes.   'But I do not', I added, 'see this as justification for revenge upon society.   He may well wish that the world were other than what it is; but this glorifying of pimps and prostitutes...even if they do represent his parents... I must say I think the Lord Chamberlain fully justified in banning him from the stage'.

Holmes made a gesture of dismissal.   'Shaw was banned from the stage because he dealt with the real evils of society. If he impels us to do away with them – and it is nothing more, after all, than what Ruskin or Morris have attempted – he is more likely to preserve our society than subvert it.   No, I think we must give Mr. Shaw a hearing, and I am fully in agreement with him on this matter of Wilde'.   His long, thin arm shot out and retrieved a volume bound in green and gold, and he riffled over the pages.   'Listen to this, Watson.   It is from an essay upon the poisoner – and also, as it happens, poet and painter – Thomas Griffiths Wainewright: of him, Wilde observes: "The fact of a man being a poisoner is nothing against his prose". Wilde has a feeling for the complexities of the criminal mind: I am not sure there are more than two of us in London who do'. He snapped the volume shut. 'Come, there is no time to be lost. The Marquess of Queensberry is a violent man, and I should feel considerably more secure in the company of a friend'.

It was then that I uttered the words that I have never been able to forgive myself for, though I blame Mr. Bernard Shaw even more. His odious cleverness had left a most disagreeable impression; and the worst of it seemed to me that he had lured my friend into a case that might destroy his unique reputation, the fruit of years of patient and brilliant effort. It was therefore with great sadness that I said: 'No, Holmes; it is as your friend that I cannot take part in this association with agitators and perverts. Have a care: "He that toucheth pitch shall be defiled therewith"'.

It amazed me to see the look that came over Holmes' face. With a pang, I recognised how deeply I had hurt him. But the die was cast: I felt that principle was involved. I ought, I suppose, to have remembered another line of Ecclesiasticus, which I had just quoted so glibly: 'Forsake not an old friend', says the same ancient wisdom. But I could see no way out of the dilemma, and I sat staring through the window as I heard Holmes walk sadly down the stairs and close the door gently behind him. Tormented by doubt, I passed what I believe to have been the most uncomfortable after- noon of my life; and when he came back in the early evening, I saw that which turned my resentment of Shaw into positive hatred. The door slammed below, and Holmes staggered into our sitting-room, holding a bloodied handkerchief to his face. I rang for a basin of hot water from Mrs. Hudson, and washed him as gently as I could, though he could not keep from starting with the pain, and bandaged up his injuries. 'Holmes', I said quietly when I had finished, 'tell me where that man lives, and I swear that I will exact vengeance for this monstrous attack'.

'Hush, Watson', said Holmes, holding up a hand. Through the swollen eyelids I could see his eyes sparkle. 'I know your devotion to me'. My heart was wrung at his words. 'The error was mine: the Marquess, you see, does not fight by the Queensberry Rules. When he heard who I was, and the errand upon which I came, he asked me, smilingly, to put up my fists "for a friendly bout" with one of his retinue. When he saw that I was giving a reasonable account of myself, he signalled to the rest of his hired bullies, and they jumped me. "Take that, you imbecile", his lordship screamed as I retreated, "and tell that man Wilde that I will serve him as I have served you". My next visit must be to Wilde, to beg him not to be provoked by this impossible creature'.

'*Our* next visit', I corrected him. 'Whatever my feelings about your client, I will not stir from your side as long as you are in peril from this mad aristocrat'.

'I thought I knew my Watson', grinned Holmes through his battered face. 'Go and whistle up a cab for me, will you?'

Holmes had been told that he would find Wilde at an hotel. As we drove there, he pointed out how significant it was that he now seemed to live habitually away from his wife. My predisposition to dislike the man was not assuaged by my first sight of him. Unlike Shaw, who carried himself like a dancer, Wilde was gross both in form and feature. But I was surprised by the grace of his gestures and the cultivation of his accent, which was that of an English gentleman; and could not but smile when he replied to Holmes' statement that he had been sent by Shaw: 'Mr. Bernard Shaw has not an enemy in the world; but none of his friends like him'. The remark was made with the easy, natural delivery of a great actor, the pause in the centre perfectly timed. What pleased me no less was its coincidence with my own opinion of Shaw, that he had somehow made idealism obnoxious. Holmes, however, did not smile, as he said in the gravest tones: 'I have to tell you, Mr. Wilde, that in essentials I agree absolutely with Mr. Shaw: you stand in the utmost danger. I have met Queensberry, as you can see' – he pointed to his bandaged head. 'He is an absolute brute, but a cunning and dangerous one. His method is to tempt his opponent into battle, then crush him with superior force. If you allow yourself to be goaded by him, and there is anything in your life which might be looked upon with disfavour by conventional society, you are doomed'.

A frightened look flickered across Wilde's eyes; but he composed himself and replied, with the same assured delivery as before. 'Your view of society, Mr. Holmes, I am happy to say, is shared by myself. It is also shared by your admirable Prince of Wales, who has suffered more than once from the censoriousness of English morals. Whenever I meet him, he asks me, with a laugh, "Ah, Mr. Wilde, what is that brilliant thing you always say?" And I answer, "Thank you sir. Which one, sir?" Which invariably makes him laugh again. And he says, "That thing about the English, Wilde". And I tell him: "The English, sir, have an almost mir—*ac*—ulous capacity for turning *wine* into *water*"'.

'Ha', I barked, displeased.

'Ah, Dr. Watson', Wilde interjected, turning in my direction. 'I had almost forgotten the good doctor. That was very remiss of me. You possess, after all, the instinct of the modern artist – the preference for colour over form. *A Study in Scarlet*: now that is a distinctly promising title. But why scarlet? You disappoint me, Dr. Watson. From the pillar-box to the omnibus, it is a proclamation of the commonplace – it is the positive *uniform* of convention – it is irreproachably…*ordinary*'.

143

'It is the colour of blood', I said with dignity. 'Or for that matter, of *wine*'.

'A touch, Watson!', cried Holmes with a smile, 'a distinct touch!' But his expression changed as he continued: 'Mr. Wilde, we are wasting time. I have to tell you', he went on, in his most serious tones, 'that you gravely underestimate the forces you are stirring up against yourself. The Prince's morals have attracted censure, and he is at the head of society. Think how little consideration can be expected by an outsider'.

'Of course', replied Wilde, in the same fluent tone, though it seemed to me that now there was an edge of bitterness to it. 'The English cannot possibly forgive the Irish. They have injured us far too deeply for that'.

'Spare us, Mr. Wilde', said Holmes, in the same attitude of rigorous severity. 'We may not all share your artistry; but some of us have read our Tacitus. *Odisse quem læseris* is an old story by now'.

To my surprise, Wilde took this rebuke with equanimity. 'At last, a worthy antagonist!', he exclaimed. 'You have no idea, Mr. Holmes, after having silenced so many dullards, how satisfying it is to be *found out*'.

'I fear', said Holmes, still implacable, 'you will find the experience a great deal less amusing than you seem to anticipate'. And he drew a picture of the likely outcome of a prosecution that made Wilde's pasty face turn even paler. By the time we took our leave, the playwright, wan and exhausted, had given his word to Holmes that, however exasperating the Marquess' provocations, he would keep his nerve and not respond to them.

Holmes left for Lincolnshire the following morning, having been called there over the case of the Lackland Treasure, which was to have such a curious aftermath, and which I may one day give to the world. It was a belief of his, arrived at after long study of Admiralty charts and parchments from the British Museum, that the medieval regalia lost to the tides by the luckless King John might have been carried ashore at a spot which he had pinpointed on the map. A local antiquarian, following his directions, had recently unearthed some jewellery in the area, and wished to have Holmes' opinion upon it. In a state of high, though characteristically repressed, excitement he agreed to examine it, but was disappointed to discover that it came from a later period. A far greater disappointment, however, awaited him on his return. When he arrived at our lodgings, grim-faced, and flung a bundle of newspapers on the table, I saw that he was fully apprised of what had agitated all London in his absence.

It appeared that, shortly after we left him, Wilde had paid a visit to his club, and there found a card awaiting him, upon which Queensberry had scrawled offensive insinuations about his character. Outraged beyond any thought of discretion, Wilde initiated a case for libel against Queensberry, who was arrested and, by the time Holmes returned, had been charged and committed for trial.

I besought Holmes to withdraw from the case: as he had given his considered advice and had it rejected, he could not now be held responsible for the outcome. It was not in Holmes' nature, however, to abandon a case; difficulties, indeed, were what appealed to the solver of problems in him. 'Shaw was right, I am afraid, Watson', he said. 'Far more is at stake here than Wilde himself – it involves the whole tenor of our moral and mental life – and, for that reason, and however we may feel about him personally, we must attempt to save him from his own errors of judgement'.

This, however, turned out to be more difficult than even I had anticipated. Wilde, when we managed to arrange a meeting with him, was in obstinate, if uneasy, mood. He fastened on the fact that Queensberry's defence intended to portray him as a corrupter of youth, in justification of which, they intended to subject his writings to a most intense scrutiny. This Wilde shrugged off.

'My entire career has been a raid upon the Philistines', he said in his most lordly manner. 'I am well armed, and seasoned in the fray'.

'That may be so', answered Holmes. 'But what of your letters to Lord Alfred? Are you aware that these will be produced?'

'These, too, are works of literature; they are hymns to a beautiful friendship'.

'If that is so, why did you pay blackmailers for the originals?'

'You think me in the wrong', said Wilde, with a touch of pique.

'What I think is irrelevant. It is what a jury may be brought to think that you must fear. If they form a representative cross-section of the British public, I can tell you in advance what they will think'. With intense seriousness, his brows drawn together, his aquiline features and ascetic frame forming a striking contrast to the pale and enervated Wilde, he rang off each point like a pistol-shot.

'First, if your letters *can* be construed as corrupting, you may be certain that Queensberry's lawyers *will* do so.

'Second, the fact that you have paid blackmail will support the inference that you have something to hide.

'Third, and most damagingly, Queensberry's lawyers have a list of young men, of the most unscrupulously mercenary type, whom they nevertheless will assert that you have also corrupted'.

'What? How can they?' Wilde's jaw fell open. 'Lord Alfred frequented their company as much as I – in fact more so, since I have so often been preoccupied with my work. It was he who introduced them to me. The father cannot

146

possibly call them in evidence without irrevocably damning his son'.

'Yes, he can. His lawyers will lead them to testify to their relations with you alone. Will *you* allow *your* lawyers to call them as witnesses against your friend?'

Wilde looked baffled and lost. Holmes said, in a softened tone: 'No, I did not think so. The inevitable upshot will be, that Queensberry emerges as a loving father, and you the corrupter of his son'.

'A loving father! Great heavens!', cried Wilde, suddenly galvanised into energy. 'As for his son...'

JHe was interrupted by the entrance of a pale youth, slender and blond, his face set in a look of petulant annoyance. The expression intensified as Wilde averted his gaze. 'What is this?', cried young Douglas, staring menacingly from Holmes to myself and back to Wilde. 'What *have* you been tattling about, Oscar?'

'I have been attempting to impress upon Mr. Wilde', said Holmes, unmoved by this display of impending tantrums, and in a low, calm voice that gave his words deadly effect, 'that he is doomed if he remains in England. There is only one hope left for him. He must go at once to Paris with his wife. From there he can write to *The Times*, declaring that he has dropped the case because he despairs of justice while your father is posturing as a model parent'.

'But that is letting him escape!', cried the young man, his face darkening with fury.

'I beg your pardon', said Holmes. 'It is letting *who* escape?'

'Queensberry, you dolt!', shrieked the son. 'This is our opportunity to damage him, to demean him, to destroy him!' He was overtaken by a paroxysm of helpless rage, his face twisted to the likeness of a gargoyle.

'There is no question of that', said Holmes, unmoving in the centre of this whirlwind of fury. 'You will not be allowed to take the stand against him. Your father's character, as such, is not on trial – unfortunately, I may say, since I have had personal experience of him'. Here he indicated the scars which were still visible on his face. 'But the legal issue is simply this: whether the words which he wrote of your friend are true. That is now the case; and I have told Mr. Wilde that, in the minds of a British jury, he is virtually certain to lose it'.

A look of momentary dismay on Douglas' face was followed quickly by a cunning smile. 'Oscar has never given a brass farthing for vulgar prejudice. He is above all that. He will fight it, and he will win'. He looked adoringly at his idol, and all Wilde's doubts seemed to fall away.

'You are right, of course, dear boy', said the older man soothingly, his courage appearing to flood back. 'You will see, Mr. Holmes: I intend to make this my most *irresistible* performance'.

Holmes shook his head slowly as he rose from the chair, but did not utter another word. Silently he turned his back and stalked from the room, while the slender boy beside the rotund dramatist smirked and sniggered in triumph. I followed my friend with a heavy heart.

'It is just possible that he will do it', said Holmes to my surprise, as we settled into our cab. 'Though I am afraid the odds against him are too great. Still – who knows? Perhaps he is the enchanter he imagines. You will come with me to the trial?'

I was aware that the Marquess of Queensberry was, through his agents, relentlessly pursuing his vendetta against Wilde; and so, still apprehensive of danger to Holmes, I agreed to accompany him to court in spite of my distaste.

There were three trials in the case of Wilde. As all were very fully reported in the public prints, I will here content myself with recalling them as they affected Holmes. In the first, Wilde was the plaintiff, alleging that Queensberry had been guilty of libel by accusing him of sodomy. As the evidence began to emerge of Wilde's relations with young men of the lower classes – relations which could no longer plead the intellectual companionship he had alleged in the case of Lord Alfred – Holmes turned to me with urgency. 'Once they drop the case against Queensberry', he hissed, 'Wilde will be arrested. I will go to brother Mycroft to have the warrant delayed. Do you follow Wilde, and persuade him to take the boat-train to Paris. It is either that or prison'. So saying, he hurried away.

As Wilde stumbled out of the Old Bailey, it was impossible for me to reach him through the throng. In a moment, he was gone; and, when I finally succeeded in tracing him to the hotel in which he had taken refuge, it was late in the afternoon. There I found him alone in his room, a suitcase, half-packed, upon the bed. But there were empty wine-bottles scattered all about; and, when I attempted to address him, I saw, to my horror, that he was in a stupor from which he could not be aroused. I was in any case too late to save him: a hotel servant came to the door to say the police were at hand. Not wishing to embroil Holmes by association, I slipped away.

It was well that I did so. An extraordinary hysteria seemed all at once to come over London. Young men of means fled in large numbers to the Continent; Holmes received desperate appeals, some from the first families in the kingdom, to save them from disgrace at the hands of blackmailers. The innocent suffered with the guilty: a youth carrying flowers to his beloved might find himself the object of obscene jeers and taunts. Young men in whose features there was the slightest hint of sensitivity began to sprout side-whiskers and moustaches. 'Everywhere I look', remarked Holmes as he gazed out of our window at Baker Street, 'I see a uniform stream of manly respectability.   It seems as if all of London, Watson, is determined to disguise itself as you'.

'Such levity is unbecoming, Holmes', I said severely. 'Heaven knows, I have little sympathy with your client; but this stampede is monstrous'.

'Precisely.   It is that which gives me hope'.

'Hope?   Everywhere one turns, Wilde is decried as a fiend.   The very theatre in which his play is running has blocked out his name'.

'Yet they continue to run the play', said Holmes, 'and his spell as an artist continues to draw crowds.   Already I seem to see the beginnings of a reaction.   Better folk, having overcome their shock, are ashamed of this vile trampling on a fallen man.   The second trial begins tomorrow.   It will be interesting to see the manner in which it reflects public opinion'.

Again Holmes was proved right.   When Wilde was, once more, reviled for his friend- ship with young Douglas, he rose magnificently to the occasion.   It was, he declaimed with passionate eloquence, 'such a great affection of an elder for a younger man as there was between David and Jonathan, such as Plato made the very basis of his philosophy, and such as you find in the sonnets of Michelangelo and Shakespeare'. Wilde's dominating presence, his musical voice, his appeal to what was finest in our civilisation, had their effect, and the gallery burst into wave after wave of applause.   Again I felt my heart beat strongly at that instinct for fair play which gave his due even to a man accused of the crimes of which Wilde was generally believed to be guilty.

But the courtroom was once again hushed for the evidence that followed.   Servants from the Savoy Hotel testified to having seen another man in Wilde's bed.   I felt my previous sympathy for him evaporate; but just then there was a plucking at my sleeve, and I saw a folded piece of paper in the hand that Holmes extended to me. Opening it, I read: 'NOT WILDE – DOUGLAS'.

'What do you mean?', I whispered.

'Exactly what I have written', replied Holmes in an undertone. 'The bed in which the young man was seen was that of Douglas, not Wilde'.

'But they must be told – the prosecution must be informed!', I said in accents of distress that brought disapproving stares from the spectators around. After pausing for a moment, Holmes whispered: 'They already know'.

'Know!'

'They know that Queensberry has coached the witnesses in such a way as to throw all the blame on Wilde and leave out the name of his son. He calls it his booby-trap. He knows that Wilde will not save himself at his friend's expense'.

My head swam. I had seen the Marquess at the earlier trial, and been repelled by what I saw. The smudges of eyebrow, the pendulous lower lip, the bowed legs and ignoble gait conveyed an impression as of some sub-human species from the pages of Mr. Darwin; and I could not now be surprised that such a creature should attempt to turn Wilde's better impulses against him. My heart was torn with conflicting emotions; and it was with a sense of relief that I heard the foreman of the jury declare that they, too, could not agree upon a verdict.

My relief, however, was short-lived. Holmes informed me that another trial was to follow; and, after a visit to his brother Mycroft, returned in a still more sombre mood than before. 'It seems they are determined on a conviction', he told me. 'The Solicitor-General himself is to prosecute this case'.

'But why?', I cried. 'What is to be gained by hounding this man?'

'It is because of Rosebery', he replied.

'The Prime Minister?   But how can this affect him?'

'Do you remember', Holmes asked, 'how, at the first trial, the court rang with laughter when Wilde's counsel, intending to speak of Queensberry, called him Rosebery by mistake?'

Amid all the welter of detail, I did seem to recall some such episode.   'What of it?', I queried.

'It was a most significant error', replied Holmes.   'The quarrel between Rosebery and the Marquess was alluded to only in passing; but in fact it was of the most serious kind. The Marquess, believing Rosebery guilty of an immoral relationship with another of his sons, followed him to the Continent, and there publicly threatened to horsewhip him. The Continental newspapers are full of the affair.   If Wilde is treated with even the slightest leniency, they will say that the British Government has done so to protect its own.   The purpose of this trial, therefore, is to place the Government beyond reproach.   Wilde's chances of acquittal are infinitesimal'.

My friend's concern communicated itself to me; and, before I could consider the matter, I had asked: 'What can we do?'

'Good, Watson', he laughed.   'We can begin by putting on these'.   And he emptied the contents of a large sack at my feet.   To my dismay, there were two filthy suits inside, blackened with coal-dust, and the segmented brush of a chimney-sweep.   Holmes insisted that I change into one of the suits, and, when I had done so, stood back and considered the effect.

'Not quite right yet, I fear', he said waggishly, his head on one side, and to my inexpressible horror smeared his handkerchief on the rim of the coal-scuttle and wiped it over my face.   'There, that is better', he said, as I blinked the grit out of my eyes, which were beginning to water.   'Now take this' – and he handed me the brush, even filthier than the clothes – 'and I will join you in our common trade'.

As we tramped down the stairs in unison, we heard a scream from Mrs. Hudson. She had cleaned the carpet only that afternoon, taking out and polishing the brass rods one by one, and I stood rooted to the spot by guilt. 'On, Watson, on!', cried Holmes impatiently. Once outside, we boarded a passing omnibus. The other passengers hurriedly made way for us as we took our seats on the upper deck. Holmes turned to look back. 'Ah, I thought so!', he chuckled. A young man with the physique of a boxer, who had been pacing up and down the street in front of our house, was standing and scratching his head as he looked after us. 'Our disguise has given us a clear start', Holmes went on. 'By the time he decides to follow us, we shall have cleared the next corner. We will alight there, pass down the side-street, and take another omnibus'. As we moved through the city, constantly shifting direction, Holmes informed me that Queensberry had his gang of bruisers constantly on the prowl; that they had made their way into every hotel in which Wilde had attempted to stay, threatening to make a scene, and obliging the unfortunate man to take refuge in the house of a friend. When we arrived there, and the servant had begun to close the door in our faces, stating that our services were not required, Holmes pushed his way past her and rasped out his name.

A stately, thin-faced woman swept down into the hallway, alarm on her features. When she had come close enough to recognise him under the disguise, she sighed with relief. 'Mr. Holmes! I was afraid you were minions of Queensberry's, and that he had succeeded in tracking down our friend. We have been most careful to keep his presence here a secret'.

'I am aware of that, Mrs. Leverson', said Holmes, and at once I recognised the name of the distinguished novelist, 'but I have my own sources of information. I have come from

Whitehall, where the word is that a supreme effort will be made to secure a conviction this time. I must advise Mr. Wilde to leave the country at once'.

The lady shook her head in despair. 'It is what I have felt from the outset, Mr. Holmes. But I have found him immovable. Let me show you something to indicate his state of mind'. She returned in a few moments with a letter in her hand. It had been addressed to her by Wilde between the first and second trials. Holmes glanced over it in silence and passed it to me. I read:

> I write to you from prison, where your kind words have reached me and given me comfort, though they have made me cry, in my loneliness. Not that I am really alone. A slim thing, goldhaired like an angel, stands always at my side.

'"Always at my side"!' I repeated. 'Is Douglas, then, here with him now?'

'By no means', replied Holmes with bitter irony. 'That prudent youth has decamped for Paris'.

'Wherever he is, Mr. Holmes', said our hostess, 'Oscar believes that his sufferings bring them closer. He has sacrificed wealth, reputation, career for him, and I fear is about to sacrifice freedom and any hope of a return to public favour. But what I fear most is that he is to be dreadfully undeceived. I shudder at the thought of the day on which it comes home to him that his sacrifice has been wasted'.

'I agree with you absolutely. It is an unscrupulous little cad: the mirror-image, in all but looks, of the father. Between them they have driven a great man to his ruin. I will do my best to make him see reason; though, as I have observed to Watson, "There is danger for him who taketh the tiger cub"'.

'I remember the tale', replied Mrs. Leverson, glancing at me. '"A Case of Identity", was it not?'

I nodded, and we followed her upstairs, where, having announced us, she left. Wilde had been put in the nursery, and there was something both desolate and Brobdingnagian about the massive author of children's fables a fugitive amid the débris of childhood. Holmes squatted, Indian-fashion, on the floor; I perched uneasily on a nearby rocking-horse. Briefly and dispassionately, Holmes outlined the purpose for which he had come. 'The appointment of the Solicitor-General as prosecutor', he stated gravely, 'is a matter of the utmost significance, psychologically and substantively. Psychologically, a jury of ordinary men, used to reverencing and even fearing authority, will be asked to condemn you by a high officer of the Crown. That in itself will produce in them – irrespective of the evidence – a powerful presumption of your guilt. Substantively, the Solicitor-General possesses a privilege which gives him an advantage over the ordinary prosecutor: the right of final address. However powerful, however impassioned, the case which your defender may make, it will be subject to belittlement and distortion at his hands. It is with his words ringing in their ears that the jury will leave to deliberate'.

Beads of perspiration had formed on Wilde's chalk-white face; but when Holmes asked his permission to reveal all of the evidence – which would immediately explode the prosecution's central contention of his corruption of youth – he obstinately refused. Holmes delicately probed at his motives. 'Your defence of the young man is noble', he said. 'But do you really think he is worthy of it?'

Wilde turned to him a face on which determination showed through exhaustion. 'Is any of us, Mr. Holmes', he asked, 'is any of us worthy of love?'

'There is only one course left to you, then', said Holmes. 'You must leave the country'.

'And abandon those who have put up my bail?', cried Wilde sharply.

'It is from them that I have come', replied Holmes. 'I should not have dreamt of making such a suggestion without consulting them. Their concern is to see you free: to do that, they would gladly relinquish any monetary claim upon you. What say you now? How does this affect your defence of your friend? Can you honestly say that you owe it to him to run this terrible risk?'

'I owe it to myself', said Wilde quietly; and for all of Holmes' arguments he refused to alter his stance. Holmes left defeated.

The third and last trial turned out as anticipated. Following certain of Holmes' suggestions, Wilde's counsel succeeded in discrediting the evidence of the hotel servants. One had brought her spectacles to court; she was forced to admit that she had not been wearing them at the time that, she alleged, she had seen Wilde. Another could not say whether the young man he claimed to have seen with Wilde was dark or fair. Having disposed of the independent witnesses, the defence counsel made a heroic speech, pleading with the jury not to destroy the career of a great man of letters on the evidence of self-confessed criminals.

Again the court rang with applause; but what Holmes had dreaded now came to pass. The Solicitor-General, making devastating use of his right of final address, denounced the appeal to art as a flimsy pretext for immorality. The jury, clearly, agreed with him, returning a verdict of 'Guilty', and the judge found Wilde 'the centre of a circle of extensive corruption of the most hideous kind among young men'. The court responded with a hum of approval; but there were a few who raised the cry of 'Shame!', and Holmes was among them.

With a snarl, he stalked out of the court and through the mob of revellers who were dancing on the pavement outside. It was the Queen's birthday, and I strove to say as much to him, but he leaped like a maniac into the traffic of the Strand, with its melée of crowded omnibuses, traders' drays, newspaper hawkers and bicyclists ringing their bells, and dived under the ancient gateway that leads to the Inns of Court. Once we had entered the laneway, the din receded; and Holmes paused, deep in thought, outside the circular church of the Temple.

As I paused to get my breath back, he observed bitterly: 'I never pass this church, Watson, without the most sombre reflections. There, at the centre of our legal quarter, lie the defenders of Christendom, hounded and destroyed on the same charge as Wilde; condemned as corrupters of morals by a hypocrisy infinitely more insidious and more corrupt. What judgement waits upon us for these crimes?'

I was determined, for his sake as well as my own, to restore him to a sense of reality. 'It seems to me, Holmes', I said briskly, 'that you have allowed your moral compass to be skewed by an understandable sympathy with your client. Public opinion is against you'.

'Public opinion? Do you refer to those creatures dancing in the street? They were prostitutes, Watson!'

'Prostitutes!'

'They consider that their trade has been harmed by men such as Wilde, and rejoice in his downfall. At the same time, the male representatives of their order were openly soliciting on the steps of the court'.

'Openly soliciting! What is this you say?'

'Only that, whatever else may have been upheld by this trial, it was not morality. Do you honestly think Douglas was corrupted by Wilde?'

'Certainly not. But there can be no doubt that Wilde was guilty. He was convicted by due process of law. I thought the prosecutor put the matter very ably'.

'You thought him sincere?'

'I have never heard the sense of outrage more passionately expressed'.

'Do you know who introduced Wilde to these dens of prostitution?'

'There was a great deal of evidence. I cannot remember every detail'.

'Wilde was introduced to that society, of which the prosecutor declared the utmost abhorrence, by Douglas, whom he is supposed to have corrupted; and Douglas was introduced to them by the prosecutor's nephew. What say you now, friend Watson, of the "magnificent fair play" of English law?'

An abyss seemed to open beneath me. Holmes walked slowly through the mellow courts until we reached the Embankment. Here, though an occasional steam-boat hooted and smoked, the noise seemed to diffuse itself as it made its way across the calm water; and the sailing-boats that passed up and down, with the pinnacled silhouette of Westminster beyond, and Cleopatra's Needle in the middle distance, gave the impression of civilisation flowing in accordance with a timeless order.

We sat on a bench; and, as Holmes took out his pipe and began to fill it, Mr. Bernard Shaw sauntered by. Seeing us, he halted.

'Mr. Shaw!', cried Holmes. 'There is one question remaining, on which I wish you to enlighten me, if you will'.

'Certainly', beamed the noted eccentric.

'As I perceive it, there is but one puzzle in this case. Douglas and Queensberry, the assorted harlots and blackmailers, the scarcely less venal advocates and servants of the Crown – all behaved more or less in character. Wilde stood apart: he might have saved himself, and did not. What can you tell me of Dublin?'

'Bravo, Holmes. I have no doubt that it is in Dublin the answer is to be found. You see, his mother told him, before the last trial, that if he ran away, she would disown him'.

'That is all?'

'That is all, in the sense of everything; he worships her'.

'The only trace of worship I have seen in him was for that worthless young hysteric Douglas. And, whatever he did, he could surely trust to her forgiveness'.

'It is a little more complicated. The father was a public and notorious lecher. Yet the mother never uttered a word of reproach. Oscar once told me of her welcoming a veiled mistress to his deathbed, remarking that if her presence could be of any comfort to him, she would not stand in the way. He was close to tears; he said that he could never forget her nobility. One of his characters says: "Every woman becomes like her mother; that's her tragedy. No man becomes like his mother; that's his". Oscar *has* become like his mother; that is *his* tragedy'. And, raising his broad-brimmed hat in salute, Shaw pirouetted along the path.

'There goes', said Holmes thoughtfully, 'our most distinguished playwright still at liberty; but he has a great deal yet to learn about the human heart'.

'You do not agree with him, then?'

'I neither agree nor disagree. This seeing of people as puppets of their past has a certain superficial plausibility. But it fails to account for all of the facts; and, the more complex the human being, the less it accounts for. No, I am convinced that Wilde did what he did in full awareness of what he was doing. And if that is so – and I find myself inevitably thrown back upon it – it is one of the most extraordinary actions that has taken place in Europe over the past two thousand years.

159

For what it means is that somebody has at last taken himself, quite literally, as a Christian'.

'A Christian!', I spluttered, beside myself. 'Really, Holmes, you must pull yourself together. This case has begun to affect your brain. As your doctor, I must insist upon a holiday. Somewhere clean and bracing, and removed from human habitation: somewhere like Dartmoor, perhaps'.

'You seem to have forgotten, Watson, what we encountered upon our last holiday in Dartmoor'.

Temporarily, under the stress of emotion, I had. How often, in my nightmares, those fiery eyes returned to me: the bloodshot, glaring eyes of the Hound of the Baskervilles! Involuntarily, I shuddered.

'No', said Holmes, leaning back and puffing at his pipe, 'It is not the moorland air that I need to clear my head. It is a solution to this problem; and I believe that I have found one'.

'It is very singular, you will agree'.

'On the contrary, it is shared by a very high authority. I have heard it said of Wilde that there is no man who exhibits more Christ-like characteristics'.

'What profane blackguard uttered those words?'

'They were reported to me as coming from the Bishop of London'.

The scene seemed to whirl about me; but Holmes did not advert to Wilde again until after he had been released from prison, and, one day, a slim package arrived for me in the post. When I opened it, I saw a volume of verse. On the fly-leaf was the inscription: 'To Dr. Watson, with the Compliments of the Author'. But who the author was I could not imagine: there was no name on the title-page, only a code made up of a figure and two numbers. Holmes, hearing me groan and sigh my puzzlement, looked aside from his newspaper with a quizzical gaze. 'Somebody has sent me a volume of verse',

I said, 'with his compliments. But I have not the slightest idea who it is. No name on it'.

'What is it about?', asked Holmes. 'Perhaps you will find your answer there'.

'I do not think so', I said, as I skimmed through the volume impatiently. 'It seems to be the tale of somebody who was hanged for murder, and there is a good deal of criticism of the conditions under which he was held. Some kind of tract for prison reform. But why write it in verse? And why the devil has the fellow not put his name to it?'

'Perhaps he is a prisoner himself. Perhaps a warder. Perhaps the prison chaplain'.

'I do not think so', I said. 'Listen to this:

> The Chaplain would not kneel to pray
> By his dishonoured grave:
> Nor mark it with the blessed Cross
> That Christ for sinners gave,
> Because the man was one of those
> Whom Christ came down to save'.

Holmes had sat bolt upright while I was reading, and now was rigid with attention. 'Give it here, Watson', he said urgently.

He glanced at the title-page, with its peculiar cipher, and read it aloud. *The Ballad of Reading Gaol. By C.3.3.* Ha! I thought so! It is Wilde. C.3.3. was his cell number at Reading. Do you not see what this means?'

'Not in the slightest'.

'What does the number 33 suggest to you?'

'It has only one association that I know of'.

'And that is?'

'The traditional age of Christ'.

'Precisely: a symbolism reinforced by the letter C'.

'Wilde hardly chose his own cell'.

'No, but its having been chosen for him would confirm his feeling that there was significance in his suffering. He is reputed to have said that he had put his talent into his work, and his genius into his life. Given such a belief, everything that occurs to him is suffused with meaning. Why else should he underline the cipher? See, he repeats it at the end of the poem'.

'You have only made the matter more puzzling. Why has he inscribed the piece to me?'

'I think I can give you the answer to that', answered Holmes, who was now looking at the opening lines of the poem. 'Do you remember that little altercation you had at your first meeting, when he criticised you over your choice of colour for *A Study in Scarlet*, and you answered him so splendidly? Well, it has evidently remained in his mind; listen to this:

> He did not wear his scarlet coat,
> For blood and wine are red,
> And blood and wine were on his hands
> When they found him with the dead,
> The poor dead woman whom he loved,
> And murdered in her bed'.

'So that is why he has sent it to me! He is making amends!'

'He is doing much more than that, Watson; and he has, in the process, borne out my view of his character. The man the world thinks of as the supreme narcissist has reduced himself to a spectator, a fellow-sufferer in a place of still greater suffering. He has subsumed his own anguish in that of another: the sign of a great spirit'.

I did not feel it expedient to express my disagreement; but Holmes came back to the subject at the time of our visit to Paris on behalf of King Edward. As we passed through the Left Bank on our return from Vincennes, Holmes pointed to an undistinguished building, and remarked quietly: 'That is where Wilde died: 13, Rue des Beaux-Arts. Do you not see its significance: a life devoted to the arts, ending in the unluckiest of numbers?'

'Unlucky only if you consider it an undeserved misfortune', I said shortly.

'But that is just the point, Watson', he replied vehemently. 'Thirteen is thought of as the number of Judas, as he was thirteenth on the night he betrayed his master. But the odd man out can equally be considered Christ; and it is to Christ that the number originally referred. The lunar year consists of twelve full months and a fraction; and it is in the course of the latter, the odd or intercalary season of Christmas, that the sun dips towards extinction before rising again. Resurrection is dependent on death, as Christ on Judas; Wilde's revelation was that human nature is paradoxical and partakes of both. The subject of his poem was both lover and betrayer, as Douglas was lover and betrayer to him, and he himself to his unfortunate wife'.

I remained silent in the face of these blasphemies, as Holmes sang to himself: 'For each man kills the thing he loves…' Our carriage, meanwhile, had reached the river, on whose glassy surface the stately palace of the Louvre stood inverted.

SIX

THE GREEN MAN'S CHAPEL

As we drove in our trap from the station, a hill shaped like a volcano emerged from the plain, its sides wooded, and a circular building on its summit turned gold by the setting sun.

'Whatever can it be, Holmes?', I cried.

'Our problem, I suspect, Watson'.

We had come down to Cornwall in response to an invitation from the Reverend Eustace Weatherby, a former fellow-student of Holmes', whom he had run into – quite literally – in the reading-room of the British Museum a few weeks previously. Holmes was balancing a pile of tomes he had received from the desk in the centre of the round room, while Weatherby was rambling amid the shelves that encircle it, a heavy volume of the cat- alogue in his hands. Ordinarily, Holmes tells me, readers make way for one another as if by instinct, but on this occasion the absent-minded cleric walked right into Holmes' collection and scattered it in all directions. At once he was on hands and knees, scrabbling about among trouser-legs and hemlines, in a still clumsier attempt to retrieve the volumes. As he was about to give Holmes' books back to him, his mouth fell open and he dropped them again.

'Holmes!', he exclaimed, in a voice that echoed under the dome and caused the readers, as one, to look up in annoyance from their desks. 'I never thought to see you here!'

'Nor will you again, Weatherby, unless you can lower your voice', replied Holmes. Already an official of the library was striding purposefully towards the pair, breach of silence and damage to property written clearly on his face. A few muttered words from Holmes, and it was agreed to keep the books for his return, while he steered the obstreperous cleric to the tea-room.

'Holmes!', cried the Reverend Weatherby, as they were seated over tea and scones, 'you are exactly the person I need to guide me'.

'You need someone, that is certain', said Holmes, with an asperity which passed over the head of his interlocutor.

'The ritual, I think, I have resolved', mused the cleric. 'But the treasure is as far to seek as ever; and, as for the murder...'

'Murder?', interjected Holmes sharply, his ears pricking up.

'Oh, you will not find the murderer', laughed the cleric, amused at the new tone that had come into my friend's voice. 'It happened in the sixteenth century. But the ritual, the treasure, the murder – all seem interconnected; and it seemed to me that if I should succeed in resolving the one, all the rest would follow. But I seem to have missed something; that is why I have come here in search of further information'.

'Not another word', said Holmes. 'If I were to listen to the details now, they would interfere with my concentration. And that I cannot afford: I am currently retained in the case of the Imperial Ballerina, which has wrought such havoc in St. Petersburg'.

The vicar was insistent that Holmes should visit his parish in time for a midsummer ritual which, he averred, bore strongly upon his mystery; and so it was that, on the eve of that day, having alighted from a local train and taken a trap from the station, we found ourselves driving over the wild Cornish moors on a golden evening, cirrus clouds fanned out high over a sun in decline on a distant sea.

We arrived at a vicarage in modern Gothic which stood on a village green beside an imposing medieval church, and were greeted by the Reverend Weatherby, an affable cleric with a halo of white hair. After a simple but satisfying meal, as we sat smoking by the fire – for the summer evening had turned a trifle chill – Holmes began: 'Now tell me about this crime of yours'.

'Not so fast, Holmes', said Weatherby, with a smile of boyish triumph. 'I must not deprive you of the exercise of those deductive faculties which I remember so well, and which Doctor Watson has so eloquently recorded'. I bowed. 'I must admit, also, that it pleases me to hold in my hands the key to the tale, as you accuse Watson of doing, until you have acquainted yourself with the facts. As I have not yet offered you any information about the place, it is impossible for you to reach any conclusions'.

'On the contrary', replied Holmes, 'I have already formed a provisional hypothesis'. The cleric's mouth fell open. 'I have noted', Holmes continued, 'the existence of two churches, the second of which, beside us here in the village, is of a size which indicates considerable wealth at the time of its building. And, as it is in the style of Decorated Gothic, I should guess that the tin-mines of the area were highly productive in the early fifteenth century'.

'Later, Holmes. Styles travelled slowly in these parts. And what, pray, do you deduce from the church you passed along the way?'

'It follows from what I have already stated. An increase in wealth led to a relocation of the church to a more convenient site. Unlike, however, the similar move from Old Sarum to Salisbury, the old church was not dismantled to provide materials for the new. I take it, then, that it is a site of peculiar interest or sanctity'.

'Amazing', murmured the cleric in astonishment. 'As you say, it was – indeed still is – the veritable sanctuary of the area. The locals had at first no wish to worship in the grandiose new edifice which the wealthy families of the area had provided for them. So it was agreed that on a single day of the year, worship should be held in the original church...'

He was interrupted by the drawing-room clock striking a wheezy three-quarters to midnight.

'But more of this later; it is time for us to witness the ritual'.

Out on the village green, the entire parish seemed to have assembled. In the centre stood ten young men with blazing torches, who had taken up careful position so as to form a five-pointed star. By the time the bell in the church tower had begun to toll midnight, what talk there was had died down. The silence and the unsteady illumination made a profound impression on me, who had just come from the noise and the glare of Baker Street.

On the last stroke of the bell, the youths began to move, slowly at first, and then with ever-increasing speed, along the endless single line of the star, so that it seemed to be graven in light. Then, when we had been hypnotised into seeing the star still moving although it had stopped, two more youths danced their way from the crowd to kneel in front of the vicar, one with face gilded and giving off a dazzling sheen in the light of the torches, the other blackened and almost invisible. Each carried a sword.

The vicar unfolded an old piece of heavy paper, and read:

Go forth upon thy ways, o knight,
Courage and faith thine armour bright,
So comes our Lord once more from night,
Where strikes the earth the sword of light.

As he finished, the two broke away, leaping their way into the space left by the torch-carriers. A rustic band struck up – just such an incongruous orchestra as one would expect to find in so remote a place: furious fiddles, sonorous clarinets and bassoons, wailing bagpipes and a great bass drum – increasing in speed, and heightening the tension, as each dancer threatened the other in ghostly mime, advancing and retreating, retreating and advancing, until it seemed they fought in grim earnest, as the drum kept their blows company. Then, suddenly, the one whose face was gilded knelt in front of the other, who raised his sword and held it suspended as the spectators, almost audibly, held their breath. Three times this happened, and at each of the strokes the band stopped, so that they seemed suspended in an uncanny silence. On the third occasion the shadowy swordsman touched the neck of his opponent, who lay stretched on the ground a moment, then rose to rousing cheers from the spectators. The ten torchmen cast their brands into the centre, the villagers rushed to heap the bonfire, and the space before the church became bright as day. As a keg of ale was noisily broached, we left the villagers to their carousal and went inside.

'If this is your mystery and your murder, I have already solved it', said Holmes

'It is my mystery, but not my murder', smiled the vicar. 'The most persistent tradition in these parts concerns a ritual which was held in the circular chapel on Christmas Day, but of which all trace has vanished. Last year, as I watched this dance, it occurred to me that this might be the missing ritual'.

'And it signifies?', queried Holmes.

'For those of us of the cloth, midsummer is the feast of the decollation of John the Baptist'.

'Decollation', I repeated, puzzled. 'It sounds like some sort of dish'.

'A dish, certainly, came into it', said the vicar with an expression of distaste; 'but in somewhat gruesome fashion. You see, "decollation" signifies beheading, and you will recall that the Precursor of our Saviour lost his at the behest of a sinful queen'.

'Was there not a play upon this subject in London some time ago?', I asked Holmes.

'As a matter of fact, there was', he replied, '*Salomé*, by Oscar Wilde...'

'Wilde!', interjected the cleric and myself in horrified unison.

'Before you rush to condemnation', said Holmes patiently, 'let me tell you what the play contains. It seems to me that the idea of Salomé's being in love with John the Baptist, and having him beheaded because he has rejected her, is a most fitting expansion of the biblical tale. The final scene, of the princess kissing the dead lips of the saint...'

'Kissing dead lips!', exclaimed Weatherby in disgust.

'I see I shall not convert you', smiled Holmes. 'But what, in that case, do you make of your ritual?'

'It is very simple', replied the vicar. 'As the Precursor makes way for the Saviour, nature bows and accepts death before grace'.

I could see that Holmes was disappointed. 'In that case', he said, 'why was the ritual held at Christmas also?'

'It reiterates the message at the birth of our Saviour'.

Holmes frowned. 'Then how do you account for the star?'

'The star of Bethlehem'.

'But that has six points', said Holmes evenly. 'This has five'.

'A corruption'.

'It seems to me', said Holmes, 'that you have fallen into some contradiction here. On the one hand, you posit a ritual of singular antiquity, handed down with peculiar reverence, and surviving even a transfer from its original location. On the other, you say that it has been corrupted in the process'.

'We must continue this discussion of detail at a later date', said the cleric, stifling a yawn and rising, 'although I must say it seems to me of no great consequence'.

'On the contrary, it is the whole mystery', muttered Holmes, as our host's footsteps retreated up the stairs. Once they were safely out of hearing, he grasped an apple from a dish in the centre of the table, split it crossways, and held up half. 'What do you see, Watson?'

I gasped in astonishment. For there, clearly visible in the core of the fruit, was the five-pointed star we had seen represented in the dance.

'What can it mean, Holmes?'

'It means precisely what we have seen, Watson. The apple was a sacred symbol for the Celts who once inhabited – still inhabit – these parts. You have heard of Avalon, which is described in medieval records as Insula Pomorum – the Isle of Apples. The beauty of apple-blossom suggested the mystery of the renewal of life, which seemed to hinge on the two turning-points of the year: the decline and revival of the sun'.

'You have solved the ritual!', I cried.

Holmes looked quizzically at the apple he had sliced in two, then offered me one half while he munched the other. 'I do not wish to alarm our vicar unduly', he said, 'but there may have been a time when it was something more than a ritual: when the goddess of the land, whose symbol was the apple, took a new mate after he had slain his predecessor. I fear our good vicar has been presiding over events which, did he comprehend them, he would find far more disturbing than anything dreamt up by Wilde'.

As we sat over breakfast next morning, the high pointed windows of the vicarage affording a view of the circular chapel on the hill, I was roused by a crunch on the gravel, and startled to see a dark face look in. The vicar, following my gaze, smiled, put aside his napkin and got up to open the door. Immediately the swarthy face disappeared from the window and reappeared in the doorway. To my even greater surprise, it was the face of an Englishman, not quite so dark now as when viewed against the brilliant light of the summer morning, yet still noticeably alien. Holmes, unperturbed, uttered some phrases of greeting in a language which brought back memories – some melancholy, some glorious – of my own past. Our visitor began to answer in the same tongue, then checked himself and exclaimed: 'But how the devil did you know I spoke Urdu?'

'Simple', smiled Holmes. 'Your posture proclaimed you a soldier, though out of uniform; your bearing – imposing, yet guarded – suggested authority amid an alien population; your tan suggested a dry, rather than a humid, climate, and its depth the north rather than the south of a warm country'.

'Lahore', answered the other with a look of shock. But he recovered himself quickly, as if by an effort of will, and thrust out his hand. 'Perran-Tremayne, late of the Second Punjabi Engineers'.

'And now squire of Perranleigh Hall', added our vicar.

'I came into the property some few months ago', said the officer shortly.

'If I had known you had returned', said the vicar amiably, 'I should have invited you to join us last night. I trust your visit to London was a success?'

'Difficult to say at this point. So ancient an inheritance as mine, you can imagine, is a very tangled affair, and the language of lawyers is more of a puzzle to me than Urdu ever was', he barked with a short laugh. 'And the same holds true, I must confess, for His Reverence's rituals. They are beyond a simple man like myself – I belonged to a company of sappers in India, and I feel more at ease with timber than with theories'.

'Captain Perran-Tremayne has been kind enough to lend us the benefit of his professional experience', said the vicar. 'But let me summon the trap, and I will explain as we go along'.

After we had stepped up into the trap, and the vicar given a flick of his whip to the horse, he informed us that the chapel on the hill was badly in need of repair. 'My predecessor shut it down, and it is now in a parlous state. I did indeed consider having it dismantled, since it is in use only one day of the year – one night, rather: it is open for midnight service at Christmas'.

'That seems an unconscionable waste', I agreed.

'By no means, Watson', said Holmes sharply. 'That is rather the beauty of the thing. It is a site that has kept its sense of pilgrimage: of a place sequestered. Nowadays, as we hurtle hither and thither by steam-train, crossing the country in a matter of hours, we feel that anything is accessible, everything known. We give ourselves no time to apprehend the unknowable...'

'My sympathies are with Dr. Watson', put in the vicar, 'but I encountered insuperable opposition from my parish. They expressed profound horror that something which had been preserved from time immemorial should be done away with. Indeed, they were highly vocal on the matter. A number of the older inhabitants informed me that the most abiding recollection of their childhood was seeing the lights behind the coloured windows reflected in the waters of the mere – for the ground which surrounds it floods in winter – as they passed along the pathway to the church. One of them, rather fancifully, likened it to a jewelled goblet rising out of the waters. Like a vision from another world, said another. Indeed, for some reason or other, the site is known locally as Avalon...'

Holmes darted me a significant look.

'...though why', the vicar went on, 'I cannot imagine. Its dedication is to Saint Piran, patron of Cornwall'.

Weatherby tied the reins of the trap to a fence at the bottom of the hill, and led us along a path which spiralled upward through the woods. These denied us a view until we had

172

come out upon the platform on which the church was set; and we looked out over a wild valley across which there sounded the desolate cry of a curlew, and beyond which we saw the distant line of the sea.

The chapel was built of white stone, in the plain Norman style; but was entered by a doorway of the greatest elaboration. Above was a carved face peering out from leaves inhabited by animals and birds. The features bore an expression at once both sinister and   sad: if I had been asked for a single word to express it, it would have been 'haunted'.   I remarked on the fact.

The vicar looked up.   'How strange that you should say that, Dr. Watson.   The locals do believe that the place is haunted – haunted by the memory of a murder which is supposed to have taken place here a long time ago...'   He paused in confusion.   'However', he went on hurriedly, 'My brethren of the cloth report similar carvings in their own churches: the subject is apparently known as the Green Man'.

Removing a key from his pocket, he pushed the creaking door open.   Once inside, we saw scaffolding set all about, and reaching to the ceiling, which did not however succeed in obliterating the very peculiar atmosphere of the chapel. Behind a simple arcade of round-headed arches shone ten small circular windows adorned with vegetation similar to that on the doorway, and which at any other time of day must have conveyed a sensation of gloom.   But at this time, with the morning sun behind it, what caught one's attention was the large window, also circular, behind the altar.   The lower half of the circle was invisible, being cut off from view by a towering altar; but the upper half showed a scene of peculiar brilliance.   Here stood a Christ in glory, robed in gold and wielding a great sword, against a background of emerald green.

Holmes let out a low whistle.   'What', he queried urgently, 'is in the lower half?'

The vicar led us into the space behind the altar, where we saw an astonishing sight. Where the background of the upper half of the window was green, the lower was gold; where the upper half showed a Christ with a sword, the lower showed an antlered Green Man with an identical weapon.

Holmes clapped his hands. The sound echoed and re-echoed in the hush of the chapel.

'Why, the whole thing is obvious. How long has the altar been here?'

The vicar gazed at him in puzzlement. 'It was erected by a predecessor of mine at the time of the Evangelical Revival'.

'Of course. It has been deliberately designed to block the lower half of the window'.

'Theologically, that is certainly unorthodox. Some would even call it blasphemous'.

'Do not you?'

'Not necessarily, depending on its interpretation. To me it is a perfectly straightforward illustration of what I remarked last night'.

Holmes' expression, which had shown some signs of interest, turned to one of disappointment as the vicar went on: 'The Green Man, representing the life of nature, is overcome by the workings of grace'.

'Hm', said Holmes in that preoccupied tone which I had learnt to recognise as the sign that his mind was working on some other problem. He had been inspecting the altar with narrowed eyes; and, following his gaze, I saw that the dark oak had been patched up with laths of a fainter hue. He then gazed at the floor, upon which he gave a scarcely audible sigh of satisfaction.

He interrupted the vicar's discourse: 'The altar had become unsafe?'

'Exactly', replied the squire, hurriedly. 'It is riddled with woodworm. I thought it best to board it up until we could undertake a more thoroughgoing restoration'.

The vicar chimed in: 'The scaffolding is the work of our squire. Having laughed me out of a fantasy of mine – indeed disproved it – he has offered to make the most pressing repairs himself, so that we can reopen the chapel for Christmas'.

'My simple ambition', said Perran-Tremayne sardonically, 'is to keep the place from falling around our ears while others weave theories about it'.

'This fantasy of yours', Holmes pursued, undaunted. 'In what did it consist?'

The vicar exchanged a deprecating glance with the squire, then went on ruefully. 'It is really very silly. You remember the doggerel I recited in the course of the ritual?'

'Something about a knight going forth to battle'.

'Yes; well, the second half of it runs:

So comes our Lord once more from night
Where strikes the earth the sword of light.

'You see, once I had surmised that the dance belonged in the church, I thought these verses might be a pointer to something hidden in it: there are persistent legends of a treasure having been buried here. So we followed the light shining through the tip of the sword of Our Lord at dawn. Captain Perran-Tremayne worked out where it must fall on midsummer's day, and we dug there. We found nothing. We tried again at the spot where the reflection must fall at Christmas, and again the result was the same'.

'You are sure you have looked in the right place?', queried Holmes.

'It is a matter of simple trigonometry', replied Perran-Tremayne sharply. 'The subject is one in which I may be

175

thought to have some professional competence; but of course you may check my figures if you so desire'.

'I should not dream of questioning them', replied Holmes soothingly. 'I was merely expressing interest in His Reverence's exposition'.

'I had hoped', said the vicar, 'that if we found the treasure, it might help us restore the church. But thanks to the Captain's generosity, that is no longer necessary. Well, I think we have seen all that is to be found here', he concluded, and indicated the door.

'Yes, I think we have', said Holmes in a tone of resignation. But it seemed to me that he was seething with suppressed excitement as we filed out of the chapel and the vicar relocked it. As he took out his pipe, and stuffed it carefully with shag tobacco, I could see that his fingers were trembling.

Replacing the key in his pocket, the vicar said apologetically: 'I am sorry to have brought you all this way for nothing, Holmes. When I invited you down, I was convinced that there was indeed a treasure buried in the church, and that you could help us locate it. Thanks to the Captain, we now know that there is none. Meanwhile, I hope you will enjoy our scenery and our bracing air – which Doctor Watson tells me you are much in need of'.

'I feel the better for it already', said Holmes, gazing out over the valley. 'But I fear we shall have to be on our way. London knows no cessation of crime. There is a train in the early afternoon?'

'The 12:25'.

'Perfect. Come, Watson, we had better pack'.

I thought I saw a smile flit across the features of the squire. 'Well, I will be on my way, vicar', he said, when he had driven us back to the vicarage. 'There is much to be attended to on my estate. Mr. Holmes, Dr. Watson, it has been a pleasure to meet you'.

But when we had gone indoors at the vicarage once more, Holmes' manner became suddenly urgent. 'What of the murder with which you lured me here?', he asked.

'Forgive me, Holmes', the vicar replied apologetically. 'I assure you I had not meant to lure you here, as you say; but now that the treasure has been proved non-existent, there can have been no murder for its sake. Both can only be the imaginings of rustics seeking to while away a winter evening'.

'You are falling into the same inconsistency as before: you dismiss the villagers' tales as distortions and fabrications, yet you consider their dance a singularly pure transmission of an ancient rite'.

The vicar gesticulated helplessly.

'Furthermore', continued Holmes relentlessly, 'did I detect a certain constraint in alluding to the murder in front of our squire?'

'Certainly, Holmes', said the vicar ruefully. 'It was all in the distant past, you understand; but it is no very pleasant thing, all the same, to have one's forebears taken for murderers and thieves'.

'Thieves?'

'Oh yes, in the view of the villagers, the Perran-Tremaynes are interlopers on a great deal of their property – half of it in fact. According to village tradition, the roles in the dance at Christmastide were taken by the heads of the two wealthiest local families, the Perrans and the Tremaynes. It was the head of the Perran family who alone knew the location of the treasure. This consisted of a pair of golden swords, which were replaced in a secret location after the dance every year. One Christmas Day – so the story goes – the then Tremayne hid in the chapel, learned the location of the swords, and killed their guardian, in some way that was made to look like an accident. A fall of stone from the ceiling, I believe it was.

177

'The killing, despite suspicions, could never be brought home to Tremayne. It was said that he afterwards attempted to force himself upon Perran's young widow, who was with child, and that his pursuit of her was so relentless that she fled away by sea, it was thought to Wales, and was never heard of again. Tremayne, invoking an earlier marriage between the families, laid claim to the Perran estate. As there was no-one to contest it, and he had been generous with the judges, he was allowed to add it to his own, at the same time taking the name Perran-Tremayne to quash any future counter-claim.

'His success, however, was short-lived. One of those he had bribed at court to advance his cause was Thomas Cromwell, a man no less unscrupulous than himself, who advocated the suppression of the monasteries to enrich his master, Henry VIII, and himself in the process. When he passed through this part of the country, he was royally entertained by Tremayne; but, noting his host's wealth, was moved less by gratitude than by greed, and used the pretext of the midsummer dance, which he had witnessed, to denounce Tremayne as an upholder of Popish superstition – and so disloyal to the King – have him executed and his estates confiscated. Cromwell himself, mistaking his master's taste in female companionship, was brought to the block soon after, and Tremayne's widow was able to have the estates restored. But in the meantime had come to pass the curse which the villagers believed attended Tremayne's sacrilege, and which they believe even yet has not worked itself out fully. A series of misfortunes has attended the family from one generation to the next, which they are convinced will only cease when an heir of the Perrans returns to take his revenge on an heir of the Tremaynes'.

'Quite as bloodthirsty a tale as any I have encountered in the fog-laden alleyways of London', smiled Holmes, 'and fully justifying the sinister interpretation which I place upon the loneliness of the countryside: as Watson has recorded in – what was it you called it – "The Copper Beeches"?'

I nodded.

'But I am afraid', Holmes continued, 'that we must now take our leave – oh, and might I borrow your key?'

'My key?'

'Yes – that question of the squire's measurements. I expect everything is in order, but I should like to be certain. We will leave it with the station-master. No, no, I insist upon our going by ourselves'.

Once we had returned to the chapel, Holmes made directly for the back of the altar and prostrated himself on the floor with his magnifying lens. He then scooped up what looked like minute grains of dark sand into a page of his pocket-book, in a state of high excitement. 'Exactly as I thought!'

'You have lost me, Holmes'.

'Come Watson, stand here'; and he placed me exactly under the centre of the window. 'Now look up at the altar. Do you not see, behind the boards nailed over it, a thin pale square?' By straining my eyes I could just make it out. 'It was the first thing I noticed. Anyone who has had anything to do with carpentry will tell you that they do not reinforce anything. Tremayne's talk of woodworm is the merest blind. My confirmation comes from this', and he showed me the powder in the paper.

'What is it, Holmes?'

'Sawdust. And sawdust, not from those deal boards which have so crudely been hammered into place, but from the oaken altar. Someone has gone to the trouble of sawing out a square, then hammering it back into position again'.

'Why on earth should they do such a thing?'

At that moment I heard a faint sound, as if someone were outside the chapel. I followed Holmes as he raced to the entrance, but there was no-one visible, and the trees screened our view of the path.

'Perhaps it was the wind', I offered, for the breezes were fresh at that level.

'Perhaps', said Holmes, as he took out our watch. 'At any rate, it is time to test my theory'.

'I am utterly at sea'.

'It is really very simple. Our vicar's theology is radically defective. The key to the matter is the dedication of the chapel to the Green Man, alias Saint Piran, patron of Cornwall. What do you know of him?'

'Hadn't he something to do with the mines?'

'He is said to have discovered tin, and to have been responsible for its mining. He is also said to have come across the sea from Ireland, where he lived in a forest among the beasts of the wild'.

'Hardly surprising', I snorted.

'Be that as it may, Watson, put these two things together, and what do you get? A saint who is associated with the underworld, on the one hand, and on the other with the animal life of the forest. It seems to me that we have here a god of nature in its dark and yet fruitful aspects. For the older peoples, light and dark were part of a recurrent cycle. It is something we have allowed ourselves to forget, living as we do under artificial illumination. We have forgotten the meaning of darkness: forgotten that our world rotates to its rhythm; forgotten that we carry it within.

'Our squire, having lived in India, will have been more receptive to the idea. He will have encountered gods who represent destruction as well as creation – both being aspects of the same process of renewal. Apply this to the chapel, and what do we get? The Green Man is a version of the Celtic divinity of darkness, seen as alternating with the divinity of light. Saint Piran is his successor, lightly baptised. This chapel is dedicated to him. Apply this to the vicar's doggerel, and who is "Our Lord"?'

'The Green Man, I suppose', said I dubiously.

'Correct, Watson: and it is the tip of his sword which marks the hiding-place of the treasure – presuming there to be any after all this time. But that is a matter we can now put to the test'.

Leaping up on the altar, Holmes pulled away the clumsy framework which held the sawn-off square, jumped down and strode to where the tip of the lower sword was now clearly outlined against the floor. Making some rapid calculations in his notebook, and marking off the distance with his pocket measuring-tape, he came to a point which he proceeded to identify with a piece of chalk taken from another pocket. At once he emitted a snarl of disappointment.

'See, Watson', he exclaimed, 'We have been forestalled'. He pointed downwards. There, on the stone, though an attempt had been made to wipe it out, were the faint traces of an earlier chalk-mark.

He was right. When we lifted the slab, we found a stone-lined vault, but it was quite empty. Holmes let out a sigh of annoyance.

Just at that moment I found myself propelled, with a speed and force that I had not experienced since my rugby days, across the chapel floor, to land by one of the columns. It was well that Holmes had done so: for portion of the roof had collapsed in a cloud of dust and broken stone that rained down on the spot where we had stood. Holmes himself had struck the column with considerable velocity, and lay stunned while I tried to revive him. I had an impression of hurrying feet while I loosened my friend's collar and, in a few moments, had the satisfaction of seeing his eyes flutter open.

'Tremayne!', muttered Holmes.

'How can you be sure of that, Holmes?', I cried. 'Did you see him? Have you got any proof?'

His reply filled me with foreboding. 'I do not need any', he said. His voice had deepened as he gazed into space, and he seemed as one possessed. Pushing me aside, Holmes rushed out of the chapel and down the hill. I was hard-pressed to keep up with him, and barely managed to spring onto the step of the trap as he whipped the horse to a gallop. I hung there, swaying, as he drove down the road to the village, and leaped down where another trap stood, its horse panting, outside the manor-house. Perran-Tremayne had reached the door of his dwelling and stood on the steps, his face pallid under the overshadowing trees. Holmes had reached the garden gate.

'Tremayne!', he called out in stentorian tones. 'What have you done with the treasure?'

'But you are dead!', came the squire's strangled voice, that wavered between disbelief and fear.

'Not this time!', cried Holmes, in a tone that filled me with horror, so little did it resemble the quiet accents of my friend. 'What have you done with the treasure?'

For answer, the squire, pale as death, bolted into the house and slammed the door. I saw Holmes race towards it, throw his shoulder against it, and, with what seemed like superhuman energy, force it open. I ran after him, heart in mouth, into the manor-house. There I witnessed a dreadful sight. Holmes had torn a sword from a display of armour in the hall, and was hacking at the panel of a door like one deranged. Before I could restrain him, he had burst it open and rushed inside. I raced after him, determined to prevent him from perpetrating some tragedy in his madness.

But my fear was unfounded. When I entered what appeared to be a study, I found Holmes resting his weight on the sword, the point of which was stuck in the floor. At his feet lay the body of Perran-Tremayne, his heart pierced by another sword which stood bloody out of his back.

'The circle is complete', muttered Holmes, a demonic satisfaction in his voice and an insane glitter in the eyes under their dark brows. Then all at once he fainted away, to slump beside the body on the floor.

I was joined in a few moments by the vicar, who had heard the clamour – as indeed had the entire village – and together we carried Holmes to a sofa and administered a cordial from a nearby sideboard. I could do nothing for Perran-Tremayne – he had died instantaneously – but, as I waited for Holmes to recover, my curiosity was piqued by a large travelling-trunk which stood open beside the desk. There, amid a change of clothing and the usual impedimenta – brushes, shaving-gear and the like – I found, wrapped in green velvet, a pair of swords fashioned out of heavy gold. They were chased with the rich patterns of ancient Celtic workmanship, in which animals and gods were intertwined with luxuriant vegetation, and set with jewels that glittered in the beam of light that crossed the study from the window: from which, far beyond the woods of the park, could be discerned the Green Man's Chapel.

A sound of coughing behind me indicated that my friend had recovered. As I turned he sat up, and to my joy there was no trace of the demonic figure I had seen stalk the squire but a few moments before. The character that sat smiling faintly on the sofa was the supremely rational, self-possessed Holmes of old. I rejoiced that he had been restored to his senses; but the question that the vicar put to him echoed my own disquiet.

'How did you know', queried the cleric, 'that it was Perran-Tremayne?'

For answer, a shadow flitted across Holmes' face, and his eyes became clouded again. He started and shuddered, as if he had suddenly recalled the series of events that had taken place, and was at a loss to account for them. I saw that he needed assistance; and I am not a little proud of the answer I then gave.

'He knew it was the squire', I asserted proudly, 'because he knew that it could be no-one else'.

It transpired that the estate was already forfeit when Perran-Tremayne inherited it, due to his debts at the gaming-tables, and that the vicar's information offered a way out of his embarrassment. His acquaintance with Indian myth, and practical knowledge of trigonometry, put him far ahead of that bumbling cleric, and led him straight to the hiding-place of the swords. Their sale in the illicit market for antiquities would have netted him a considerable fortune. Thus far, all was obvious; but when I was alone again with Holmes, I ventured to repeat the question which had been put to him by the vicar.

'Holmes, how did you know that the roof was about to collapse? You hurried me away an instant *before* it happened'.

The answer that came back to me chilled my blood.

'Because I knew it was going to happen'.

'You mean you had reached it through a chain of deductive reasoning?'

'No, I mean that I knew. I knew because it had happened before'.

'I thought you had not been there before', I said, puzzled. 'When you accepted Weatherby's invitation, did you know of this matter already?'

He looked at me solemnly out of his deep-set eyes. When he spoke, his voice was steady. 'I have never been there before', he said. 'Not in my present existence. But that I have been there in some fashion, I cannot doubt. Here, stop that restless pacing; sit down and let me tell you what happened at the moment I pushed you under the arcade.

'I saw what was going to happen, because it had happened before. It had happened before, and it had happened to me. I saw all that in a flash, as the uneasy feeling I have had since I came in sight of the chapel, a sense of darkness and oppression that has been gathering force within me since, forced its way into consciousness like a breaking wave. I knew what was going to happen; I knew it had happened once before and in that place; I knew that as I lay there, under the fallen rock, that once before I had seen Tremayne's face above me, and that, after that glimpse, I died'.

'Holmes!', I protested. 'The shock has disordered your brain. As your physician, I cannot encourage you in this delirium'.

'My mind', replied Holmes calmly, 'has never been clearer'. And it was true that the light of reason shone in his eyes, and that of the dreadful mania which I had seen in him earlier there was not the slightest trace.

'I have two separate hypotheses to account for my experience', he said, his speech as lucid and ordered as ever. 'Though it may be that both are involved. The first is one you have heard me expound before. You remember how, at the conclusion of the episode you have titled "The Empty House", I spoke of the individual representing the entire procession of his ancestors'.

'You compared it, as I recall, to "trees which grow to a certain height and then suddenly develop some unsightly eccentricity"'.

'Of which you were sceptical'.

'I did find it rather fanciful; I still do'.

'Well try this for fancy, friend Watson. I am descended from West Country squires; and one of my ancestral families, which came originally from Wales, is Perran'.

I cleared my throat and made as if to speak, but he waved me to silence.

'The second hypothesis', he went on inexorably, 'is that, instead of being visited by some ancestral memory of a long-ago crime, I actually *was* involved in it before. This may strain your belief more than anything I have previously said to you; but it is an hypothesis considered not only credible, but unquestionable, in a very large part of the globe. In my stay among the Tibetans I found that they experienced it as the basis of all reality: a conviction they share with the Hindoos of India and the Buddhists of China and Japan. Namely that we live, not one, but many, lives'.

'Pooh!' I exclaimed. 'Hindoos and heathens: subject peoples whom we have vanquished through our superior civilisation. You cannot seriously suggest, Holmes, that we have anything to learn from their grotesque idolatries?'

'I have noticed this before, Watson', Holmes replied wearily. 'I have witnessed it all too often amongst our administrators in alien lands. Though I have encountered some notable exceptions. But for your average imperial official, the reverence that others pay to the symbols of their faith is routinely dismissed as idolatry'.

'Is it not so?'

'By no means. When I passed before the shrine in my Himalayan retreat, I was bidden to incline my head: not to a graven image, nor yet to the being represented, but to the potential realisation, which it symbolised, of my own spirit. Anything less like idolatry I cannot imagine'.

'But why must you go to India for an explanation? Surely what happens here is explicable in terms of what we know here?'

'But it is, Watson; it is. The ancient inhabitants of this land maintained exactly that same doctrine of transmigration. The classical authorities are at one in attributing this belief to the Celts'.

'That may be all very well for the Celts, Holmes; but you can hardly expect an Englishman to believe it'.

'Why not, pray?'

'Because one cannot be certain what one was in a previous life: whether one was... well, you know...'

'A bigamist? A mass murderer? Out with it, Watson'.

'Oh dash it all, Holmes, one cannot be certain whether one was – you know – a gentleman'.

'You are saying that reincarnation is an affront to respectability', Holmes laughed. 'Well, perhaps it is, Watson, perhaps it is. But so is incarnation: as a medical man, you will have had ample experience of how we enter and exit this life. However, you will admit that our problem remains; and, unless you can find a better answer, mine is the only solution that I can see'.

'But I can', I protested. 'I have found a perfectly coherent answer; you simply have not given me the opportunity to expound it. My explanation is that you had worked out a rational solution to the problem before you pushed me aside, and that nasty bump you received has driven it out of your head. It is a clear case of hallucination arising from concussion. No, not another word', I said, as he made to frame a reply. 'As your physician, I have arrived at a diagnosis; I must now insist that you follow my prescription'.

Through the Reverend Weatherby, we were given the name of a landlady of good repute in the nearby seaside town of Perranporth. All this happened less than a week ago; and we have been here since, in one of the most glorious bouts of summer I can remember. As we entered the town, Holmes remarked, 'You know, Watson, there is said to be a chapel here buried under the sands. It is dedicated to Saint...'

'Hush', I said. 'It is vital to your cure that you rest and not refer to what has passed'.

He was silent then: as he has been, to a great extent, since. Despite my best efforts to keep him entertained with tales of my practice, he falls into occasional fits of bemusement. I pen these notes – with some difficulty, it is true – in a deck-chair on the broad sands of Perranporth, while Holmes, in an outlandish costume striped black and white, bathes in the eddies of the tide. A few moments ago, I caught him looking blankly out to sea, where a pool of light fell out of the clouds, as if through high windows, dazzlingly onto the water. He stood immobile, gazing as though under enchantment, so long that I began to think him in a trance. Then, just as I was becoming seriously concerned, he turned and smiled to me in reassurance. From where I sit in my deck-chair, notebook on knee, trousers rolled up and knotted handkerchief over my head, I wave back cheerily. He can always rely on me.

SEVEN
THE TROYTOWN
MURDER

Holmes never again, I am happy to relate, alluded to those morbid fantasies which fell from his lips whilst his brain was disordered. They were, I am convinced, the result of delirium; and yet what has happened since in the world at large has produced effects still more unreal, still more grotesque, than anything we could then have imagined; and which may yet sweep away all we have clung to in the name of civilisation. There are times when I think we may never recover; times when I look back to the reign of our beloved King Edward as to a golden age. And yet it was no sense of foreboding, only personal sadness, that I stood bareheaded among the crowds at Admiralty Arch and watched a Tsar of all the Russias and an Emperor of Germany ride with the new King of England in Edward's funeral cortege. How could I have guessed that these cousins, who sent friendly telegrams to each other in English signed 'Nicky' and 'Willy', would within a few short years be at the head of opposing camps in the greatest war the world has ever known? The cataclysm is still raging, the outcome as yet undecided. At times it looks extremely dark; but let me, while it is yet fresh in my memory, chronicle an episode in which it touched us very nearly.

I entered our old rooms in Baker Street to find Holmes intent upon a microscope. He made no answer to my cheery greeting: which, to tell the truth, was entirely forced. I had just been summoned from my hospital work, where I had been visiting bed after bed in a vast ward, trying to give hope where in fact there was none. We older practitioners had been called in to tend the men who were well enough to be brought from France, and so avoided the worst horrors of the medical scene there; but in our daily rounds met enough casualties who would never walk, or see, again, to drain our own spirits.

On Holmes' failure to return my greeting, I subsided onto the sofa, poured myself a stiff drink, and settled down to wait for him to address me. When he did, it was to administer a shock greater than any I had received in the course of the day. Quietly summoning me to the microscope, he gestured for me to take the seat he had vacated, and I gazed through the lens at two bullet casings on which the marks were identical.

'These were fired from the same rifle. There can be no doubt of it'.

Holmes' tragic demeanour showed that he, too, had arrived at the same conclusion. He gesticulated helplessly. 'The one on the left is the one which killed Sir Hector Bruton'.

'Sir Hector!' The heavy type in the newspaper of the evening before had gone unregarded save for a glance as I fell into my pallet at the hospital, too exhausted to read even of the murder of Britain's rising general, recently promoted to the supreme command.

'And the other?'

'Was fired this afternoon on a range in Whitehall from the rifle believed to have murdered him'.

'Why, it is an open and shut case!', I cried. 'The two are one and the same'.

'The trouble is', responded Holmes, dropping his bombshell, 'that it opens and shuts around our young friend Geoffrey Clavinger. The rifle belonged to him'.

I was speechless with horror. Young Clavinger was the son of Anna Ponderby and Roger Clavinger, who, my readers will remember, had come together at the end of the case which I have titled 'The Last Pre-Raphaelite'. He had sat in these rooms many times with his parents, the picture of quiet, well-bred English youth. No less likely murderer could be imagined. And yet...and yet...

'I see your thoughts have taken the same turn as my own', said Holmes. 'I have had the court-martial put off for forty-eight hours through the intermediacy of Mycroft. It is the best we can do. During that time we must see him, and uncover any evidence that will save him from the firing-squad three mornings from now, if the bayings for his blood emanating from the War Office are any indication of the mood there. Once the military put him on trial, nothing can save him. And a military trial it will be, since he is currently in uniform'.

'I will arrange leave from the hospital'.

'I have already done so in your name. Anna and Roger were here earlier with Mycroft. They were absolutely distraught, and unable to tell me anything which might save their son. My brother is useless outside the committee-rooms of Whitehall. We are now his only hope. It seems that everybody else in England wants young Geoffrey dead'.

I was forcibly reminded of this reality as our carriage drew up at Paddington Station, to be met by news vendors screaming with the peculiar hysteria of wartime England. 'Minister Demands Action on Murderer – Calls Legal Proceedings "Unnecessary"'. 'That man has a great career ahead as saviour of his country', muttered Holmes. 'If it ever comes to that, heaven help us all'.

I had passed the drive reviewing what I knew of young Clavinger, as my companion was wholly silent, wrapped as tightly in gloom as he was in his ulster and deerstalker cap. I recalled the spirited child who had run up our stairs, preceding his parents, garbed as a pirate with eye-patch and cutlass, or as a prince of the desert in flowing robes and kaffiyeh, and daring Holmes to identify him. As he grew from childhood to manhood, his departures from conventional society grew less colourful – though, to my mind, scarcely less fanciful – as he came to believe with his parents in the remaking of human nature, and with them attended every first night of Mr. Bernard Shaw.

Then, at university, his ideals took a new direction – or perhaps it was simply a return to the old – as he was thrown in with the gilded youth who had grown restless amid their Edwardian and Georgian comforts and spoke of redeeming the spirit of England, if necessary by fighting gloriously in her cause. It was a mood he would have grown out of quickly enough; but when the Great War erupted, he had enlisted with his friends in a moment of exaltation, and been rapidly drawn into its vortex.

When he came back on leave the following year, I scarcely recognised him. He sat with his parents in our living-room, but now looked older than they: as in a sense he was, having lived through horrors beyond their imagination. The boyish look was gone; in its place was a man sharp-featured and hollow-eyed, who spoke in a low monotone.

'In the beginning it was a lark, Mr. Holmes, like wearing uniform around the quad – that sort of parade-ground, fancy-dress atmosphere'. A wry gleam of irony lit up his eye as if he recalled his childhood frolics, then vanished as disillusion returned. 'We took leave of our friends in a frightfully superior tone – they still, as we felt, in the trammels of adolescence, where we had broken free and asserted our manhood. We were heroes off to combat – players of the ancient game of chivalry – knights preparing for the joust.

'In the event, we were thrust into mud-coloured uniforms, to protect us from snipers, and into mud-filled trenches, to protect us from machine-guns. And we were left to rot there, week after week, except for forays out across no-man's land intended to give us a sense of accomplishment, but which accomplished nothing but senseless butchery before we were driven back to our trenches, or at most gained a few meaningless yards.

'We wait upon mass-slaughter by machine. There is very little resembling personal combat, and nothing at all resembling chivalry. Artillery pounds our half-subterranean homes, machine-gun fire rakes them, we cower against the threat of annihilation. Meantime' – and here his voice took on bitter irony – 'the newspapers speak of the Great Push, the sudden, brilliant move that is to turn the war around. For us, this means that thou- sands of coffins are brought up in lorries and unloaded behind us. We know for whom they are intended, and try not to advert to them, try not to breathe in the aroma of fresh pine when the wind is from that quarter. Then the night arrives on which the order comes through for the Great Push – but the enemy's spotters have seen what we have from their balloons, and, in the event that they have not done so, a huge barrage meant to soften them up advertises the location of this Great Push, and gives them ample time to bring up reinforcements. So the Great Push is halted, we are driven back on our lines at enormous cost, and the coffins used – when they *can* be used'.

He paused with a look of peculiar horror in his eyes, as if he were gazing into a vast distance, and had become lost in it. I tried to bring him back. 'What do mean, when they *can* be used?', I asked.

'I mean, Dr. Watson, that such is the power of modern weaponry that it makes people simply disappear. Individuals we have known through school and university – in an instant they cease to exist. There is nothing left to bury – nothing to prove that they are dead. We hope against hope that we are mistaken – that they have been taken in battle, until the vain search, month after month, of the lists of prisoners-of-war forces us to face the unspeakable truth. What does it mean, when a friend is obliterated in this fashion? A chap whose family you have met, with whom you have shared golden afternoons, who can be reduced to helpless laughter by a classical quotation in the tone of a pompous don – what does it mean when an acquaintanceship which has ripened through the years is wiped in an instant from the face of the earth? How can you write to his family – a sister, perhaps, whom you have remembered through long nights in the trenches – and honestly say he has died gallantly? He has simply been expunged. This is not even death as we knew it.

'And, if we no longer die, no more do we live. Behind the lines are brothels, which we are bidden to use with as little thought as we take rations. Women are brought up to these establishments in a stream as steady as the coffins. It is as if a mechanical society seeks to give us the illusion of having lived before we die. Those of us who would never have patronised such a place, or perhaps only done so in some undergraduate initiation, now do so as a matter of course. We do it to drug ourselves, to purge away any decent feelings we may yet retain, so that life itself becomes meaningless, and we are anaesthetised for a meaningless death. I sometimes wonder if we can ever again recover the feelings by which we used to live. I fear not; and that is what I fear most'.

I was astounded by this revelation. 'My God, man, you are living like an animal'.

'Not even that, Dr. Watson. An animal mates or kills by instinct, out of need; we do so automatically. We have come to resemble the machines that pound us to pieces. We no more hate than we love. We have acquired a contempt for the society that uses us so – for the dealers in munitions whose profits accrue from pulverised bodies, for the ghastly mania of politicians who routinely send hundreds of thousands of young men to their doom, and for the institutional religion which is simply another face of this organised destruction. We listen with mockery, on a Sunday when there is an intermission in the battering, to the parson, who is the colonel's brother, tell us God is on our side. There is only one side, and that is the side of humanity. We in the trenches are convinced that those we call our enemy are at one with us in this. We are certain that a negotiated settlement – a return to the *status quo ante*, without vindictiveness or punishment – will be acceptable to the men of both armies. We *must* desist before what is left of this civilisation destroys itself. I do not know if we shall ever be able to return to what we once thought of as normality. But we have no alternative but to try: this *has to* be halted'.

'And how do you propose to do that?' Holmes spoke for the first time. 'Against you is arrayed all the prejudice of the civilian population, played upon by politicians for their own ends. You have forgotten that this war has brought people to authority who could never have attained it in time of peace. These can keep their position only by rabble-rousing; behind them are the military command, bewildered as you are by what is happening in the field, and desperate lest this be discovered. Even you would be appalled at the incompetence I hear of from Mycroft. He keeps his position only by pretending to share their aims. They babble of victory; but there will be no winning, only losing – by the side which first succumbs to exhaustion. Anyone who speaks the truth is a traitor. The voice of sanity cannot, will not, be heard'.

'It will', muttered the young-old man who sat before us. 'Something will be done to bring it to their attention'. And he walked out of our rooms like an automaton.

All this came back to me as we settled into a first-class carriage and sped towards the market-town in Devon closest to where the murder had taken place. The diatribe in our rooms had supplied motivation in plenty; but that at least, I thought, was Holmes' secret and mine. That this was an illusion was quickly proved when Holmes tossed over the latest newspapers on the case.   Clavinger, they stated, was a known agitator against the war: clearly, he had spoken to his brother-officers in the same terms as he had spoken to us. Armed, he had entered the grounds where General Sir Hector Bruton, who had just been appointed to supreme command of the army in France, had lived.   He did not deny this, though he claimed that he had wished merely to remonstrate with the general.   What was not in dispute was that Sir Hector had been shot dead, and tests were being conducted to establish whether the murder had been carried out with Captain Clavinger's rifle.   I groaned when I came to this part: we already knew the answer.

'Well, Watson?', asked a grim-faced Holmes.

'The case seems very dark against him', I said, 'particularly in view of what he said when parting from us a few weeks ago.   "Something will be done to bring it to their attention".   It looks as if this is it – that by this desperate act of folly, the poor young man wished to register his objection to the war'.

'And yet he denies it', said Holmes.

'What does denial mean in such cases?   Remorse, probably: sudden realisation of the consequences of his crime. An awakening, too late, from the alienation in which he has lived'.

'There I disagree with you.   Such an awakening, as you call it, would have led in this case to confession.   Clavinger is the most truthful young man I know.   No, this is the one ray of hope I permit myself'.

But when we got inside the cell, after unfriendly scrutiny of our papers at one prison checkpoint after another, Holmes behaved like a man possessed.

'Why did you do it?', he screamed, his ascetic figure and waving arms making him resemble some gigantic bird of prey.

'But...I didn't do it', quavered a horrified Clavinger.

'*Then who did?*', demanded a demonic Holmes.

'I...I don't know', stammered Clavinger. 'I went into the grounds in the hope of remonstrating with General Bruton. I lost my way, lay down to get over a dizzy spell, came out again and was arrested for murder'.

'Quite rightly too!', snarled Holmes. 'Your rifle was the one that fired the fatal bullet. It was a known fact – scores of witnesses will testify to it – that you harboured a grievance against the higher ranks of the army – a grievance you took out in this horrible and senseless crime. All the evidence convicts you, and all you can say to counter it is that you could not have done it because you were *taking a nap*. What have you to say for yourself before sentence of death is passed upon you – a sentence you so richly deserve?'

For answer, the pale young man stared blankly into space. 'I have known I was doomed from the start of this nightmarish business', he murmured. 'Perhaps it is better so – to die quickly and cleanly instead of waiting in suspense for some ghastly fate in the trenches'.

With these words he slumped back on the pallet which was the only furnishing of his cell. All at once, Holmes was kneeling by his side, an arm around his shoulder, his flask unstoppered. 'Here, take a sip of this', he said. 'You had to realise how desperate is our situation, how impossibly weak your defence – a military prosecutor could tear it apart in seconds. Now, I want you to tell me everything that happened, omitting nothing, however seemingly irrelevant'.

'There is nothing to tell, Mr. Holmes. I entered the grounds, as I say, in the hope of speaking to General Bruton about the course of the war. He has – that is to say, had – a reputation for decency far above that of the other generals; and, in my desperate state, I felt that if there was anyone in the high command who would listen to me, it was him. I had had a couple of weeks' leave with my parents further down the coast, had rejoined my unit, as we passed in front of the estate recalled that this was where he lived, made an excuse about having a message to deliver, and had myself dropped off. The unit was due to halt in the village; and I was confident I could appeal to Sir Hector – give him the men's point of view, leave him to mull it over, and rejoin them. Instead of which...'

'Go on', said Holmes, tersely.

'The road runs close to a rocky coast, rising into cliffs, which at this point jut out into the sea. There is only one approach to the house. As soon as I got there, I found that this avenue was heavily guarded by sentries, who would be bound to ask for my credentials. So I retraced my steps alongside the estate wall until I reached a stile, which was unguarded. This surprised me, until I climbed over and discovered why...'

'The maze', muttered Holmes, who had been perusing the county guide on the train.

'Exactly', nodded the captain. 'It is composed of high hornbeam hedges, well-grown and sturdy. A couple of minutes' wandering in it convinced me that it was impassible. One of its windings led to the edge of the cliff, along which there ran a narrow ledge. I attempted to make my way along this; but after turning a curve saw that it gave out within a couple of yards. As I attempted to retrace my path, I made the mistake of glancing down. The roar of the surf put me in mind of the guns in France, and I felt dizzy and weak. Somehow or other I dragged myself back, and lay down for a moment. I believe I passed out. When I came to, I blundered my way back to the stile, where my rifle was where I had left it – I thought I had better approach unarmed, in case I was shot by mistake. I was heading back to the village – I noticed, by the way, that the sentries had vanished and that there seemed to be some sort of commotion up the drive – I was heading back to rejoin my unit when I was overtaken and arrested for murder'.

'Is there anything else you can tell us – anything at all?', pursued Homes urgently. 'The fainting-fit, for instance – have you any idea how long you were out?'

'Not the slightest', confessed the young officer. He paused, then continued with some hesitation. 'The one thing I did notice has nothing to do with the crime, and I am afraid you may think it rather silly. Directly opposite the stile was a stone cottage set back from the road behind a large herbaceous border, in full bloom and beautifully tended. It occurred to me that this was the England we were supposed to be defending, and I thought in a flash of bitterness how far that was from the truth. At the same time, I felt a kind of pang: it did represent something we once knew, and are in danger of losing forever'.

To my surprise, Holmes did not interrupt these sentimental ramblings. His tone had become distant. 'Well tended, you say?'

'Exquisitely, Mr. Holmes. The thought occurred to me how content I could be, after all that has happened, to retire to such a place if I survived the war...'

'Hm', said Holmes. 'I do not wish to give you false hope – your situation is still extremely serious. Nothing may come of it; but I see the smallest pin-point of light. I believe it is possible – just possible – that a solution may be found. I will go now, to follow up this clue you have given us. Take heart, and try to remember anything else that may be of use'.

A firm handclasp, and Holmes and I were in the car which Mycroft had had put at our disposal, speeding in the direction of the dead general's home, which was but a few miles distant. There was little of the sun's light left as we pulled up by the roadside which young Clavinger had described. As he had told us, the estate lay on an outcrop of rocky cliff, with a boundary wall pierced by a single stile. In seconds Holmes was on his knees before this with his magnifying lens.

'It is true', he muttered, as if to himself. 'The rifle stood against this wall. The rains of the night before have taken the imprint perfectly, and, thank goodness, it has not been obliterated since'.

But once he had climbed over the stile, he emitted a snarl of rage. 'A stampede', he hissed. 'It has obliterated any traces that might have helped us. And with regulation army boots too. Halloa, what's this?' Like a ferret, Holmes followed one set of tracks that wove uncertainly into the maze, then turned to the right, and led to the verge of the cliff. He followed this for some distance along the sheer ledge high above the surf on the beach far below, while I stood back, as much put off by the height as by the fresh gusts of breeze that threatened to dislodge anyone foolish enough to venture along that unguarded precipice. Holmes came back, following the tracks with narrowed eyes, then emitted a low cry of triumph as he ran about, like a bloodhound following its trail, on hands and knees. When he had finished, he looked up and cried: 'Absolutely true, Watson, in every detail. Clavinger walked along the ledge, hoping to get to the house by that route; then, finding it impossible, made his way back here and collapsed in a dead faint. The traces show that he fell on the grass with considerable force. A medical examination will no doubt reveal bruises compatible with these marks'.

But when Holmes arrived at the manor, he was faced with a barrier of disbelief and scorn. The guard at the head of the driveway raised his eyebrows when he saw the name on the pass provided by Mycroft, then waved us through with a shrug. I was stunned by the sheer drama of the setting. The house, an irregular Jacobean building of red sandstone, which glowed dully in the late evening light, stood on the very edge of the cliff. In front lay formal gardens, their yew hedges clipped into geometrical shapes; and in the centre of these rose a low mound topped by a banqueting-house. Between them and the road lay the gigantic maze. Holmes had read out a brief account of its antecedents on the train.

'Excavation has revealed that the house was built on the site of an ancient fort, outside of which were some traces of a labyrinthine defence-work, known as a Troytown. When it was chosen for a dwelling in the Jacobean period, these were converted into a horticultural labyrinth and the name taken over for the manor. The original Bruton, created baronet by James I, derived his family name from the Brutus who, according to the medieval chroniclers, made his way from Troy and landed on these shores to become, as an equally reliable etymology has it, ancestor of the British'.

I smiled at these quaint conceits. The Briton of today, ruling an empire which spans the globe, no longer need claim descent from ancient Troy.

'Ah, but that is just where you are wrong, friend Watson', said Holmes, answering, as usual, the thought I had unwittingly expressed rather than any words I had put it in. 'We regard these people as childish; in fact they were anything but. We have historicised architecture, and no longer plaster classical orders on a medieval building; we have reconstructed the sounds of the classical languages, and no longer pronounce them as English – but that is where we have lost something vital. We no longer think of the present as continuous with the past, as our ancestors did. We have been deceived into thinking ourselves superior by the doctrine of evolution and our own technical progress; and where has it got us? Into that mess of mechanistic slaughter young Clavinger decried. We forget that in all vital respects we are still the same: the same blunderers, with the same lusts and the same ambitions.

'The man who named his house Troytown, who brought ancient Europe and ancient Asia into a single system, made no such mistake, nor did his descendants. Generation after generation there has been a head of the family – a Sir Hector, a Sir Paris or a Sir Aeneas – through whom they were linked in imagination to the matter of Troy. For the past three centuries, they have served their country in obscurity, until the emergence of this latest Sir Hector, a career officer whose reputation with his men was generally thought to be behind his recent promotion to the highest command in France. It was considered by many an attempt to marshal opinion behind a dangerously unpopular general staff'.

All this was called back to mind as we came in sight of the Jacobean house, with the sunset glowing on its diamonded windows and deepening the shadows of its classical pilasters; but it was quickly driven away again by the sight of the reception committee awaiting us at the entrance. I recalled that the sentry at the gatehouse had cranked up a telephone after letting us in.

In front of the building stood a formidable array of uniformed staff officers, some of whose faces I recognised from the newspapers. Holmes descended to a chilly reception, in which hands remained firmly clasped behind backs. Their leader, a tall, thin general with greying fair hair, I knew as the one who had already been designated Bruton's successor, who was popular among politicians as one who would get their job done at any price, and unpopular among his men for precisely the same reason. He said in a gravelly voice: 'Be good enough to follow us, Mr. Holmes'.

We were marched, for that was my impression, surrounded by officers who had fallen in to front and rear of us, silently, to what seemed to have been the dining-room, and was now festooned with maps. General (soon to be Field-Marshal) Ackerman seated himself opposite, and the others sat around us, I felt, like a ring of steel, their eyes glaring hostility at us like so many bayonets.

'Mr. Holmes', stated General Ackerman, in a voice as of remote thunder, 'we have received a Cabinet order to co-operate with you in every way, and, being men trained to follow orders, we obey them. I do not know what influence you exercised to have this command laid upon us, but I do not mind telling you that there is not a man around this table who does not think your presence here a waste of time. An irresponsible waste of time, I might add: because every day we spend in this investigation, men are being lost in their thousands across the Channel'. He gestured through the window at the darkening sea.

'Hear, hear', cried a swarthy officer seated at Ackerman's right, whom I recognised as General Lowther, and who gazed at us with the fascinated hatred of an venomous snake. Ackerman paused to allow us to assimilate this salvo, then continued: 'Yesterday evening, General Bruton was enjoying an after-dinner cigar alone in the banqueting-house which overlooks the entrance to the labyrinth. As he did so, he was approached, from the only direction left unguarded – that is, the labyrinth itself – by a known malcontent, who is also known to have been armed. This man's rifle has been confirmed as the murder weapon *by your own report*, which has been communicated to me by telegraph'. He waved the paper in our faces. 'Now what, I ask you, is the point of wasting the time of the busiest men in this land, at a time when its very existence is imperilled' – here he received vigorous nods from all around the table – 'in seeking to save this man from the consequences of his crime?'

'Simply this', said Holmes imperturbably, 'that he did not commit it'.

Around the table jaws dropped in disbelief. But Ackerman was master of the situation. 'And what revelation, may I ask', he demanded with withering sarcasm, 'can justify this contravention of the physical facts?'

'His footprints', replied Holmes. 'They bear out Clavinger's contention that he never came through the maze'.

'His *footprints!*', repeated Ackerman, with the ominous disbelief of a sadistic schoolmaster. 'His *footprints!* Do you seriously believe that any military court, in the face of the evidence I have cited – and I may as well tell you, that, given the seriousness of the offence, it will be chosen from among the officers in this room – do you imagine that any military tribunal, presented with these infantile excuses, will hesitate to convict?' I could tell from the scornful bellow of harsh laughter that greeted this sally that his supposition was too well founded.

Holmes, however, was unperturbed. 'Who discovered the body?', he demanded abruptly. There was a moment's hesitation, then the swarthy Lowther spoke up from Ackerman's side. 'I did', he replied.

'Under what circumstances?', pursued Holmes.

'I was about to join Sir Hector', said Lowther, 'and was making my way up the winding path to the banqueting-house when I heard a shot. Naturally, my first thought was for General Bruton; but I found him beyond help. He had been killed instantly by a shot through the heart – giving every evidence, I may as well say, of having been aimed professionally'.

Holmes appeared to ignore the implications of the last remark. 'Did you see or hear anything untoward at this time?'

'Only a faint sound as of running steps from the labyrinth, as if someone were attempting flight in that direction'.

'How can you account for Captain Clavinger's making his way through the maze and back, considering that he was totally unfamiliar with it?'

'I expect he had studied it in some book'. The general's face was perspiring, but tight-lipped with the scorn of one who had had not much traffic with books, or much time for those who had.

'There is no such book'. Holmes opened the county guide he had read to me in the train. 'This states that the plan of the maze has never been committed to paper – that it is known only to the lord of the manor and his gardener, because of a prediction that when the maze failed to shield its master, the family line would come to an end. How can you account for this?'

'It is not for me to account for what happened; it is for Clavinger, who is on trial. But since you ask, it may have been beginner's luck. As every fighting man will tell you, stranger things have happened'. There were vigorous nods around the table. 'And, as you see', he went on, 'the prediction has come to pass. Sir Hector had no heirs'.

An uncomfortable silence followed. Holmes said: 'I must speak to Lady Bruton. Can this be arranged?'

General Ackerman answered: 'I will see that she is summoned to the study next door. But I must ask you to be brief. She is in a state of great shock'.

At this, and with a scraping of chairs, the meeting broke up. Holmes' interview with the widow was short and fruitless. She was a tall, imposing figure with an aquiline countenance and raven hair. She was dressed in black, but dry-eyed and composed. She had been in the house when the shot was heard. Yes, there were witnesses: she had been assigning the work of the following day between the house servants and the military personnel that the large influx of guests had brought in its train.

No, she did not know of anyone who might have wished her husband dead. I thought her eyes hardened as she answered; and she continued: 'I may as well tell you, Mr. Holmes, before you hear it from others, that ours had been a marriage in form only for some years past. I am sorry that

Hector is dead, but I will not pretend to inconsolable grief. May I go?'

'After one more question, Lady Bruton. Where is the gardener?'

I thought a saw a look of fear flicker across her face. But if so, it vanished in an instant. 'He is on military service. For the duration, we are making do with his retired father'.

'Who lives in the cottage opposite the stile, I take it?'

Again I noticed that look, as if of incipient fear. 'Exactly, Mr. Holmes. You are very observant'.

'Thank you, Lady Bruton. When I see a garden so splendidly tended, I take it that the owner is professional'.

'If that is all, Mr. Holmes, I will have you and Dr. Watson shown to your rooms. They are not exactly luxurious, but they are all we have to spare'.

We were shown into spartan apartments on the servants' floor, where I fell asleep immediately, worn out by the events of the day and my hospital rounds of the night before. It was early next morning when I was woken by Holmes. 'Come, Watson, we have only one full day, and must waste no time. I procured this bread and cheese from the kitchen; there is a decanter of water on the dressing-table. You can eat while you dress, and then we must be off to the gardener's'.

As we made our way along the path to the cottage, I marvelled at the abundance which careful cultivation had brought into being in such a small space, so that it was a palette of pinks and reds and blues; while at the back of the house, which a passageway through the building displayed clearly, could be seen currant bushes neatly arrayed and ripening into fruit. Holmes' peremptory knock brought an old man to the doorway, commanding of feature though leaning on a stick. From Holmes' rapid glance at this instrument, I could see that he had already dismissed its owner as an actor in the tragedy of the maze. 'South Africa?', he asked in a rapid calculation which involved the injury that required the stick, the age of its owner, and the roll-call of imperial war. 'Bloemfontein', growled the veteran; then added in a graceless tone, 'who is it wants to know?' On hearing Holmes' name he was unimpressed: he had already had visits from some of the generals across the way, who were, his tone implied, personages of far greater consequence than any civilian from London.

'I have some questions to ask', said Holmes, 'which I think it would be more comfortable for you to answer sitting down'. A graceless gesture of invitation followed, whereupon we were introduced to an old woman as 'the missis' – grey, severe, and unsmil- ing like her husband, but with an air of nervousness that I put down to her lack of experience with guests outside her class. She resumed her knitting, on which she had been concentrated, by a window with a view of the road.

'This is where you normally spend your days?', asked Holmes.

'Don't see as 'ow we could spend them anywhere else', said the man, who answered to the name of Simms.

'Then you will have had an uninterrupted view of the stile opposite two days ago?'

'Could've done. What if I did?'

'A young soldier placed his rifle beside it before entering the grounds, and picked it up again upon leaving. Did you see anybody else touch the weapon in the meantime?'

'Can't rightly say as 'ow I did', said the veteran, with an imperturbable stolidity that barely masked a quiet enjoyment of putting the London toffs in their place. His wife, however, dropped a stitch in her knitting and had to unravel it, her face bent over the work darkly.

'For God's sake, man!', exclaimed Holmes. 'You sit here all day, looking out at the road, and if by any chance you are absent for a moment, your wife sees all that passes. A strange soldier leaves a rifle at the stile, goes inside for a time, comes out again and picks it up, and you tell me nobody noticed! I tell you that someone took up the rifle, carried it into the grounds, used it to commit a murder and left it back again; and throughout all this, you tell me, you saw nothing! This is no time for playing games – a young man's life is in the balance!'

'If thee saw so much', said the old man with implacable hostility, 'then thee saw the pixie what made away with the rifle. But there's gentlemen up at the 'all what tells me your clever young swell's a traitor and a murderer – and it's them I believe, seeing as 'ow they're men who've served their country, as I've done myself in my time, and proper proud I am of it too'.

I could sense Holmes' exasperation as the only avenue that offered hope of saving Clavinger's life was relentlessly barred. 'You speak of serving your country', he hissed; 'Is this a lie like all the rest?'

The old man raised himself from the table with a fearful glint in his eye, and would, I am sure, have struck Holmes with his stick; but at that moment a piercing wail came from the back room – the cry of an infant, whom the angry exchange had woken – while the voice of a young woman called for help. 'I am a doctor', said I, and went to her assistance, only vaguely conscious that the old man with the raised stick had attempted to block my way. On a bed in the room behind I saw a blonde and voluptuous young woman who was, I thought, under normal circumstances the beauty of her village. But she was now, with an expression of distaste, holding at arm's length an infant who was roaring lustily. As she thrust it into my arms, my sense of smell informed me of another reason it needed urgent attention.

'Tell them they'll have to warm the milk again', she remarked in a peremptory tone. 'Mine is not flowing'. From the colour chosen for the infant's swaddling, I guessed it to be a boy.

'What an adorable little lad!', I cooed, in my best bedside manner, which I have known to work wonders on innumerable young mothers, bewildered and exhausted by their new charges. 'Coo, coo, coo – there!', and I held out a finger for the infant to grasp, which it did, with some abatement of noise. Pleased with myself, I proceeded to another line that I have never found to fail. 'I am sure', I said dotingly, 'he is the image of his father'.

The result was consternation! The young mother shrieked aloud, and burst into tears. The infant, terrified, joined in with a roar even lustier than before. I looked from the young mother's drawn face and tear-streaked cheeks to the older man, now crouched in an attitude of menace in the doorway. His face was a dark mask of hate. 'Thee'd best be off', he spat ferociously. 'The poor lad has no father'.

Now I saw it all! The absence of a younger male, the young woman cared for by the older couple: clearly, she had lost her husband in the terrible battles then raging in France – and I had unwittingly stirred the still-warm embers of her grief! Deeply mortified, I bowed my way backwards out of the room, leaving bedlam behind.

'You have certainly done it this time, Watson', said Holmes, as we retreated down the path, with a glimmer of what I thought was malicious humour. 'Bedside manner, indeed!'

'I...I..', I stammered. 'How was I to have known?'

'How indeed?', asked Holmes, in the same sardonic tone as before. 'How but by consulting your intelligence before allowing your emotions to carry you away?'

Rebuked and abashed, I slunk after him to the house. I was not surprised when he told me he had some enquiries to make in the village, that he thought he could make them more effectively without my assistance, and suggested that I take a picnic lunch to the nearby beach – 'you need the rest' – and sunbathe there until four o'clock, when he would meet me at the manor again.

From the library I borrowed a copy of the *Iliad*, and took it with me down the winding path, overhung with pines, to the cove, where, turning my back on the fateful house above, I gazed over the summer sea and tried to puzzle out again the verse I had construed in the schoolroom many years before. To my surprise, it had turned into a different poem. Far from the glorious tapestry of gods, demigods and kings held up to us by our schoolmaster, I found a pointless squabble between one general and another. Even in the passages I had learnt to admire most – as Helen on the walls of Troy, scanning the enemy lines for a glimpse of her brothers, now, unknown to her, dead – I found a dreariness and a waste that I had not adverted to before. Depressed, I closed the book and soon fell asleep under the shadow of a rock. I dreamt that Homer's eye-painted prows had pulled in on the strand, their occupants spilling ashore to barked commands very different from the stately diction of the classics. Then the strange warriors were marching straight in my direction: their horsehair helmets had changed into *pickelhauben*, and the harsh tongue they uttered was German. They had made a landing on this very beach! I was helpless to move; before I could warn them the enemy would have wiped out our general staff and won the war at a single blow!

The helmeted figure bending over me turned into Holmes in his deerstalker, as I awoke with a start. In his hand was his watch, open to show that the hour of four had passed, and on his face a look of the utmost urgency. 'Come, Watson, we have work to do, and hopefully shall have taken our citadel by nightfall by means of the same guile as is described in that excellent tome beside you. Pick it up and come!'

As we climbed the path to the clifftop, Holmes told me of his investigations. He had visited the village pub in the guise of a tourist from the city, and it was not long before his liberality with drinks, and apparently innocuous questions about the effects of the war on the village, brought results.

'You recall how we were told that the gardener's son had been drafted for service? This is true only in the most literal sense. General Bruton took him on as batman, in which capacity he was enabled to remain with his parents. In the village, which has already suffered a number of losses, there was considerable resentment of the fact that, while their sons were sent to fight and die in France, this young man was allowed to live at home and serve in the hall – where, if I am not mistaken, we shall find him now'.

He went on to say that he had followed his session in the hostelry with visits to the local clergyman and the midwife; but before he could go any further, we had arrived at the manor. To the duty officer in the hallway, Holmes presented the Cabinet order, secured by Mycroft, which gave him the right to exact co-operation from all military personnel, and demanded the presence of Corporal Alfred Simms. The officer looked at his companion, shrugged, and sent him to fetch Corporal Simms from the garden. He came in, brushing from his hands the soil which proclaimed his occupation, then followed a stern-faced Holmes to the study. Holmes locked the door and ordered me to stand against it with my revolver drawn. The soldier, whose features proclaimed his relationship to the young woman in the cottage, paled visibly as my friend spoke.

'You have once chance only. There will not be another, and there will be no bargaining. If you attempt to lie to me, I shall know instantly. You see the names on this permit: I will go to their bearers immediately, over the heads of your military superiors, should you attempt to deceive me. None of them will save you: this is a country, thank goodness, which still observes the rule of law'.

Holmes spoke clearly and unhurriedly, allowing each sentence to sink in. 'Two days ago, as you sat in the parlour of your parents' house, you saw a young man in uniform leave a rifle at the stile opposite. You took the rifle, and being the only man alive who can do so, your father being incapacitated, swiftly crossed the labyrinth. On the other side you saw General Bruton smoking a cigar. You fired the rifle once, shooting him through the heart' – here the young man made an inarticulate noise, which Holmes silenced with a gesture – 'and carried the rifle back through the labyrinth, replacing it at the stile. You did this because you saw an opportunity to avenge the honour of your family: Sir Hector was the father of your sister's child. You therefore had motive, capacity and opportunity. You, and you alone, can be proved to have murdered your superior officer, Sir Hector Bruton: a crime which carries the penalty of death by firing-squad. From what I have seen of the high command, it would not surprise me if they decided to carry it out tomorrow morning'.

Judging by the beads of perspiration on the young man's brow, it was evident that Holmes had estimated the generals correctly.

'You are right, sir, about the first and the last: I brought the rifle in and I took it out again. But not about the middle. I never killed Sir 'Ector'.

'Why should I believe you? Give me one reason not to call the officer at the door outside, and put you in charge for premeditated murder'.

'I will give you one, sir, and a good one too. Sir 'Ector was ready to marry my sister, and make her Lady Bruton. All of us was fair off our 'eads, sir, that our 'Elen was going to be a lady, and one o' they gentry'.

The news astounded me; but I could tell from Holmes' calmness of demeanour that it was not unexpected to him. He persisted without any change of pace. 'Have you got any evidence of this so-called betrothal?'

'No, sir, can't say as 'ow we 'ave'.

'Let me put it to you this way, then. Do you seriously expect that, having admitted to taking the rifle and replacing it, any military tribunal will find you innocent of the killing as well? You may have been given assurances in private, but you will see very quickly that these will not be honoured in public. Courts-martial tend to believe senior officers; there is no appeal; and sentences are carried out within twenty-four hours. You have less than that time to live unless you talk, and talk quickly'.

Relieved to be given the opportunity to tell his side of the tale, the young corporal fairly gabbled out what had happened on the fateful evening. He had taken the rifle through the labyrinth to the house, outside which, in the dark, he had seen General Lowther in what he fancied was intimate proximity to Lady Bruton. General Lowther, indignant at being interrupted, had demanded to know what he was about. On hearing his story, he had slowly disengaged himself and asked for the rifle, promising to take care of it himself.

Simms was at the entrance to the labyrinth when he heard the shot, and turned to find Lowther, panting, behind him. 'There has been an awful tragedy', he gasped. He had told Sir Hector, he said, of the relationship between himself and Lady Bruton, whereupon the baronet had snatched the rifle and shot himself through the heart. Simms was bidden to leave the rifle back where he had found it, and say nothing to anyone, 'or you will find yourself in the front lines in France – and you know where that leads, my lad. Remember that in the army, credibility is graded by rank, and say nothing of what you have heard and seen – or think you have heard and seen – to anyone'.

'Nor 'ave I sir, though I was griefstruck by Sir 'Ector's death – our family 'as served 'is for generations. You've got to believe me, sir'.

'I do', said Holmes. 'but there is one more question I must ask you. Tell me what you know of the relations between your sister and Sir Hector'.

'We'd all been sorry for Sir 'Ector, 'e having no child and no-one to leave the estate to, Troytown being a special place and all that. Well, when 'Elen went into service at the 'all, and found herself hexpectin', 'e was for marryin' 'er and carryin' on the line – divorcin' 'er ladyship'.

'I don't suppose Lady Bruton took this very well'.

'No sir, there was rare 'igh words between 'em. But Sir 'Ector, nothin' would please 'im but to 'ave the whole thing settled before 'e left for France'.

'There was not much time for that'.

'No, sir, the lawyers was to have come from Lunnon yesterday. But you see, sir, there was no need of 'em'.

'So Lady Bruton retains the title and the property. Ample motive, I should think, for murder'.

Which is precisely the point Holmes proceeded to make to her ladyship, who was next to be interrogated in the study. She denied nothing of what the corporal had said, save that she was accessory to the murder.

'But you will be tried as such, you realise that. Your only hope is that you tell me everything now'.

'There is nothing to tell', said the widow wearily. 'Nigel was an old friend: a contemporary of Hector's at Sandhurst. We had been…close…for some time. I told you that my marriage had broken down. When my world seemed crumbling, he was a tower of strength to me. But I did not imagine that he would stoop to murder for my sake'.

'Or for the sake of the property', said Holmes quietly.

The widow shook her head wearily. 'None of this matters any more. He will have to stand his trial, I suppose. Yes, I knew in some part of me that he had killed Hector. But so did a lot of others'.

'Others?', asked Holmes.

'Oh yes', she replied with returning animation. 'Hector was steeped in the family tradition of service, and he was possessed of an old-fashioned sense of responsibility for his men. He wished to save lives by playing a holding game: everyone knows that America will sooner or later enter the war. But his brother-officers believed that the public needed victories, whatever the cost. There were furious altercations every night. It was after one of these that Hector retired to the mount, and Nigel...did what he did.

'I knew from the silence that followed the killing that many at the higher levels suspected what had happened, but said nothing. It suited them, you see. And I suppose it suited me'.

Holmes went in search of General Ackerman to arrange for the arrest of Lowther. But that was not to be. Since she made an excuse that no gentleman could question, I allowed Lady Bruton to leave the study: from whence, as it transpired, she went straight to Lowther's office. Suddenly a shot rang through the house, and we entered to find his head slumped over the desk, a widening pool of blood slowly covering the map of France. So paralysed were we by the sight that the first intimation I had of Lady Bruton's escape was Holmes' hissed: 'After her, Watson!' I, being closer than he to the door of that crowded chamber, quickly pushed my way to the corridor, to see her poised in the window-seat at the end, from which there was a sheer drop to the sea. 'Lady Bruton!', I called beseechingly, but my cry seems to have been the final factor that impelled her into a decision and out over the edge. Her body was recovered by boat later that evening.

The general staff was quietly triumphant. Their policy could now go forward without question. They saw that the murder was reported as a crime of passion in the newspapers, and the case officially closed. Holmes was resigned to the outcome. 'An investigation of our armed forces is politically impossible at this time, Watson: Mycroft has told me as much. He is also willing to take on young Clavinger as assistant, to do what good he can in these evil times. We have at least saved his life, which is what we set out to do. That is the best we could have hoped for'.

'It is best for young Helen, too', I rejoined warmly. 'Her son will inherit Troytown, and the line of the Brutons continue'.

'I fear not, Watson', said Holmes. 'I told you I had checked with three sources: the public-house, the clergyman and the midwife. The clergyman showed me that the space for the father in the baptismal certificate had been left blank; he seemed to imagine that it was out of discretion that it was not filled in with the name of Sir Hector. But the midwife informed me otherwise. Young Helen had at first given her to understand that the father was some local lad who had been shipped off to France. But the discovery of her employer's interest in her gave her the idea of palming off the child as his, with some twaddle about its being premature. Sir Hector, clearly, was in no mood to question the joyous discovery that his family line would go on, and with it the tradition which meant so much to him. By the way, I must thank you for setting me on the right track'.

'I?', I said, bewildered.

'By showing me that Helen Simms had no natural feeling. If a mother cares for the father of her child, she will cherish it, as I imagine you can confirm from your own experience. Instead, she treated the child as a nuisance, and handed it over to you. Her tears were not for the death of its father, which Sir Hector was not, but for the opportunity to become a great lady that had come within her grasp and so suddenly been snatched away. I do not doubt that when she is well enough to do so, she will abandon the child and resume her adventures in some more promising place – London, probably, as the magnet for all the adventurers of the Empire'.

'You mean she will cut her hair short, and embark upon a career?', I asked.

'By no means, Watson. Helen is not a modern woman. I mean that with her looks and guile, she will find some man to attach herself to, the richer and more influential the better – perhaps a series of them – and raise herself in society by that means. Love is beyond her range'.

So it transpired. Young Clavinger reported afterwards that Helen Simms had decamped in the direction of London, leaving her parents to bring up her child: which, under the circumstances, was perhaps as well. He informed us that Troytown was derelict, its maze a shapeless ruin.

My last sight of it was on the morning after the double suicide which closed the case. At breakfast Holmes was nowhere to be seen, and after finishing my own I crossed the forecourt where horses were being brought around from the stables and ridden off down the avenue. I climbed the winding way to the top of the mount, where I found Holmes smoking his pipe and gazing out to sea.

'Do you recall, Watson', he asked, without shifting his gaze from the glimmering band of water that separated us from the Continent, 'the scene in which Achilles drags the body of Hector backwards behind his chariot?'

'Vaguely', I admitted, taken aback, as always, by his capacity for apparent irrelevance in the face of the happenings of the night before, which still cast a shadow on my own spirits.

'In Homer, he drags it three times around the tomb of his dead friend, Patroclus, who had been killed by Hector. But in Vergil, Achilles drags the body of Hector three times around *the walls of Troy*; and Vergil tended to follow the older tradition'.

'I do not see what difference it makes: either way, it sounds barbaric'.

'Hardly more so than what is now happening in France. No, dragging the body around the tomb of his friend is something we can understand: it is personal revenge. Dragging it round the city, on the other hand, is something far more primitive, and more horrifying to the spectators on its walls, since it presaged their own deaths'.

'I hardly follow you'.

'We still speak of a maze as a "Troytown". The city was seen as a labyrinth, the windings of a magical defence. Its magic was unwound when its hero was drawn round it backwards'.

'Forgive me, Holmes', I asked, 'but what has Greece to do with our current situation in France?'

'Simply this, Watson: that the fall of Troy was an event permitted by the gods. A city built by the gods, it was abandoned by them when its time had come'.

He gesticulated with the stem of his pipe towards the sound of the horses dying away on the avenue. 'I wonder whether that is not what we now hear. One by one the historic houses of England are being abandoned, as the families who ruled from them for centuries are obliterated. Once upon a time we liked to think that the spirit of Troy had taken refuge on these shores. I cannot but wonder if it is now poised for flight'.

I shook my head, baffled. I could never follow him through these morbid meanderings. He stood, tapped out his pipe and placed it in his pocket. 'I do not know what it all means, Watson, or indeed whether it means anything. There was a poet of the eighteenth century who saw all life as a labyrinth, with the thread of its purpose hidden from us. We know as much of these matters now as we did then'. And quietly, almost to himself, he recited:

The ways of heaven are dark and intricate,
Puzzled in mazes and perplexed with errors:
Our understanding traces them in vain,
Lost and bewildered in the fruitless search;
Nor sees with how much art the windings run,
Nor where the regular confusion ends.

EIGHT
BLOOD AND IRON

Blackened guns lay in tangles of shattered steel along the road, while the masses of poppies that spattered the fields were splotches of blood under a louring sky. Here and there, dead trees stood up like skeletal fingers out of the wasteland. Watson, who has always been sensitive to emotional impressions, turned to me and said: 'You know, Holmes, I am not a vindictive man; but I should dearly love to have in my sights the barbarian who began all of this'.

I said nothing, struggling at the wheel as our two-seater lurched against the ruts and windings of the country road. Nor, having driven all day through the devastated landscape, did I answer after we had turned onto the cobbles of what had once been a courtyard. Three sides of it lay in ghastly ruin, but the fourth, its candlelit window glowing brightly in the gathering dark, still eked out an existence as an inn. Within, odd sets of glass and silver glittered under heavy oaken beams; and, after we had disposed of a simple meal, I swirled the brandy slowly in my glass and replied: 'You really think so, Watson?'

He had evidently been wool-gathering, because when he came to with a start, he had not the faintest idea what I was talking about. What he describes as superior mental powers are frequently only the ability to concentrate on a single train of thought. 'You referred to the Kaiser, I presume, when you said you wished to have him in your sights?' His reply was even more emphatic than before. 'It would give me the utmost satisfaction to shoot the blackguard as one would a pest'.

'Would it now, Watson? And how, pray, do you think your action would alter what has occurred?'

'What I mean to say', he went on, becoming flustered, 'is that if I had had him in my sights before this whole dreadful business began...'

'You imagine', I finished, 'that you would have pulled the trigger. Well, friend Watson, permit me to doubt it. You see, I have been in precisely the situation you name'.

'You mean...'

'Yes, I have stood, pistol in hand, as close to the Kaiser as you are to me now'.

For once Watson was silenced. I put down my glass. 'What I am about to tell you, Watson, is in absolute confidence. If it were to become generally known, it could, even now, create the most frightful unpheavals of public feeling in both countries'. He nodded his assent.

'Let me begin', I said, 'by taking issue with your use of the word "barbarian". It is indeed the Kaiser who is responsible for it, describing his own ruthlessness in such terms; and it has been repeated, with equal ruthlessness, by the propaganda minions of our own government. Not the least of the tragic effects of this war has been the tarnishing, in the eyes of the English people, of a great civilisation'.

'Oh yes, Watson', I continued, holding up my hand. 'There was a time, a far happier time than this, when I believed that it compared very favourably with our own'. From his nettled look, I could see that he was not convinced. And so I told him of how, after Oxford, I had continued my studies in Germany. I had gone there as much to forget Caroline Musgrave as to improve my grasp of the language and so gain access to the vast sci- entific literature which was rolling off the presses there. I said nothing of the former motive to Watson; but I told him of the shock of surprise with which I had stood in the domed cathedral at Aachen, the city of Charlemagne. Here, amid the octagon of arches, the gleaming mosaics, is Byzantium in the north: the Roman idea in Germany; the first manifestation of that vision which was to reshape medieval Europe in the image of ancient Rome: that Carolingian renaissance of which our own Alcuin had been one of the great luminaries, and in which ancient manuscripts were copied in the first wave of what was later to become the tidal flood of the Renaissance.

From here I went south to the university city of Tübingen: that lovely castled town on the curve of a river, where willows overhang the banks by the tower in which Hölderlin, romantic poet of a classical vision, lived and died. Here, in the closeness of a small community, I soon came to know many of the students, joining them on summer nights as we floated on lantern-lit boats, the lights of the town sparkling above us while we sang the songs of romantic Germany. On these occasions, one thrilling contralto stood out against the rest. It belonged to Hildegarde von Wasserburg; and I, who have always loved music, and in particular the introspective music of the Germans – as Watson has noted in 'The Red-headed League' – soon found myself in conversation with her. She told me of her interest in the English influence on romantic Germany; and, as she wished to practise her English and I my German, we took to meeting frequently at the student cafés whose tables spilled out onto the town square beneath the castle.

Word of my exercises in deduction had spread, and one day a student came to our table who wished me to read his character from his appearance. Conversation at the nearby tables stopped; students from the other cafés crowded around; but the thing was absurdly simple. The ragged greatcoat which suggested the impoverished theological student, son of some rural clergyman, was belied by the ramrod back and jutting chin of the military aristocrat, whose false beard did not quite conceal his duelling-scars. A curt order in his own Prussian dialect – 'Attention!', I snapped – had him automatically clicking his heels, to the roars of laughter, prolonged as it seemed to me by dislike, of the locals who had put him up to it.

Hilde explained the laughter, and the popularity I had gained as a result, as we climbed the winding way to Burg Hohenzollern. The mountain, the Mons Solarius of the Romans, stands up out of a chequerboard of forest and tillage, an isolated outcrop of the Swabian Alps. Above it clouds soar; and to the walls of the farmhouses round about it cartwheels have been fixed, as if in recollection of the solar worship of the ancient peoples of the area, German Alemanni or Celtic Suevi. 'It is from this region, the Swabian Jura', Hilde said along the way, in her faintly accented English, 'that the three great imperial lines of Germany have arisen: the Hohenstaufen, who went on crusade and, knowing Arabic from their dominions in Sicily, spoke to Saladin in his own tongue; the Hapsburg, who have sat in their imperial capital of Vienna for five hundred years; and last the Hohenzollern, who rose from mastery of this mountain to leadership of a united Germany'.

We had come out on the platform on which the castle is built, or rather rebuilt, around its medieval chapel. 'The rest was recreated after we merged with Prussia', she informed me. I seemed to recall that the Württemburg we stood in had taken the Austrian side in Bismarck's successful wars for the leadership of Germany; but on surrendering to Prussia had been allowed to retain a certain independence as a kingdom.

'Yes', she observed meditatively; 'but there are some who, even now, feel that our destiny does not lie with Prussia – a bleak frontier territory, altogether less rich in tradition than our own, which some of us think of as the true heart of Germany. You heard the laughter when you exposed that Junker popinjay. But I must warn you', she remarked, looking around her quickly, 'it is dangerous to speak of such matters. The

Prussian secret police are everywhere, especially in the haunts of the students, where they seek to identify their enemies among the next generation'. She seemed about to say more, but restrained herself, though I thought I saw her eyes mist over as she gazed out over the vista of cornfield, meadow and woodland far below.

As autumn came on, and the outdoor tables were folded and put away, the interiors of the cafés, with their great potbellied stoves and their windows misted over, had become still more crowded and noisy, so that one had to shout to make oneself heard. I had been of some assistance to my professors in the matter of the Catullus Palimpsest, which made the scholarly world of Germany ring, so that our conversations were now continually interrupted by demands for the display of my powers. In the midst of these, the defeated Prussian student slipped in a challenge that I should prove myself as capable of assuming as of unmasking a disguise. So it was that I posed as a visiting scholar, and took in the faculty so successfully that my antics at high table – my snarling pedantry and deflation of pomposity – became an undergraduate legend. But, melancholy as I had become, I no longer shared the high spirits of youth, and grew weary of these inroads on my time: so that we took to meeting in Hilde's room under the gables of the old town. She had the poetry of the language at her fingertips; and, as so much of it is readily convertible into the world's great music, the illustration of a grammatical point would lead to quotation, and so by a natural progession to her singing, while I sketched out the chords on the well-worn piano under the sloping ceiling. Many times during that winter, grammar was forgotten as we modulated from one impassioned song to another. There was one in particular that stands out to my mind: she sang *Frühlingsglaube*, it seemed to me, with a particular depth of emotion, as if she sensed the frost that had seized hold of my feelings. To me it was as if that song of hope in the return of spring – of an endless blossoming, touching even the remotest valley – held out the courage to believe in the renewal of life; and I remember to this day the lift of her voice on the urging to forgetfulness of grief:

Nun, armes Herz, vergiss der Qual...

Her piano stood beside a window that looked out onto the river; Hölderlin's tower was visible beneath us; and, as she spoke quietly of his sunset world, with its sense of unthought-of possibilities about to fade out of reach, there were times I imagined she was holding out prospects for us both. In her gaze at me from time to time, the gentle face behind the gold-rimmed spectacles, I thought I sensed an invitation. I seemed to recognise in her glance that signal whereby female desire, masked by female pride, asks only to be asked; but she was too shy, and I too mistrustful and numb at heart, for anything to come of it.

I had spoken of these happenings in the most general terms; but Watson's empathy with the sex had divined the currents that swirled beneath the surface of my narrative. 'Dash it all, Holmes', he cried, 'don't you see how she felt about you? No woman takes that kind of trouble over a man she does not care for. For a man – at least a man like yourself, Holmes, if you will pardon my saying so – who inhabits the world of abstraction, so impersonal a sharing of interests may seem possible; but in the case of a woman, it denotes interest of the most personal kind. The unfortunate girl was in love with you'.

'Was she indeed, Watson', I murmured, 'Was she indeed? Attend to the sequel, and you shall see'. And I went on to tell of how I left the town abruptly, without a farewell, since anything I might have said could be only be an empty

225

formality or a placing myself in a false position. When I returned to the same area some years later, it was in a very different role. I had read of research being carried out in a chemical laboratory in Stuttgart that seemed to me to have potential application to the detection of crime, and managed through my brother Mycroft to get myself invited there. Stuttgart, then as now, was one of the great centres of German industry; yet it maintained a pastoral aspect. Only a fraction of the city was built over, and vineyards were to be found at the centre. My hotel room was adorned with a crucifix, suggesting the decorative sensibility of a monastic age, and recalling to me a visit with Hilde to the former monastery of Maulbronn, where the quiet echo of the fountain in the cloister seemed to gather around itself the time of another age. Immediately I banished her from my mind – by now I had established a discipline over my thoughts on which a medieval monk might have prided himself – and sat up late over my scientific papers, formulating more exactly the questions I wished to ask on the morrow.

But the morrow brought me back to the past far more quickly than I could have anticipated. I had found my way to the laboratory and been presented to its director, tweeded and goateed, who in turn introduced me to his assistant and, he expected, eventual successor. 'By far the most original mind at work here', he assured me, and from the shadows behind him stepped...Hilde. She was slimmer and lither; the flaming hair had darkened to old gold; and she came forward now surer of herself, with a certain steeliness, even, and took my hand.

'What a surprise!', I cried.

'Not for me, Sherlock', she replied. 'I remembered you immediately your letter arr- ived, but thought I might surprise you a little as you liked to surprise all of us at Tübingen. Indeed, it was your example which led me to abandon philology for science. I could not live in word-spinning while, as your example showed me, there was so much to be done in the practical world; and I consider myself honoured that the work in which I have participated has brought you back here'.

I examined her hand with professional detachment as I released it, noting that its chemical stains and burns matched my own; and in her eye I read a similar dedication. After she had shown me round the laboratory, and we had met its staff over a lengthy lunch in a nearby bierstube, she took me to a set of rooms that she had engaged for me in a side-street of the old city near the Stiftskirche. What remained of the afternoon was taken up with settling me in; and, after a sumptuous evening meal – it included wine sauces of a kind that I associated more with France than Germany – washed down with some fine local vintages, she invited me for a glass of schnapps to her own apartment, which was nearby. I agreed willingly, as our conversation had been wholly professional. She had acquired a freedom of manner which I had rarely found among my fellow-countrywomen, and which I attributed to the self-confidence which came from establishing herself in a career of her own. But this was to take a form which surprised even me.

Once in the room, through whose cross-paned windows the light of the street entered, she lit a pair of candles on the table, poured the liqueurs, emptied her glass in one rapid gesture, and excused herself. When she returned, she had discarded her last shred of... reticence.

With the same lack of inhibition she sat astride me. I put out a hand to resist; but she said: 'I have always known there was someone else; yet I have always been drawn to you. I wanted to do this long ago, but did not dare. I do not ask that you love me; but in whatever way you may want me, I am yours'.

I felt that it was all wrong: that I should leave instantly and not come back. But I could not hurt her pride; and besides...

'You were saying, Holmes..?' Watson's voice, a trifle curt, interrupted my reverie.

'What's that? Oh yes', I resumed. Translating the episode for Watson, in such fashion that he should be left with his impression of my superhuman detachment, was no simple matter. 'I was saying that the woman I now encountered was one whose intellect and interests matched my own, and that I felt an increasing closeness to her'.

He gave a sigh in which relief mingled with regret. 'You know, for a moment I fancied you were about to tell me you had fallen in love'.

It was, indeed, something I avoided telling myself. I held myself to the belief that my one true love was Caroline, and this was something different. Hilde made it easy for me by asking for no declarations, by encouraging me to think of our couplings as, in her phrase, 'healthy lust', too long suppressed. In this manner, she became an obsession to me, a dependence that, in its own way, was as degrading as that accursed passion of mine for cocaine. In the laboratory, we preserved a professional detachment; but our nights and weekends were delirious. We rarely left her room: the hurried sorties we made to the nearby bierstube, usually late at night, were followed by a return to make love once more. There were times when she had to go away: to report, as she told me, to the sponsors of her laboratory; but I found that her absence only whetted my desire; and on the weekends following, we often did not emerge from Friday night until Monday morning.

It was on one of these Sundays that I heard a pounding outside. Draped in a sheet, I went to answer. As I opened the door, a familiar voice growled: 'Chemistry, hmm?' Mycroft waddled in with a silver-headed stick; and, as he flicked an item of silken underwear from a chair and rested his bulk on it, I realised that only the greatest of emergencies could have brought him this far from his accustomed haunts.

'Sherlock', he grunted urgently, 'I must speak to you alone'. I turned to Hilde, who sat shielding herself with the bedclothes, and told her I would return to my lodgings. There Mycroft launched into the mission which had brought him so far from home.

'You are aware', he began, 'of the situation within the imperial family?'

'Who is not?', I shrugged. There could hardly have been a child in Germany who did not know of the dramatic conflict between the generations. The old Kaiser Wilhelm, who with Bismarck's help had become the first German Emperor, had allowed his chancellor to rule in his name with an iron hand. His son and heir, Friedrich, however, had different ambitions. He was married to the daughter of our Queen; both thought alike; and there was little doubt that when he should come to the throne a constitutional monarchy, on English lines, would replace the current military dictatorship. Bismarck foresaw this, and lost no opportunity of vilifying the Crown Prince and Princess; but it was clear that his days were numbered.

Then fate had taken a terrible turn. It was reported that Crown Prince Friedrich was afflicted with an infection of the throat. At first it was pronounced benign; but when it was diagnosed, beyond any shadow of doubt, as malignant, the prospect opened up – for Germany, for England, and for Europe at large – was catastrophic. For Friedrich would be succeeded by his son Wilhelm, whose feelings about England were altogether different.

This prospect was realised in what became known as the Year of the Three Emperors. By the time Wilhelm I died, his son was no longer able to speak; and, three months after he had watched his father's funeral cortege pass through mounded snow from the Charlottenburg Palace, Friedrich himself was dead. His body was not yet cold when his own son, now Wilhelm II, sealed the death-chamber in the hope of uncovering his mother's correspondence with her English family. In this he was unsuccessful: she had had it spirited away to Windsor, with English assistance – an adventure which I may one day relate – but his hatred of his mother's homeland was unrelenting. He blamed her for having weakened and enervated his father with her ideas of a civilian monarchy; for his part, he commanded and swore in the best Junker tradition.

As Mycroft recalled these details to me, I interjected:

'The withered left arm...'

'...has led him to overcompensate. With his powerful right hand, the stones of his rings turned inward, he squeezes the hands of visitors until tears start to their eyes, then smilingly releases them.

'But the full rage of his feeling of impotence is concentrated on England. He envies us our wealth, our empire, our naval might'.

I turned from my evocation of Mycroft to Watson: 'You recall his visits to England, I presume?'

'The yachting at Cowes?'

'Precisely'. There was nothing the Prince of Wales took more pride in than his reputation as a sportsman; and nothing, in turn, endeared him more to his people: his wins at the Derby sealed his popularity with his future subjects. But he had taken a particular interest in yacht-racing, where he was able to participate in person, and which he did every summer at Cowes. The Kaiser made this a matter of rivalry, and, with a budget the Prince could not match, built a larger and more powerful boat, beating him on his own ground and driving him out of the sport.

'The problem appears to have been', Watson observed, 'that he did not know how to lose'.

'Worse still', I replied. 'He did not know how to win. Nothing gave greater offence in England than his glorying in victory. It marked him out at once as lacking the sporting instinct, and therefore not a gentleman – a status to which he yet, in some curious fashion, aspired. For him, to be an English gentleman was the supreme social cachet, and he wished to be taken for one with all his heart and soul. But of course the thing was impossible. Not only did he crow over his win; he infused it with political animus. He spared no pains to let the world know that his victory in a yacht-race over his uncle was a foretaste of the coming naval supremacy of Germany over England'.

'All this was apparent to the Prince of Wales, who had known him from childhood. He was convinced that his nephew's rivalry was a species of mania, and never spoke of him without touching his forehead. But he found few to agree with him. Politicians less knowledgeable than the Prince were convinced that he exaggerated the threat – perhaps out of rivalry on his own side. Wilhelm, after all, was a young and powerful Emperor, while Edward was an ageing Prince with no discernible political influence. Our diplomats, moreover, reported from Berlin that Bismarck – the real source of power – was sequestered on his country estate, and that his son, whom he had groomed to succeed him, was handling day-to-day business at the Chancellory. They reasoned that this would not be the case if ought were amiss.

'The Prince's reply was that Bismarck was above all a master of timing. He had attacked the Austrians only after detaching them from potential allies; then, in a lightning campaign, defeated them by the use of the railway and the breech-loading rifle. Austria was forever excluded from influence in northern Germany, which was now unified under the leadership of Prussia. Once again detaching potential allies, Bismarck shattered the French, adding Alsace and Lorraine to the new German Empire which he proclaimed at Versailles – a master-stroke of political symbolism. The

Prince was of the opinion that inactivity in Bismarck was a sign he was biding his time, and that Wilhelm's indiscreet sabre-rattling was a truer indication of German intentions.

'Having failed to find a sympathetic hearing in the Government, the Prince had turned to Mycroft, who always respected his instincts about people, and who had accordingly travelled to Germany to see me, to my unutterable astonishment.

'"I?", I asked. "What can I do about it?"

'"You can do what I cannot do", replied Mycroft: "act. You can speak the language; you can dress up in disguises. You can go now to Berlin in this uniform I have brought in my gladstone, of an officer from Württemburg, and infiltrate military society in Berlin. You will be on the watch for the chance remark, the momentary indiscretion, which betrays the intentions of Bismarck and Wilhelm"'.

'He would brook no excuses; and so it was that he saw me off on the next train to the capital, into which I descended with no little bewilderment.

'Imagine a city in which London – the palaces, galleries, cathedrals, the pomp and state of a splendid imperial capital – were combined with the industry and excitement of a Manchester or a Birmingham – indeed of both: for Berlin was now greater than either. Imagine a London in which, behind the fashionable avenues, courtyard after courtyard opened out into workshops and factories. And, to complete the picture, think of these compounded with Aldershot: parade-grounds, barrack-yards, brilliant uniforms everywhere. In the centre, over the war-chariot of the Brandenburg Gate, floated the red standard of the new empire, blazoned with the black cross of the Teutonic Knights. It was a heady, unimaginable brew of imperial, industrial and military power: it bubbled over with a sense of impending greatness, an excitement, that made Mycroft's dingy office at Whitehall seem tame indeed.

'I realised the power of my uniform on the first evening. I had wandered into a café; and seeing no table free, was about to depart. But at that moment a civilian who had been sitting nearby stood and, leaving his coffee half drunk, picked up his bill and waved me obsequiously to his seat. I quickly adjusted to the nasal bark, the *Potsdamer Ton*, which marked one out as born to command, and was unquestioningly accepted as a member of their own caste by the officers in whom I found a swelling of pride, a quickening of morale as they realised that military virtues, and not the hated, weakling, civilian values, were to be rewarded under the new Kaiser, in whom all this display of power was concentrated.

'Mycroft had provided me with a means of approach to him in person. He had given me a fictitious uncle in Württemburg who was an inventor; and to make this tale plausible had provided me with some War Office plans for a repeating rifle, redrawn in German style. These were for a prototype which had since been superseded, but they should suffice to gain me an audience with the Kaiser, who prided himself, without cause, on his knowledge of weaponry.

'I spoke of these plans to my new-found friends, one of whom promised me an introduction to a relative, a senior officer who enjoyed access to the All-Highest, as the Kaiser was known. Arriving at the restaurant fixed for the meeting, I found indeed a group of senior officers waiting for me, but their manner was cold and curt, quite unlike that of the excitable young subalterns I had been drinking with. They patted me down for weapons, motioned me to a back room, and slammed the door behind me. Inside, I saw sitting, alone at the table, none other than – Bismarck'.

Watson gasped.

'Oh, there could be no mistaking him. There was the craggy face with its tufted eyebrows and its immense moustache. He wore his general's uniform and puffed on a large cigar; his spiked helmet lay on the table, amid several empty beer-steins and the remains of a gargantuan meal. The man's appetite was legendary; and it extended in other directions as well. He had once been unscrupulous in his pursuit of women; and on his watch-chain I noted the onyx medallion which was a memento from a Russian diplomat's wife. He had, too, been a reckless duellist, and his daring had not left him with youth. The tale was told of the would-be assassin who fired at him point-blank on a Berlin street, only to have the old man turn, seize him and hand him over to the guard. This aura of the life he had lived clung about him as about some dangerous animal.

'This master of the shock tactic had left me at a loss for words. He had brought me face-to-face with history in his own person, and I could see that he revelled in the paralysing effect he had had upon me.

'He waved me to a seat. "Those plans", he said softly, in his curiously gentle voice, "let me have them".

'"Yes", he remarked after a rapid inspection, "I thought as much. Obsolete. Not that the All-Highest would know the difference".

'I was taken aback by this want of respect for the Kaiser; but what I heard next astonished me still more. "There is no need for you to seek an audience with the Kaiser; I can tell you everything you wish to know – Herr Holmes.

'"Oh yes, it is useless to deny it. I know you are here to ascertain the Kaiser's intentions, to discover whether he and the warmonger Bismarck will between them set all Europe aflame. In one direction, indeed, the fears of your Crown Prince are amply founded" – here he paused to tap his head – "the man is a mental case. But I fear him as much as you do – even more".

'"*You* fear him!", I gasped, incredulous. "But why?"

"'Because he will destroy everything I have lived for.   He will destroy my Germany.   I have never feared war, as the history-books will tell you, when war was needed: when it was the only way to unite this country under Prussia.   But the pages that follow will tell you how generous I was to vanquished Austria, which has since become our ally.   For the same reason I have cultivated friendship with Russia, since a war on both fronts, with it and the France we have humiliated, would be a nightmare.   And so I desire friendship with England.   Oh, I do not deny that ultimately England will become our enemy: already our industrial production threatens your markets.   But this will happen naturally and peacefully: our new Germany needs time to grow.   This madman is already provoking Russia, and boasting of a navy which will take on that of England.   And all because he does not like his relations!   This ridiculous personalisation, this inability to practise diplomacy – in the hands of a man who, thanks to me, wields immense power – is a disaster of stupendous proportions.   Especially if he has not a Chancellor who will restrain him".

"'We understand", said I smoothly, "that you have groomed your son to succeed you".

"'That is exactly", cried the old man, slamming his fist on the table, "what this nincompoop resents.   He speaks of us as Carolingians, mayors of the palace waiting to supplant the legitimate rulers.   He does not understand that, for his dynasty to survive, it needs the guidance of heads wiser than his own.   And that is why he has to go".

"'Go?"

"When your Queen was here, I told her I could keep her grandson under control: I did not wish to alarm her unduly.   But if he removes me – which his grandfather had the wisdom not to do, but he does not – Germany is lost.   No, do not smile, Herr Holmes, this is not merely an old man's vanity.   With

235

me out of the way, he will appoint a Chancellor subservient to his commands – or rather whims. All he knows of battle are those staged manoeuvres in which he is invariably allowed to declare victory; but already he thinks himself on a level with his mighty ancestors: a Friedrich II or a Great Elector. He is in love with the idea of war; once he controls the Empire, he will be taken seriously, and that idea become reality. That is what we must at all costs prevent'.

'"*We?*"

'"Yes, destiny has placed you in my hands, Herr Holmes. What would happen if I were to hand you over in that uniform, exposed as a British spy? You see. Now listen to what I have to tell you".

'He paused. "You know what the Berliners say is the biggest business in Germany?"

'I had heard the gibe in the cafés. "Bismarck and Son, because they have an emperor as travelling salesman".

'"Correct". He barked a short laugh in which scorn was mingled with satisfaction. "The man cannot sit still; and his latest craze is to celebrate the glories of his family with a great hunt at his ancestral castle".

'"Burg Hohenzollern?"

'"You know the place?" He asked this with a peculiar glint in his eye.

'"I have visited it", said I carelessly.

'"You are about to visit it again", he replied. "Those men who brought you in here are trusted lieutenants of mine. They will accompany you to the station" – he took a watch from his uniform pocket – "from which a train with connections to Stuttgart will leave in half an hour. To the south of Burg Hohenzollern rises the plateau of the Swabian Jura. Into this is cut a valley impassable on all but one side; and here, tomorrow morning, the Kaiser will go hunting. He will dismount at the entrance to the valley, into which the single path is winding and steep, and, carrying his rifle, ascend it. His retinue will be at some distance: in all matters, he has to be first. At a point where the path turns round a cliff, you will be waiting. In your hand will be a revolver with a single cartridge. Before he can raise and aim his rifle, you will have fired your shot. At that moment, my problems and yours – and the problems of our respective nations – will have come to an end".

'I was dumbfounded. "You wish me to assassinate the Kaiser?"

'"Come, come, Herr Holmes, we are not children. The man is a sick animal. Tens, hundreds of thousands of precious lives ride on one useless one. A single shot, and the menace is removed".

'"And if I refuse?"

'"I have you arrested here and now".

'"Instead of having me arrested tomorrow and charged with the murder of the Kaiser…"

'"Herr Holmes, I implore you to think this through. A war with England would undoubtedly result. Why should I remove that strutting imbecile if the conscquences are to be the same?"

'"…or having me quietly removed later".

'"Mr. Holmes, try to see the matter impersonally. I could have you eliminated at this moment if I wished, and nobody would ever trace you. I do not kill you, not because I am afraid to, but because your death would serve no purpose. It is in my interest that you go free, and report to the estimable Mycroft, and his masters in Whitehall, what I have done for them. The peace of Europe will have been secured, thanks to you and me; and, believe me, they will be grateful".

'"But how am I to escape? You have said the valley is impassable".

'"My officers will follow the hunt, immediately after the Kaiser.   As soon as they see that he is dead, they will set up a hue and cry in the wrong direction.   If, however, he is still alive, they will shoot you on the spot.   Your body, in the uniform of Württemburg, will be identified as that of a crazed Swabian separatist, which will give me a handle against those trouble-makers.   You may either die uselessly, in the cause of my internal policies, or perform the utmost service for your country.   All that stands in your way is that tinge of moral scruple I see in your eyes.   Yet even you can hardly think it criminal to fire in your own defence.   And, believe me, that will be necessary.   Our imperial master will have no compunction about shooting you on the spot".

'He saw that I still hesitated.

'"Very well, Herr Holmes.   I see you yet hold back. And so let me make the issue still clearer.   You leave me no choice.   Should you fail, you will never again see a certain young lady.   On the other hand, if you succeed, I may be inclined to permit it".

'"*Permit* it?"

'"You are noted for your logical capacity, Herr Holmes: though to tell the truth, I begin to wonder why.   Has it not occurred to you to ask how I know your identity?   Think: who is the only person in this country who has seen you and your brother together?"

'I tried to hold back the unthinkable; but the dam burst, and realisation flooded over me.   I felt sickened, faint.

'"Hilde?"

'"Precisely: she is one of my agents.   She has been in place for some time".

'His words seemed to fade into the distance; my head swam.   I saw it now.   The clumsy seduction, the clinging fondness: all was a clever arrangement to bring me under control.

'"She has developed a certain feeling for you. If you wish to see her again, it can be arranged".

'Burning with rage and shame, I realised that I was capable of throwing away everything – morality, country, the peace of Europe – in order to possess her again. Then I took hold of myself: it was a bluff. I remembered the Ems telegram, which the man in front of me had edited so as to make it appear he had slighted the French emperor, and so goad him into war.

'He saw my disbelief, and produced a paper from the breast pocket of his uniform. When Mycroft called me away, I had asked a few moments to say farewell to Hilde, and run to her apartment, but found it locked. I knew now where she had been: at the telegraph office. I had scribbled her a note, saying I had to travel at short notice on a family matter. For the first and only time, I added that I loved her. It was this note that Bismarck now unfolded. "A mistake, Mr. Holmes", he said. "Never put anything in writing. I have done it myself; let me advise you against it". And he flung the paper into the fire.

'Bewildered, I allowed myself to be driven to the station in the company of Bismarck's officers. As if in a trance, I heard the whistle shriek and the train lurch forward; and, as it ploughed relentlessly on across the bleak Brandenburg plain, unmodulated by hill or valley, the red sun dazzled my eyes until it sank, inexorably, into blackness. I attempted to forget my misery in slumber, but could not; and when I looked at my face in the mirror next morning, saw a sleepless and unshaven desperado who seemed fit for anything. As indeed I was. Through my mind, as remorselessly as the wheels of the train, there circled the logic of Bismarck's reasoning: whatever befell me, his master's death would be of benefit to my country no less than his. This remained true whatever happened to me; and, for myself, I no longer cared whether I lived or died.

'The train halted. There was the station I remembered, full of magical associations that had now turned to ashes. Then the carriage drive, the journey under guard on horseback, until I was ordered to dismount under the cliff behind which I was to await my target. I had not been there very long when I heard an imposing stride. It was the Kaiser himself who marched in my direction, resplendent in uniform, stiffly, like a statue of himself, one shoulder higher than the other, the upturned moustaches bristling, rifle clasped in his one powerful hand. As he caught sight of me – the bloodshot eyes, the bleary face, the crumpled uniform – a strange thing happened. I had thought – insofar as I was capable of thought – that the issue would resolve itself without any conscious volition on my part. The Kaiser would raise his rifle to fire; I would fire in my own defence; one or the other of us would fall. But nothing happened. My quarry, as sometimes happens with animals, seemed to recognise in me his executioner, and, as happens with animals, stood as if paralysed. He waited for me to shoot, but I could not do so; could not in cold blood let loose destruction on another human being. My indecision can only have been for an instant, but it seemed to go on a long time. High above the rustling of the trees in the valley, I heard the exquisite song of a lark. It seemed a message from another world, a world far beyond our petty squabbles. And then, all of a sudden, it was too late. I heard the voices of the Kaiser's companions as they crowded behind him on the path. I heard the clink of their spurs, saw the glitter of their uniforms through the leaves. And now the Kaiser himself seemed to come back to life. The brutal, authoritarian features took on a look of the most extraordinary vindictiveness. "Here! Here! Help!", he bellowed, and began to lower his rifle. I knew that if I shot him within sight of his followers, they would be left with no alternative than to cut me down. I fled through a tangle of trees and undergrowth. I heard the command being given to fan out and beat the area systematically, and realised that my time was limited. I soon came to the rock-face that bordered the valley. It looked impassable; but desperation led me from one sheer foothold to another. I had just reached the top when my hunters arrived at the bottom. A bullet zinged past my head; another grazed my foot as I rolled over the edge. Somehow I managed to cross the mountains and make my way into Switzerland.

'The rest is history: it is Bismarck's nightmare come true. Did I do wrong? Should I have pressed the trigger? Would a Bismarck at the Chancellery have averted the catastrophe which ensued? If I could have known – but how could I have known? And how, not having the means of knowing, could I have lived with myself afterwards?'

Watson paused a long time. We were the last patrons in the restaurant, lit only by the candle which had burnt down to a shapeless mass on the table. At length he bestirred himself and said: 'I beg your pardon, Holmes. I spoke hastily earlier'. Then, after another pause, he observed: 'At least one thing has been accomplished by this frightful calamity. No single individual can ever again wield the same power for evil'.

NINE

TWILIGHT IN BABYLON

We approached Cologne along that curve of railway track which crosses the Rhine and over which the cathedral looms like a sculptured mountain, and here I took my leave of Watson. In France his war experience had been of the greatest value to me, as we surveyed the wreckage of battlefields; but in Germany his vociferous disapproval of the entire nation, which now extended to its women, could only have been a liability. He was easily persuaded to book passage on a select steamer following the great river south into Switzerland; and it was with considerable amusement that I saw him ignore my parting wave. Already, despite his diatribes of only a few hours previously, he was engaged in lively conversation with a handsome widow of pronounced Teutonic features whom he had met upon the landing-stage.

My lightness of heart did not proceed alone from the knowledge that I had provided him with a pleasing diversion, but from the conviction that the river cruise would help restore Watson's health and spirits. There had been indications, as we traversed roads punctuated by large craters, giving the whole the sense of a lunar landscape, that my dear friend's stamina was no longer what it had been; and that his spirits, more susceptible to emotional impressions than my own, threatened to sink under the horrors of the wasteland. There was, as well, another factor to be considered. I had been sent on a mission to Germany where it was best, indeed imperative, that I merge into the local population, a task impossible in the company of so unmistakable an Englishman as Watson. Indeed I feared that, had he known of it, his spirits might have sunk beyond recovery. For even I, who over decades of discipline have learnt to banish the personal equation from my calculations, found myself faced with a darker prospect than any I had known before: with the stage set for a drama the final act of which it was unlikely I should live to see, and which, it seemed to me, might well involve the destruction of all civilisation.

Already, much that we had thought of as permanent had passed away. The Romanov, Hapsburg and Hohenzollern dynasties had disappeared, and their empires been dismembered. Germany had lost huge tracts of territory to France in the west and Poland in the east. The country assembled from the victories, not only of Bismarck, but of Frederick the Great, had been dismantled; and, whatever the historic justice of these reversions, they had been carried out in such fashion as to leave a lasting impression of wrong. Germany had won the war in the east, and appeared not to have lost it in the west. Its generals had called an armistice while their line remained unbroken, handing over power to a civilian government which bore the odium of their surrender. The hate-mongering on the other side, which grew out of military incompetence, did the rest. This produced a mood of animosity in which the confiscation of German territory was compounded by demands for unrealistic reparations which were to make up the staggering losses of the war. To add insult to injury, this punishment was imposed in the Hall of Mirrors at Versailles, where the German Empire had been proclaimed.

'Serves them right', averred Watson stoutly, as he read this news from his *Times* at Baker Street; and he was bewildered and angry when I pointed out that a mirror-image is only an apparent reversal; in reality, it is exactly the same thing. I quoted Mycroft on the fall of Napoleon, when the victorious nations had refrained from punishing the French people at Vienna; and how that wise restraint had kept the peace of Europe, by and large, for a hundred years. But Mycroft had not succeeded in having a similar solution accepted at Versailles; and, having failed to arrest that catastrophe, charged me to visit Germany, observe the effects of the treaty, and report back to him in the hope that, even at this late date, leadership might take the place of demagogy.

The first thing I did as Cologne disappeared behind me was take my bag into a lavatory and there change into German clothing, to which I added a goatee and pince-nez, becoming the very picture of such an academic as had terrorised the students of Tübingen long before. Entering a compartment which seemed to hold a cross-section of German society, I saw that this, in all essentials, had not changed. Space was immediately and deferentially made for the presumed intellectual: who, having stowed his bag above, sat down with suitably curt bowings amid his audience. I nodded at them to continue their conversation, for I had seen from the outside that they were engaged in a heated debate, and soon found that, as I had hoped, it was the current state of the nation that occupied them so passionately.

I pass over the details, as Watson seems incapable of doing, and give the gist of the argument, which went on all the way to Berlin. It began with an older, clearly once well-to-do, couple complaining of having the savings of a lifetime wiped out by inflation. They were dismayed that the new democratic government openly declared the economic dislocations beyond its control. These, of an age with myself, had seen a fragmented Germany unified into a great power; they were stunned by what had happened, and could not comprehend it. A young widow was in like case: she was on her way to find work in the cabarets of Berlin; I divined from her pinched look and desperate eyes that she would take any which was offered. She declaimed vehemently against the disaster of the war, which had destroyed a happy family – her own little girl having been left behind with her parents – and hoped the new government would rebuild the country along lines which would make a repetition impossible. A demobilised soldier, with damaged leg and tell-tale stick, nodded vehement agreement; but argued that this could not come from such a system as prevailed at present. 'Socialism', he stated, 'that is the answer – the brotherhood of man. In the trenches, we sent messages across the British lines, and had friendly answers in return. They were men, it was obvious, like ourselves, and we began to wonder why we were instructed to kill them, and they us. The answer quickly became apparent: our orders came from the officer class, representing the rulers of this society'. Here he glanced sardonically at the older couple. 'When there are no more class divisions, when we recognise our solidarity with the workers of other nations, there will be no reason to meet them on the battlefield'.

'Pshaw!', interjected a young man with slicked-back brown hair, who had come striding into the compartment at an intermediate station, and, without greeting anyone, arrogated a seat by the window and stared out of it with lordly contempt until this moment. He was tall and athletic, and wore a type of uniform I had not seen before, neatly pressed and sporting an armband with the device of a crooked cross. 'Sentimental nonsense!'

'I beg your pardon?', asked the veteran, taken aback.

'We all admire what Lenin did in Russia', said the young man. 'His seizure of power was brilliant. But this universal brotherhood he invokes: what does it amount to? It is, if I may say so' – and he glanced at the veteran's leg – 'a cripple psychology. We aim to give Germany back her pride'.

'It was pride', observed the injured man dolefully, 'that began the war'.

'There is nothing wrong with war', replied the youth smoothly. 'What matters is how and for what it is waged'.

The veteran now became openly angry. 'What can someone like you know of war? Have you lived in a rat-ridden hole for months on end, to be thrown against killing-machines by self-interested generals...?'

'What do *you* say, Herr Professor?', interjected the young man – clearly accustomed to the tricks of debate, and side-tracking a question he could not answer – turning to me with an insolent, patronising, smile. 'Though I wonder why I ask: I imagine someone of your calling knows of war only from dusty archives'.

'On the contrary', I replied. 'I have worn the uniform of the Reich, and spoken to the great Bismarck himself'.

A collective gasp greeted this announcement.

'You see', smirked the youth, rapidly changing tack. 'A man after my own heart. If that old boy had been around, what we see today would never have occurred'.

'It would not have occurred', I countered, 'because it would not have begun. We spoke of precisely this eventuality, and it was what he feared most. That conflict should be resorted to, when Germany could amass power peacefully, seemed to him the ultimate catastrophe'.

The young man blenched. 'But Bismarck gave us our Germany on the heels of a victorious war'.

'Precisely. He fought a war only when he knew it could be won, and was – I quote his own words to me – "generous to vanquished Austria". He knew that Germany could ill afford to be surrounded by enemies on all sides'.

'Generous to the vanquished!', protested the youth. 'There you have it all. And besides', he went on, 'we were *not* vanquished; we were stabbed in the back by the civ...'

I shook my head involuntarily; and he turned on me with passionate vehemence. 'Say what you will', he spat ferociously, 'it is action that counts. We will save Germany's soul – in blood if need be; no watery goodwill about it. I will say this for the occupant of the Kremlin: having once taken power, he has known how to hold on to it – not much brotherhood there!'

The wounded veteran visibly cringed. Then a slowing of speed, a shout, a halt and a hiss of steam announced our arrival at the Tiergarten. I dusted off the smuts which had accumulated on my frock-coat, and bowed to my companions in the stately fashion which became my apparent profession. But, as I left the compartment, the uniformed young man called a challenge after me. 'Come and hear our leader this evening, Herr Professor', he cried, 'and judge for yourself whether destiny has not given us another Bismarck'.

I alighted on the platform to see an obviously English gentleman, complete with bowler and umbrella, walk alongside the train with worried look, peering at the arrivals, and passing me by without a glance. When he had reached the end of the train, and turned back again, I approached him speaking in German.

'Please, can you tell me where is the Hotel Astoria?'

A start of shock passed through my interlocutor. 'As it happens, I am staying there myself', he said slowly, with narrowed eyes. Then, recovering his composure, he said: 'I shall be happy to take you there as soon as I have found somebody I am expected to meet. Excuse me'. And he turned away.

I tugged at his sleeve. 'This person you have to meet – is he by any chance an Englishman dressed in an ulster and deerstalker cap?'

He turned around to me open-mouthed, fear in his eyes. By now he was convinced the secret police were on his track. He paused to look at the photograph of myself I held in my hand; and, glancing from me to the likeness, at last recognised the resemblance. 'Phew, Holmes, you gave me quite a fright.

Blankley, Foreign Office'. He held out a hand, which I ignored, bowing instead.

'I have established, I hope, that my disguise carries some conviction. Which is more than I can say for yours'.

'Oh, I am not meant to be incognito. I am here as the agent for a British publisher, in which capacity I meet my German counterparts and monitor intellectual opinion. At the moment, I am sorry to say, it is a trifle turbulent'.

'So I gather', I replied drily. I pointed my stick down the platform. 'Can you tell me anything about those people?' The sleek young man of the compartment had joined a group of others in similar uniform. Above them floated a banner with the broken cross, which I found oddly disturbing.

'Oh, them?', he laughed dismissively. 'They're only the Nazis. A fringe group who like to pretend they're ancient Teutons. No-one takes them seriously'.

'Whom *do* you take seriously?'

He looked at me as if I had come from another planet. 'Why the people, of course, who want to follow the Russian example and turn Germany into a great socialist state. If that should happen, all of Europe would go under. The war, as I presume you are aware, has created a great deal of discontent'.

'I know about that', I said impatiently. 'But I should like to know more about your... Nazis'.

'National Socialists. Street agitators. The leader is a demobbed N.C.O. left high and dry by the peace: a common enough type, who in this case has developed messianic delusions. You would not credit the gibberish he spouts – lacks even the superficial plausibility of socialism. He's to speak here this evening to his supporters – a prize collection of mal- contents and ne'er-do-wells...'

I cut through the babble. 'Blankley, how would you go about squaring the circle?'

The official stared at me as if I had taken leave of my senses. 'Squaring the circle? Everyone knows it can't be done: it's a phrase to denote the impossible'.

'Nevertheless, it can seem to have been done'. I pointed to the banner. 'That crooked cross – what do you know of it?'

'They call it the swastika, and revere it as an ancient Aryan symbol. To me it is the black cross of Prussia dressed up in a lot of mumbo-jumbo'.

'It is a great deal more than that, Blankley. It is, as you say, an ancient symbol; and I have seen it in India. It combines the solidity of the square with the motion of the circle. And that is what, if I am not mistaken, its bearers have attempted to do by calling themselves National Socialists: combine the rootedness of nationalism with the energy of socialism – at least in theory. In practice, as you have pointed out, it cannot be done, since socialism claims to have superseded nationalism. I should like to see how they resolve this dilemma'.

He raised his eyebrows a fraction and smiled indulgently. 'Well, by all means go and take a look at them, Mr. Holmes; they are one of the sights of Berlin. But they amount to nothing more than riffraff playing warriors and spouting semi-educated piffle. So at least I am told'.

'Told? You have not listened to them yourself?'

He looked at me with weary distaste. 'Holmes, I have been sent here by the government of my country to take counsel with the leading authorities in this. I have better things to do than dive down side-alleys in search of guttersnipes. I do not exaggerate when I say that I am on familiar terms with the some of the greatest minds in Germany'.

'It is not by great minds that revolutions are set in motion. I have met a man who knows what he wants, and is transformed by that knowledge'.

All pretence of affability had been wiped from Blankley's face: he was the expert challenged on his own ground. He remarked, with barely-contained anger: 'Go to their fancy-dress ball, if it amuses you. You will excuse me if I do not accompany you; I have work to do'.

'I should not dream of imposing upon you', I replied, and parted from him after securing the address of the evening's gathering. After a hasty supper in a beer-cellar I made my way to the hall. On its steps was my interlocutor of the train, while in the street below his comrades were engaged in scuffles with small knots of protestors. 'Herr Professor!', he exclaimed in delight, clearly pleased at this accession of intellectual respectability. 'What are they doing?', I asked, pointing my stick in distaste at the milling mob. 'Oh', he said archly, 'we are fighting off some people who would deny us our right to free speech'.

Inside the building was a large, barn-like auditorium. A band blared martial tunes; and the audience, reserved at first, joined in. The platform was draped with a huge banner. On a background of red stood the black cross of the Reich with, in an empty space in the centre, the *Hakenkreuz*. For some reason it made the hairs bristle at the back of my neck; but before I had time to analyse my reactions, the band stopped all of a sudden, and a ratty-looking man in cheap spectacles came out on the platform. A brief, low-key introduction was followed by a dimming of illumination to leave only a single spotlight, in the glare of which the main speaker strutted onto the platform to enormous, rhythmic applause. A man of middle height, inclined to stoutness, which his belt had been tightened to conceal, an untidy lock of dark hair fell over his forehead and was accompanied by a toothbrush moustache. His whole appearance suggested caricature; but he held himself with the utmost seriousness, acknowledging the howls from the auditorium, which called on him by name, with a stiff upward salute of the right arm and the posture of a Roman emperor. It occurred to me that he was wholly unaware of the incongruous figure he struck; and he accepted the applause gravely for some minutes until, with a sweeping gesture of the hand, he cut it off, and was left with silence, which he allowed to grow before he launched into his tirade.

When he addressed his audience as members of a common folk, a full-throated howl of exultation erupted. Again he let it develop, basking in it till it rose to a crescendo, then, again, imperiously cut it off. Slowly and in a soft voice, misty-eyed, he recited the history of his sufferings. The first, in his eyes, was to have been born on the wrong, Austrian, side of a border town, on the fissure between the lesser and the greater Germany: the heroic fatherland forged by Bismarck in the crucible of war. With the fervour of an exile cut off from the promised land, he saw this as a country still essentially Teutonic, unlike his native Austria: which, he lamented, had been mongrelised by lesser breeds.

Quietly, caressingly, he flattered his audience; and, having worked them into receptive mood, expounded his theory. Socialism, he held, as commonly understood, did not go far enough, since it posited a conflict between the classes. His socialism was a socialism of the entire people, the purified folk. It was an intensification of nationalism; and it had this advantage over socialism: that instead of reducing the members of his audience to equality of status, he raised every one of them to nobility. For him, every Teuton was an aristocrat, every German a junker. Through a clever manipulation of terms, he had succeeded in squaring the circle.

At least for those seduced by his rhetoric. Those who were not, it appeared, were to be subjected to intimidation. Now he worked himself into a frenzy as he recited his second source of sorrow, with the passion of a man aggrieved. A simple soldier, he had been in a hospital for the wounded when the terrible, the unimaginable news had come through. He and his comrades had won the war; but they had been betrayed by the civilians who signed the peace. His eyes grew misty once more as he painted a picture of the Kaiser hounded from his throne by jackals, deracinated internationalists, traitors to the folk. Yet there was no talk of restoring the ignoble exile who even yet, mouthing vituperation of the same kind, cowered in safety among the generous Dutch. The speaker saw Wilhelm as already a figure of the past, already dead to his people, while he himself was his mourner – and, it was clearly implied, his successor. The new Kaiser would be, not the prisoner of caste, but the leader of all his folk. It seemed there could be no question as to who this Caesar might be, as the mob leaped to its feet in thunderous applause at the hysterical peroration. The band joined in the din with further martial strains: for what he had called for was a renewal of war: a war which would purify the spirit of the folk and realise its expansionist destiny. I shuddered at the recollection of the scenes Watson and I had witnessed along the way.

Absorbed in my reverie, I scarcely adverted to the fact that the speaker was proceeding down the hall, surrounded by his uniformed bodyguard, amongst whom was my companion of the train. The latter whispered something in his leader's ear, with the result that he halted directly in front of me, looking me over with a suspicious eye. 'Professor?', he barked, in a compound of hostility and insecurity. 'A simple person', I stammered, appalled by the self-interested politicians who had allowed this conflagration to begin, and even now were feeding its flames, 'a simple person who longs for the return of leadership'. To my horror, he took this as a personal compliment, for a moment turning on me an oafish grin that seemed designed as a smile of Olympian benevolence. Then, just as suddenly, it was wiped away as the blue eyes went blank, the face turned inward, and he marched away among his minions with a curious marionette walk. When I tried to gather my impressions, they resolved themselves into a phrase: that evil is impersonality. He was incapable of encounter with another human being as such: he had seen me momentarily as a possible enemy; then, reassured that I was not, that I was part of the raw material of his power, dismissed me from existence.

Outside, as the speaker drove away, my youthful acquaintance awaited me in a state of high excitement. 'Our Leader liked you', he gabbled, 'I can tell'. I was distracted from these effusions by the sight of his companions lashing out at some passers-by. 'Surely these', I expostulated, 'are no longer interfering with your right of speech?' 'No', he laughed, 'that is not the problem. The problem is that they do not look...German – you know what I mean', and he gave me a sidelong smile.

'Suppose they *are* German?', I asked sarcastically.

He failed to catch my irony. 'Believe me, Professor, we know these things. And besides, if a mistake were to be made, it would only reinforce our reputation for terror. You heard what the Leader said: we are a new humanity, beyond pity. We do not ask it for ourselves, and we do not listen when others ask for it. We must not be deflected by weakness from our duty to the Folk'. His face shone with the rapture of the fanatic.

Exhausted by my journey, and by the emotions that the meeting had aroused in me, I feel into a deep sleep; and when I awoke late on the following morning, I realised why the swastika banner had disturbed me so greatly. It ran anti-clockwise. When I had last seen this symbol at Benares, it was in the form of two swastikas placed side by side: the first clockwise, following the course of the sun and representing a steady illumination; the second its opposite, standing for the changing cycle of the moon and its inevitable descent into darkness. Each, the Hindoos realised, was an aspect of life; but it was destruction alone that was glorified by the Nazi.

I sat over coffee on the Kurfürstendamm, this time having to wait for a seat, while outside on the pavement sat limbless and eyeless veterans, begging. It was no longer the proud military town I had known in my youth, no longer echoing with the pompous strains of marching regiments. As I continued along the street, the very different rhythm of a jazz piano floated up from a basement nearby; a young woman lurking in the stairwell emerged to take my arm. I saw it that was the countrywoman of the previous day's train, her haggard features caked with makeup designed to make her appear seductive. I disengaged myself, I fear somewhat ungently, as the memory of an ancient betrayal rose to mind.

To rid myself of the memory, I walked on and on, soon finding myself in the broad avenue that runs through the Tiergarten. Initially, I found myself refreshed by the clean air of the forest, but then the words of last night's speaker came floating back. Savagery, he asserted, was the direction of the future; civilisation as we knew it had failed. As the Roman Empire had come to an end, as the Holy Roman Empire had followed and been followed in turn by that of Bismarck, so the task of the present age was to forge another Reich. It would necessarily be born in terror, he asserted; had not the rule of the Church had been ushered in by a like terror, by intolerance of the purposeless world which had gone before?

By now I was under the lime-trees, walking past the great public buildings of Unter den Linden, church and library and university. Some workers were digging up the pavement, and in place of the dark soil that underlies the London streets, what streamed from their shovels was the glitter of sand. All at once a succession of images coalesced. I recalled those towns on the great open plain of the north where quaint gabled dwellings and brick churches lurched at odd angles as they

subsided slowly into the unstable medium beneath.   I
remembered a remark of Hilde's that Prussia was distrusted in
the south because, its foundations being so shallow, some
doubted whether it was part of Germany, the true Germany, at
all.   I thought of the deserts from which nomads have
harrowed cities from time immemorial, fertilising new growth
only after centuries of desolation.   By now I had arrived at the
island where the imperial palace stood empty, converted into a
museum like its neighbours, so that there was a singular
aptness, now, about the name Museum Island; and here, in the
darkened halls, I found grim reminders of the twilight of
civilisations.

My attention was arrested by a gallery given over to
pictures in tiling: they represented fierce, tawny animals – a
bull, a lion, a dragon – against a background of brilliant sky.
Some of the tiles, gleaming and new, were clearly restorations;
others, cracked and with their colours dulled, were evidently
the originals.   I peered to read the sign, which told me they
had come from the Processional Way of Babylon; and all at
once I reeled with shock.

A few times in my life, I have had the experience of
something having happened before and being about to happen
again.   Suddenly, as if in a waking dream, I seemed to march
down that processional way, and through a towered gate into
the city of Babylon.   I walked, certain of my route, along the
familiar streets and willow-lined canals, until I came to the
great brick mountain of the ziqqurat.   At the base of this I
entered a doorway, descending, by narrowing squares of steps
that echoed the structure above, into a basement. Here,
avenues lined with clay tablets stretched off on all sides into
the gloom.   What surrounded me of the present – the
approving murmurs of grave scholars, the *wie schöns* of well-
dressed women, the delighted cries of children at the toy-like
vividness of the animals – had faded into a vast distance.   I

was in the great library of Babylon; and involuntarily, as before, I took the complex of turnings and twistings to an alcove that I remembered as mine. As I sat, I became aware of my purpose there: a project of unimaginable proportions. And yet it seemed to me elementary, a question of logical analysis. The essential clue I had taken from the nature of names. There had been episodes in my life where my name had been uttered as if in incantation by a lover, by virtue of which I seemed to have been accorded a veritable identity. If, I reasoned, there was any analogy between the human and the divine, the same must hold true on that plane. The divinity, if personal, must be possessed of a name; and it seemed to me to follow that, if our intelligence were divinely bestowed, we were intended to discover it. And so I proceeded systematically, through every possible combination of syllables: some at once so alike and so divergent as the emphatic shadows of two trees in the summer sun, or the manes of two horses streaming in a bitter wind, or the outline of the same letter as written by two different hands. Since every character in the syllabary had a numerical value, philology and mathematics were interchangeable; and since, further, proportion is the basis of the harmonic interval, my explorations had taken on the quality of a classical musicology, the key, as it seemed, to a cosmic symphony. Some, even then, thought my project blasphemous: an opinion which has been preserved in the traditions of a people who lived among us as exiles.

And they said, Go to, let us build us a city and a tower, whose top may reach unto heaven; and let us make us a name.

I must take issue with the version of my tale which involves mere bricks and mortar: the result, no doubt, of conflation with the ziqqurat which towered above my library. Yet it does, in its fashion, enshrine certain truths. Already, my project had taken many weary years, in the course of which I had abnegated personal relationships. Absorbed in my tower of words, I went without sleep; I became haggard; obsessed with my superhuman task, I lost all pity for the common fate of humanity.

The tower had reached such a height that it took a whole year to hoist the necessary materials to the top. These, in consequence, became so precious that they cried when a brick slipped and shattered, miles below; while they remained stonily indifferent when a worker fell over the edge.

I had indeed become indifferent to all else: to private feeling no less than to my public duties. I was high priest of Marduk, god of the city, and responsible for the ceremonials of the temple above, celebrations of the majestic harmonies of the skies: the performance of which, it was believed, kept the city itself in harmony. But my detective adventure in the vaults below had absorbed all my energies. I had ceased even to remember the life which had gone before, so absorbed was I in the rituals of my art.

I lifted my stylus to cut into the wet clay of the tablet. I had always loved the smell of books. I worked quickly now: my project, I sensed, close to its end. I had the feeling one has when a word one has always known, but which has escaped the memory, is about to flood again into the chambers of the mind. At that moment my lamp went out. I relit it, poising my stylus again over the tablet. To my horror, I could no longer understand what I had just written. Sometimes, on the verge of sleep, a word which is over-familiar – the name of one's native place, for instance – takes on a momentary quality of strangeness, and one turns it over and over again until it resumes its reassuring ordinariness. So it was with me now. I closed my eyes and was aware of the stench of the lamp. Against my eyelids the characters I had written came up in reverse, light against shade; but still they held no meaning. Then someone opened a door high above, and from the streets came a wave of shouting. The door clanged to; running footsteps echoed down the stairs. Into the circle cast by the lamplight panted the colleague who was my one remaining friend, whose concern for me had never slackened – a thickset, bull-necked individual who, it seems to me now, bore no small resemblance to Watson. His face was covered in perspiration. Slowly and deliberately, he enunciated what I suppose he thought were words. But what emerged was a burst of some uncouth and hideous jargon. My speech had the same effect on him. He pointed despairingly upstairs.

In the world above, a storm of unprecedented proportions had burst. Jagged streaks of lightning lit the avenues; then they were plunged into deeper darkness. The canals had risen in flood. We visited the sub-priests of each ward, pleading with them by means of signs to keep fluent the vast articulations of the city. But I was no longer listened to; and, by the time the storm had exhausted itself, and the morning star pulsed softly in a green sky, water was pouring in sheets from the rooftop gardens, down the slanting walls and in streams along the paved avenues. We hurried back to the library, but by now the flood was roaring in a waterfall down the staircase and, far below, washing shelf after shelf of tablets, the memory of ages, into mud.

I do not know when or how the killing began: perhaps from the imagined malevolence of laughter in a strange language. Passers-by were put to the test of tongues; to escape one such mob, my companion and I fled down separate streets. Somehow I escaped from the city; I have never gone back.

In the course of my subsequent wanderings, I found myself one evening on the banks of a broad river, beside which the trunks of the willows were grey to where the water had reached them. A woman called to her child, who was playing in the oblique dusty light. Something in her intonation, something in the name she uttered, touched on a past neither of us could subsequently recall. Through her, I learnt that what is truest in our lives is not amenable to intellect, but is involved with instinct and intuition. If this is true for the visible world, must it not be so *a fortiori* for the invisible? I provided patterns for the carpets she wove, coming back, always, to the design of the city. Here were the cross canals, the square pools, the trees that lined them in what had once been the wonder of the world. I reduced our city to that pattern of perfect order I had hoped to uncover under the ziqqurat. But always, now, I saw to it that one thread was misplaced.

I came to with a start, to find myself back in Berlin. Again I stood before the tiling of Babylon, its sun-coloured animals outlined against sky-blue. Around me the crowd gasped and murmured once more; and I made my way through them in a daze. On the broad stone platform which lies at the approach to the building, I came face-to-face with a young woman whose features bore an expression of deep shock, as if she were the victim of recent grief. Immediately I was drawn back to the present. What sorrow, I wondered, attended her? Had she suffered the loss of a loved one? Or, like myself, had she been overwhelmed by the meanings proclaimed by the silent past?

Leaving the island, I sat on a café terrace beside a bridge where the sunlight, reflected from the lively waters of the Spree, glittered on the underside of the arches. Here I attempted to make sense of my experience. In Germany they provide little paper circles between saucer and cup to absorb any spillage; and I still keep the stained coaster on which I wrote down the three hypotheses that then occurred to me. They read as follows:

'I. TRANSMIGRATION.
'II. HEREDITY.
'III. ASSOCIATION'.

'I. TRANSMIGRATION'. This would assert that I *had* once lived in Babylon, in accordance with the belief of the Hindoos that our souls inhabit successive bodies. It may seem strange that I should even consider this; but readers familiar with my distinction between the impossible and the improbable will not, on reflection, be inclined to dismiss it. To deny what can neither be proved nor disproved is as irrational as to assert it. However, since that, in my present state of knowledge, was what it remained – something that could neither be proved nor disproved – I put it aside, and went on to the next.

'II. HEREDITY'. You may recall that, in conversation with Watson in the account which he has titled 'The Empty House', I advanced the theory that individuals carry within themselves the entire tree of their ancestry, and that this bears fruit in otherwise inexplicable action. Ancestral memory, I have sometimes thought, may be passed on in latent form, to germinate after millennia like the grains from Egyptian tombs. Amid the tree of my own ancestry is a branch whose name, I am told by antiquaries, is cognate with Marduk. You may recall, in the adventure I have described as 'The Lion's Mane', how I stressed the 'strange outlandish blood' of the swarthy Murdoch. The legends of the Celtic peoples speak of voyages between the Mediterranean and the Atlantic: a matter which, as you will remember, intrigued my interest in Cornwall until it was distracted by the affair of 'The Devil's

Foot'. What had occurred to me on the Museum Island, according to this hypothesis, was a flash of latent memory triggered by the sight of a street familiar to some ancestor. But this second explanation was no more susceptible of proof than the first; and so I went on to the third.

'III. ASSOCIATION'. This third hypothesis was the simplest of the three. It presupposed that my depression and apprehension of the day before had found an unconscious echo in the fragments from the ancient city and the babble of tongues all about. This hypothesis was, of the three, the least tinged with that colouring of romance with which I have so often reproached Watson. It was, moreover, capable of being tested; and I resolved to do this the following morning by returning to the museum and seeing if, given similar stimuli, similar hallucinations – for that, on this theory, was what they were – would make themselves felt.

But when I stood once more in front of the Babylonian tiling, I experienced – nothing. Here again glowed the patterns on which the eyes of Herodotus had rested; here again there clashed around me the varied tongues of the earth; here again I was heavy with foreboding. But nothing I heard or saw, no concatenation of associations that I could conjure up, would act as my 'open, sesame'. The wall remained nothing but that, stood blank and opaque before me, the path it had opened momentarily into a real or imagined past now barred, it seemed, irrevocably.

At last, giving up the vain attempt, I resumed my interrupted tour of the day before. In the course of a leisurely exploration of the island, I paused before the serene and noble features of Nefertiti. She seemed as exalted, as oblivious to her surroundings, in this former imperial city as once among the pools and palm-trees of the doom-laden capital of Amarna.

And then, as I circled the statue, I stood still in shock. Every picture I had seen of her portrayed her in profile, so that the face seemed complete. But now I saw that one eye was hollow, giving her an unfinished, inhuman look. As I recoiled from the sight, a voice spoke beside me, a contralto I had once thrilled to. 'Strange, is it not', remarked Hilde, 'how one sees only one side of the portrait? And yet there are two: do you not think the same thing can happen in life?' And then, as I remained silent: 'All I ask is that you should listen to me; afterwards, judge for yourself'. I could not deny the justice of her appeal; nor could I, to tell the truth, quite control my excitement as I stepped into the motor-cab that took us to her apartment in the Uhlandstrasse.

We sat on either side of a table on which stood a shaded lamp. And there I listened in silence while she revealed an aspect of her story which presented it to me in an entirely different light.

Bismarck had done well to warn me of his ruthlessness. He had acquired compromising material on her brother, an army officer who was deeply implicated in a Swabian separatist movement: which feared, with all too much justification, that alliance with Prussia could only lead their homeland to disaster. Bismarck had threatened to have him shot unless she did his bidding: a threat which he had carried out upon my failure to assassinate the Kaiser.

I was appalled. 'To think I could have saved him, at the expense of that worthless creature's life!'

She shook her head. 'I am convinced he would have been sacrificed in any case. The old man played on the feelings of both of us. I am glad you escaped'.

'Glad! Why?', I cried involuntarily. She smiled. 'How can you ask such a question? I divined that there was a struggle in you, that some shadow stood between us which was not amenable to argument. I could not appeal to you through reason, so I determined to do so through wantonness. It was assumed, I assure you: I have never been so mortified as when I made that first move. If I could not have you in spirit, I wanted what you could give me in any way possible. And so here I am, again to ask you nothing – no, not even forgiveness – but to give you, in return, understanding and peace of mind'.

I had listened absorbed to her narrative, as one after another the barricades that I had constructed against her had given way. A question suggested itself. 'Your finding me today: was it coincidence?'

She shook her head. 'The fall of Bismarck left me at a loss – it was he who had funded the laboratory you found me in, and ensured that you would hear of it. I now decided to apply what I had learnt to the restoration of art. I have worked ever since on the Museum Island; it was there that my assistant recognised you yesterday'.

I was still more bewildered than before. 'Recognise? But how? How did you, for that matter?' I gestured towards my frock-coat of Teutonic cut, towards my goatee, my pince-nez: all of which helped to provide, as I thought, the authentic image of the German professor.

For answer she laughed; then rose and went to her bedroom. From the bedside table, I saw her take a silver-framed photograph, which she handed to me. There I was, exactly as I had accoutred myself today. It was the photograph my fellow-students had insisted I have taken at Tübingen long ago, wearing the disguise in which I had passed myself off as a visiting scholar.

I laughed, but was left with one last puzzle. 'All this does not explain how I was recognised by your assistant…'

At that moment there was the rattle of a key in the lock, and I saw the sorrowful young woman I had encountered on the steps the day before, now with a questioning look that quickly turned to smiling radiance.

'She has seen that picture every day of her life', said Hilde evenly. 'She was all I had left after my brother was taken away: our daughter'.

'*Ours?*'

'Yes, Sherlock: yours and mine'.

TEN
THE SKULL OF HOLBEIN

It was a winter's morning on which we had woken to see Baker Street covered with a crisp fall of snow. 'Excellent, Watson', said Holmes as he looked out through the curtains, surveying the street and measuring, with a practised eye, the depth to which the wheels of a passing cab were covered. 'I make it three-and-a-half inches. Just enough to discourage the elegant idler, who will not wish to risk his patent-leather shoes; but not enough to keep the enterprising cabbie at home. Perfect for the National Gallery: we shall have it, if I am not mistaken, to ourselves'.

As so often, his deduction proved correct; though it was with a pang of regret that I followed him up the steps and under the pillared portico, when the fragile blue of the sky beyond Westminster promised a bracing walk along the Thames. Inside, the halls echoed to our footsteps as Holmes, ferret-like, led me from one painting to another in a train of association that marked the movements of his agile and retentive mind. At last he stopped before that double portrait of Holbein's which is known as *The Ambassadors*.

'It is the strangest painting in history, Watson', he stated, with quiet intensity. 'In fact, it would not be too much to say that it *is* history'.

'Whatever can you mean, Holmes?', I cried.

'Describe what you see, Watson', he commanded.

'All I can see', I replied slowly, 'is two men standing on either side of a whatnot covered with bric-a-brac'.

'Bric-a-brac: hmm', he said thoughtfully. 'Well, it will do for the moment. Describe the two'.

'The one on the left', I began, 'reminds me of Henry VIII...'

'Reminds', he interjected sharply.   'In what fashion, pray?   Features or dress?'

'The costume', I replied, 'is such as one sees in portraits of our much-wived monarch.   The face, bearded, has a similar sensuality, but less marked and with a thoughtful cast.   It is a touch exotic – Latin, perhaps'.

'Excellent, Watson.   And the other?'

'Similar in features, but more ascetic – self-contained, a suggestion of authority.   This, combined with his dark robes and white collar, suggest a cleric – a supposition strengthened by that strange square hat...'

'A biretta'.

'...which I have seen, I think, in portraits of the Roman Catholic priesthood – Cardinal Newman?'

'Splendid, Watson.   Now take these facts in conjunction with the title, and what do we get?   Two envoys, obviously foreign, one clerical, one lay – you see, already we have a polarity – whose costume suggests the age of Henry VIII. We know that Holbein painted that monarch, whom you have spoken of as much-married; and the most significant of those marriages was the one which led to the break with the Church of Rome.   And it was indeed in that connection that our ambassadors were here in England'.

'You mean they were emissaries of the Pope?'

'The cleric in the picture had indeed served in that capacity; but his companion was ambassador for the king of France'.

'Of France?   What had the king of France to do with our king's break with Rome?'

'Everything, Watson.   You see, without his intervention, there might never have been a Reformation in England'.

'You astound me, Holmes.   Are you saying that one of the central events in our history was the result of accident?'

'Not accident, Watson; like all history, circumstance. The mission of the French en- voy came just after Henry VIII had married Anne Boleyn in secret, and the threat of excommunication hung over his head. However, the envoy's brother, who was ambassador to the Vatican, was negotiating a marriage between the French royal family and that of the Pope. This created an axis of power between the papacy and the French monarchy; and it was understood that Henry's tolerance of that marriage would be matched by papal tolerance of his own. Instead, however, the Pope recognised French territorial claims in Italy, and the French, in return, supported the religious policy of the Pope. Henry had mean- while had Anne Boleyn crowned queen, and the stage was set for the break between England and Rome'.

'Do you mean to tell me, Holmes, that a mere painter – a decorator of canvases – was privy to these state secrets?'

'That a painter should have known of these manoeuverings may indeed seem unlikely, Watson', he replied gravely. 'But we must remember that Holbein was a friend of Thomas More, Lord Chancellor of England, who was to be arrested the following year...'

'The following year?'

'Oh yes, Watson, the year is unmistakable. There it is, with the painter's signature – *IOANNES HOLBEIN PINGEBAT* – in the shadows of the floor. See: 1533. I can tell you, moreover, that the painting represents ten-thirty on the morning of April the eleventh'.

'This is too much, Holmes!', I protested. 'How on earth can you deduce that?'

'It is simplicity itself. It is established by a perusal of what you have spoken of as bric-a-brac. Amid the assorted clutter on what you described as a whatnot are two sundials, one of which indicates the date and the other the time'.

'All this is no doubt most interesting', said I, nettled. 'But it seems to me that you still have a long way to go to prove your hypothesis – that the subject of the painting is king Henry's divorce. All the evidence you have adduced so far is merely circumstantial'.

'*Touché*, my dear Watson. But pray recall that bric-a-brac is my forte; overlooked rubbish my treasure-trove. You will recall the clay from the running-shoes in "The Three Students", or the abandoned blotting-paper in "The Missing Three-Quarter": in each case the key to the problem. Because they are overlooked, they are allowed to carry messages which would otherwise have been destroyed. Such trivia are the building-blocks of the deductive artist: a fact that you, as my chronicler, have demonstrated on numerous occasions'.

I smiled, mollified; and Holmes went on to the final points in his demonstration. 'See the books on the lower shelf. They are open, and may be read. One is a hymnal with the verses of Luther. Surely you see the significance? Catholic representatives are placed in juxtaposition with the great luminary on the Protestant side. Behind the book lies a lute with a broken string, the classic image of division. Here we are informed of the rift which then threatened Christendom. You will scarcely doubt, now, the painter's awareness that he was witness to an historic moment, and that this indeed is his theme'.

That is what I like about Holmes. He always gets it right. I, on the other hand, am the fool. No, do not deny it: I am the court jester, the intellectual dwarf who serves to emphasize the stature of his master. I have long known this: how could I not be aware of it? You have seen this inequality from the start. 'I am inclined to think...', I begin in *The Valley of Fear*. 'I should do so', interrupts Holmes.

And so I am the fool. Yet I am the source of your knowledge. If you imagine you know Holmes, it is only through me. Oh yes; it has not escaped notice that, on the rare occasions when Holmes himself takes up the pen, he falls into that very vice of romance, as opposed to strict analytical reasoning, for which he excoriates his chronicler. Think about that: I am all that you know about him. And what does this tell you about me? Surely that the emphasis on my folly is deliberate. But let us proceed.

Holmes continued: 'Yes, an historic moment, Watson: the moment at which the Middle Ages ended and modern England began. Henry's divorce involved repudiation of Rome and its Latin ritual. For support against the Pope, he turned to Parliament, enriching its members with the monastic estates – and incidentally enhancing a power which was to achieve parity with that of his successors. He rooted us irretrievably in our own language, our own land and our own legislature. Everything we now are can be seen to have flowed from that moment'.

'You do not think the painter foresaw all this, surely?', I queried dubiously.

'I am never quite sure how much the artist sees', replied Holmes. 'By his intuitive grasp of the moment, he may see far into the future. By the depth of his gaze, he may see truths far beneath the surface'. Again he gave his quizzical smile.

I was thrilled by these words of his. That is what I like about Holmes. He always gets it right. The fool, you see, is possessor of a wisdom which is not the wisdom of the world. It is a wisdom which expresses itself in pratfalls and pitfalls: he constantly teeters on the brink of disaster, the edge of annihilation. He is the clown who unites in himself all the talents of the circus. The audience gasps in terror when he climbs to the high wire, and there threatens to fall off while the more superficially skilful of the duo sets him right. But who will doubt that it is the clown who needs the greater virtuosity, whose play upon the theme of acrobatics is the cadenza of a master violinist?

You think this vanity in me. You see this as resentment of my subordinate role, megalomania of the lackey who parades in his master's uniform. Attend; and you shall hear.

'You consider, then, Holmes, that the artist is a prophet?'

'Undoubtedly, Watson. How else could the painting be what it is? Here are two figures, companions and friends: the one masterful, colourful, dominant in the affairs of this world; the other subdued, shadowy and devoted to another. Yet both are ambassadors: both carry a coded message. The moment they embody far transcends mere politics, even ecclesiastical politics: the split in Christendom they imply is a split in the European psyche. It is a split, not merely between Protestant and Catholic, but between book and ritual, between literalism and symbol, between reason and feeling'.

I smiled, for I knew this to be true. That is what I like about Holmes. He always gets it right. I determined to apply the final test. 'My goodness, Holmes!', I exclaimed. 'Someone has defaced the painting!'

A strange, blurred shape, long and blunt-headed, not unlike the distended snout of a shark, had been splashed across the foreground of the picture, rising at a sharp angle from the left.

'That blot at the bottom of the picture, Holmes', I asked, 'that formless diagonal which, arising from the floor, appears to disarrange the entire careful composition of which you have spoken – what do you make of it? Is it an addition? Has another, later painter, begun a new composition on the same canvas?'

'By no means, Watson. Here; stand to one side'.

I did so, and gazed at the painting from the oblique angle to which Holmes directed me. From here, the snoutlike shape became rounded, and filled out to the dimensions of a human skull. 'What can it mean, Holmes?'

'It is the final summation of the theme. The painter was absorbed in the contemplation of time; here is his final judgement upon it: that all things pass away. Having recorded the moment in loving detail, he was seized by a sense of its passage, and drew this dark graffito across its base. Everything else in the painting is impersonal; this is not. It is a point of view'.

'Then why not say so?', I cried. 'Why make it so oblique, so difficult of access, so cryptic?'

'You of all people, Watson, should not need to ask me that'. And he met my eyes in a smile.

It was one of his most brilliant deductions, requiring every ounce of that intellectual acumen with which I have credited him. For he realised the facts of our association. He knew that there are two of me. I am the Watson portrayed, and the Watson who portrays. Watson the first, with his lumbering slowness, is the creation of Watson the second. So is his friend and colleague, the indefatigable reasoner Sherlock Holmes. We are, both of us, creations of a point of view; or, if you prefer, a voice. I am that voice, the singer both of myself and of Holmes. I am the person he recognised in front of *The Ambassadors*; and I, in the end, am all that you know.

You may think this Watson an intruder; but he is no more an intruder than that enig- matic shape in the painting. You may insist that he is not to be found in the original tales. Are you so very sure? May not his – my – point of view be hidden in like fashion? Is it possible that you have missed it?

Let us look at the evidence. I have spoken, in these later retrievals from the dispatch-box, of my dislike of Bernard Shaw: let me direct you from these to a tale which is indisputably canonical.

I refer to 'The Priory School'. This adventure, you will recall, concerned the kidnapping of a pupil, who was traced by Holmes to a ducal castle in northern England, and to the duke himself, whose suppositious secretary and in fact illegitimate son had had the legitimate heir held in bondage. Is it possible that you did not see in the red-bearded duke, with his pallid face, a portrait of Shaw, whose family name proclaims an origin in north Britain? Far-fetched? But the scene of the crime, of which I was careful to provide a sketch in my own hand, and which I alluded to again and again, was distinguished by a grove named the Ragged Shaw – as Shaw the person was noted for that anti-social raiment of his. And all of us had heard the rumours of illegitimacy which clung about him, and which Shaw counteracted in a manner resembling the horse-shoes in the same tale: mimicking cattle-tracks to mislead pursuers. For his apparent candour, his plethora of family anecdote, his suborning by co-option of would-be biographers, all were designed to do exactly this: *to cover his traces with the appearance of a stampede.*

My opposition to Shaw was a matter of conviction. His lack of faith in himself expressed itself as a lack of faith in the individual as such, in an advocacy of collectivism. And the worst of it was that he was a Celt; and that, to my mind, involved loyalty to oneself and to the past.

Recall the case of the Musgrave Ritual, that tale of a family whose loyalty preserved the crown of the last Celtic dynasty in England. I underlined the theme with the butler's wooing of a maid with the Cornish name of Tregellis, and his abandonment of a Howells of fiery Welsh temperament. It was a tragedy that reached its culmination in his burial alive by her: 'what smouldering fire of vengeance', I have Holmes ask, 'had suddenly sprung into flame in this passionate Celtic woman's soul?'

Consider what I was: of Scottish birth and Irish ancestry, I had my way to make in England. Do you think it an accident that Watson longs for the shingle of Southsea? It was there that I became – or rather learnt to masquerade as – English.

Being a medical man, I had to build up a practice: something I could only do by making myself acceptable to society. Do you think that was simple? Oh, I was accepted up to a point: I matched them in their sports, you see, and that was something they could understand. But in matters of the intellect... when I dared to discourse of Carlyle, when I spoke of a Scottish identity in the realm of thought, a local newspaper wrote of me as a frenzied clansman. Always, you see, there was the residual disdain, the never-quite-hidden condescension for the outsider.

The outsider? Being what I was, I was aware of history; and who, I asked myself, in that light was the outsider? There is one fleeting reference to this in the adventures of Holmes: in the tale 'Black Peter', I speak of the 'Saxon invaders'. But I am more explicit elsewhere; and again I gave you a clue. I wrote that, of all my work, that which I might alone elect to preserve were the *Tales of Long Ago*; and among these is a searing account of that invasion:

'"You will own this island before you have finished", said I.

'His eyes sparkled as he gazed. "Perhaps", he cried; and then suddenly correcting himself and thinking that he had said too much, he added –

'"A temporary occupation – nothing more"'.

And yet I did not dislike them: I merely wished to call things by their names. Here is what I say in the same tale: 'They are brave, hardy, and very pertinacious in all that they undertake; whereas the Britons, though a great deal more spirited, have not the same steadiness of purpose'. I go on to speak of the Celts' 'more fiery passions being succeeded by reaction'. What else is this but the character I attribute to Holmes?

And yet, I insist, I did not dislike them; indeed, there was much in them that I admired. They were complementary to us, you see: they had the faults of our qualities and the qualities of our faults. Again and again I have spoken of them and of ourselves in terms of a polarity: between deliberation and volatility, between steadiness and spirit, between conscience and imagination. Let me direct your attention once again beyond Holmes. In 'A Physiologist's Wife', I speak of the conflict between the Celtic and the Saxon soul. The latter is represented by the physiologist of the title, who applies scientific detachment to all things. He gives the Celtic woman he loves back to the Celtic man she loves; and, though he dies of a broken heart, maintains his detachment. Of course, there is an element of caricature here; but it is an exaggeration which emphasizes what I admired in them above all: the Saxon capacity for self-control, the quiet stoicism which can rise to the utmost nobility of spirit.

Again, is not this Holmes? How many times have I spoken of his impassivity, only to make it obvious that it is only apparent? That it is at its most acute when his feelings are most actively engaged? Holmes, then, is the best of both peoples: Celtic volatility under Saxon stoicism. Have I not alluded to this in 'The Red-headed League', where I have spoken of his duality: of his extreme exactness as a reaction against his tendency to poetry? Or, in 'The Crooked Man', of the composure with which he veiled his 'keen, intense nature'? But at heart there is no contradiction. The best traditions of both met in Arthur: in history, defender of the Celt against the Saxon; in legend, more powerful still, model of that chivalry which united the values of both peoples.

I gave you clues in plenty. In 'The Bruce-Partington Plans', the apparent criminal, who is described as the most patriotic and the most chivalrous of men, is named Arthur. Again, in 'The Beryl Coronet', the action is made possible by the gallantry of the young man who, aware of the true identity of the criminal, takes upon himself the blame for the crime of his adoptive sister. This embodiment of chivalry, this character who is not what he seems, is another Arthur. The artist hides away his signature in a corner of his picture; should I have made it plainer? And I gave Arthur's character to Holmes. Oh yes, it has not gone unnoticed that Holmes, in his battle against evil, in his taking upon himself the punishment of wrongdoers, in his detached courtesy towards women, is the last knight-errant. What then was left for Watson: for the character I attributed to myself? I have spoken of my companion's multifarious disguises. I have shown him as a jaunty young workman, as a snarling pedant, as a drunken groom, as an Italian priest, as a lady with a parasol. I have spoken, in the adventure of Black Peter, of the five separate refuges in London 'in which he was able to change his personality'. This ability to change personality is a vital aspect of his character: why else, but that it was a necessity for me? For the deepest of all the disguises was reserved, not for Holmes, but for Watson: Watson was my most elaborate creation.

To survive in their society, I had to adopt their camouflage: I had to move among them as one barely visible. I hurrahed them on in their games, and in that scramble for empire which, they would have had one believe, was simply one more of them. In Watson, I took upon myself the stolidity of the Saxon: though modified, again, by the emotionalism of the Celt. We are interchangeable, you see, Holmes and I: I simply gave him the flashier role.

And yet...and yet...the fool, in the end, touches greater depths than the king. The king's jester was originally the king's substitute: the mock-king who, at a time when the sun dipped to the horizon, after a brief season of mock-rule, was sacrificed. The sacrificed god, the divine fool, is king of the intercalary darkness. The king is the ruler of conventional time; the fool, the ruler of the time which is outside time: the time of emptiness and the time of ecstasy: the time of desolation and the time of illumination: the dark night of the soul and the full noon of God. But Holmes is still talking: let us attend to him.

'I was saying, Watson, when that glassy look came into your eyes – I was saying that the painting represents time: the time that can be measured and the time which cannot. It is the second which stands behind and is the ultimate reality. It is time in its transcendental dimension.

'You have asked me what the painting meant, Watson', he continues. 'I tell you, it is a mirror in which we see ourselves. Like the sitters, we are forever fixed in an historical moment – in our case, a moment of gasogenes and fogged streetlamps and hansom cabs rattling over cobblestones. But in his mirror the artist has given us a pointer to a dimension outside itself, a counterpoint to our ultimate queries'.

'A mirror?', I echoed stupidly.

'Oh yes, Watson, a mirror. In it all things appear and all things pass away. Why else do you think I have brought you here?'

As always, he has got it right. But the question is one the world fears. It is terrified by any deviation from the ticking of its clocks; when it is of that meaningless regularity that it should most be afraid.

I not only worked my way into English society, I was one of its acknowledged institutions – as long as I kept away from the question. They did not notice, or chose not to notice, what was implicit in my work – until I sought the certainty of Holmes in my Watsonian blunderings after the truth. Much has been made of my gullibility in matters of the psychical. Yet has it not occurred to you that there are charlatans amongst materialists even as there are among spiritualists? That the appeal to the supremacy of reason can also be a species of prejudice? That apparent rationalism may be an attempt to banish what one secretly fears, and so ultimately irrational? When a scientist keeps an open mind about the improbable, it is hailed as detachment; when a psychical investigator does so, it is reviled as folly.

And that was what happened to me. Dominance, in the Anglo-Saxon world, is dependent upon the sense of – no, the assumption of: they are two very different things – superiority. As long as I maintained that facade of knowingness, I was showered with honours. As soon as I displayed doubt, I was cast into the exterior darkness. And yet that is where by nature all of us lie. They did not wish to know who *I* was, because they did not wish to know who *they* were. All any of us is left with, in the end, is what the Middle Ages described as a *docta ignorantia* and classical Greece the knowing what one does not know. Holmes is knowledge, Watson ignorance; which of us more nearly approximates the human condition?

Human meaning is arbitrary; and it is the fool who knows it. Outside Rome stood a sacred grove in which a criminal was king. He took his throne by murdering his predecessor, and was murdered in turn by his successor. As long as he lived, his legitimacy was unimpeachable. What else are our kingdoms, our empires? The creations of successful adventurers: intimations of order, nothing more. At the heart of Rome itself – that ultimate manifestation of order – was the chaos of Saturnalia, when the world turned up- side down. Kingship is an agreed fiction: as the fool remembers. We who have eliminated that festival have attempted to forget it. It is no coincidence that the puritan, the critical as opposed to the creative mind, strove to abolish its last vestige in Christmas. Our puritans are with us still, seeking to calculate the mystery with their slide-rule of dogma – upon which no two of them can agree. At the end of the day, we are Watsons all. It is not that chaos is an interval in cosmos; it is the other way round. The answer passes away; the question abides. 'What object',

I report Holmes as crying in 'The Cardboard Box', 'what object is served by this circle of misery and violence and fear? It must tend to some end, or else our universe is ruled by chance, which is unthinkable. But what end? There is the great standing perennial problem to which human reason is as far from an answer as ever'.

Many of my adventures with Holmes have been described as mysteries; but strictly speaking this is a misnomer. There is only one mystery in existence, and that is existence itself. All the rest is mystification.

I rest my case. I, after all, am merely Watson; you, my dear reader, are Holmes. Speaking of whom, I hear him call from the next gallery. I must away: the game's afoot.

'Watson...*Watson!*'

www.ingramcontent.com/pod-product-compliance
Lightning Source LLC
Chambersburg PA
CBHW051248260626
47162CB00002B/669